BRIDE OF THE LIVING PROOF
Neighborlee Book 7

Michelle L. Levigne

www.YeOldeDragonBooks.com

Ye Olde Dragon Books
P.O. Box 30802
Middleburg Hts., OH 44130

www.YeOldeDragonBooks.com

2OldeDragons@gmail.com

Copyright © 2021 by Michelle L. Levigne
ISBN 13: 978-1-952345-19-7

Published in the United States of America
Publication Date: May 1, 2021

Cover Art Copyright by Ye Olde Dragon Books 2021

Welcome to Neighborlee, Ohio.

Where? Somewhere on the North Coast of Ohio, south of Cleveland, right off I-71, north of Medina, in the heart of Cuyahoga County.

What is it? That's a little harder to explain.

Neighborlee is a place you need to experience.

The most important thing you need to understand: Neighborlee is *magic*. Some people say the town is alive. It exists to protect the weird and wonderful (and sometimes a little bit scary) from the cold, practical, material world.

More important, Neighborlee protects the outside world from the weird and wonderful that come to visit … and sometimes come to stay.

First stop: Divine's Emporium, a four-story Victorian house sitting on a hill overlooking the Metroparks. Whatever you really need, you can find at Divine's. Even if you don't know what you're looking for when you walk in the door. The shop is often bigger inside than it is outside. Angela is the proprietor. Please stay on the first floor. You don't want to find out what is hidden and locked safely away upstairs. Like Aslan, Angela is good, but that doesn't mean she's safe. And neither are the secrets and wonders and doorways to other worlds that she protects … and keeps securely locked.

Come in and explore. Meet the people who help Angela guard Neighborlee. Share their adventures of magic and wonder, danger and sacrifice. You never know who or what you'll run into as you walk the streets and listen to the stories of their lives.

Chapter One

I need to back up a little bit. I ended the last volume of "confessions" of the activities of the guardians of Neighborlee by glossing over the events of the last few weeks of January and ended with the arrival of Jane Wilson, owner of the newly opened New Day Spa, *aka* the Ghost, retired guardian of the inbred, lazy town of Fendersburg. But more important than that: former resident of Neighborlee Children's Home. A Lost Kid.

By the time I ran into Jane in the Spindelmutter Building, doing her final inspection and signing the lease papers, we were coming to some semi-firm theories about the changes that had occurred in Neighborlee thanks to the battle at New Year's. I had some breathing room in some areas, because Daniel was semi-mysteriously out of town, for reasons only partially explained. I'm talking Daniel Sheridan, head of Sheridan Communications, the conglomerate that had bought the *Neighborlee Tattler.* He had turned out to be a fan of my comedy and wanted to be friends. (Don't believe me? Read the previous two confessions, how he invited himself to my Star Trek club Christmas party, and then glommed onto me for self-defense against Sylvia Grandstone at the New Year's Eve overnighter at Eden, the community center.)

Some of Daniel's errands out of town had to deal with humongous PR problems, thanks to the Grandstone family. They had been trying for years to forge and force a marriage alliance via Sylvia and Daniel, in very transparent hopes of taking over the growing Sheridan communications empire, and all that lovely money. It turned out that Daniel had an entire team devoted just to denying and quelling all the false stories of secret rendezvous and trysts and love letters/texts/emails between him and Sylvia. When Sylvia royally messed up her assignment for the Rivals at New Year's Eve, and got herself killed, the Grandstones apparently went into a scorched earth policy to defend their good (hah!) family name, and try to convince people Daniel had broken Sylvia's heart. Supposedly she had fled the country to get him jealous with a string of love affairs. Seriously? A *string* of them, picking up a dozen boy-toys in as many exotic locations in less than three weeks since Sylvia's body vanished from the Neighborlee police morgue?

So yeah, Daniel had big problems to deal with, to protect his family and his family's empire, and his sanity.

Funny thing. Thanks to some self-defense snooping by our friendly Artificial Intelligences who lived in the ether, namely London Holiday and her boyfriend, Sherwood, we were getting clues Daniel was dealing with some personal problems not exactly related to the Grandstones. Or if they were related, he had some sneaky, highly skilled connections and friends in high places who were good at hiding from our friends who could get into almost anywhere. Even without the oversight of my favorite computer genius, Athena Longfellow and her fellow insane geniuses, Wallace and Cosmo. After all, they were the core of the group that built the social media phenomenon, FlopDrop, as a college assignment.

Daniel's absence was more a relief to me than a worry. Even though I did worry. Because yes, despite being the Evil Overlord who took my academic sports beat and stuck me with the (gag!) lovelorn column, *Talk to Terry* ... I kind of liked the guy.

We had bigger concerns. Neighborlee's defensive power field was fluctuating. We hoped it would grow back, and stabilize. The first big clue was ...

Winkies.

I had been able to see them occasionally, little sparks of magical power, masquerading as fireflies. But only me. Not Felicity or Kurt.

Now the winkies were swarming. I saw them throughout town, not just at Divine's Emporium. Fireflies aren't that unusual, thanks to the proximity of the Metroparks. But this was just over halfway through January. In an Ohio winter.

Good thing? Sign of improvements? Or just a warning sign of impending trouble?

Because remember, the nasty interdimensional invader we had been fighting conceivably could also tap into the same otherworldly power flow that shielded Neighborlee, helped heal the guardians, and fed the winkies.

More important, Kurt and Felicity could see winkies now. When Stanzer came to the shop for a meeting of the guardians the Friday before I met Jane, he saw them. The Hounds, his interdimensional guardians, could see winkies too. But apparently the two breeds of magical critters didn't really like each other, so the Hounds stayed away from Divine's and the winkies stayed away from Stanzer.

That probably was good, because too many interdimensional species in one place just seemed like a trouble magnet, to me. Kind of like having too many Infinity Stones in one solar system. All that energy bouncing around had to generate magical noise. We wanted Big Ugly to stay asleep, deeper and longer.

Athena joined the meeting when she got out of class that Friday afternoon, and she saw the winkies too. This time, not a good thing. Encountering the winkies awakened memories for her, incidents of the darker side of Neighborlee weirdness. Specifically, when someone had opened a doorway into otherness, my freshman year of college. Athena had nearly been smashed by a runaway car, caught in the crossfire aimed at me.

Worse: she remembered events leading up to the death of Stephanie Miller. Bethany's mother. Guardian.

To say Athena was angry that her memories had been manipulated wouldn't exactly be accurate. We talked about it for a while. She had experienced and seen and been protected enough by what the guardians had to do, what Angela could do, she was more disappointed than angry. A little nauseated. Irritated, with an underlayer of guilt because she understood why. Followed by irritation with herself for feeling some relief that she -- and Bethany -- had been given as close to a normal childhood as anyone with guardian DNA could have, living in Neighborlee.

Athena lingered after the others went home, to ask her questions and confront Angela and me with her memories. Ford hadn't been there for the meeting. Chances were good he would have sensed the storm brewing in Athena from the moment she walked into Divine's, saw the winkies, felt their power, and the defensive walls in her memories started toppling. He would have been involved in the discussion, but he and Charlotte were out of town on some errands. He was involved in the memory blocking, because Angela wouldn't have done that to Athena without his and Charlotte's permission.

Right that moment, it was just Angela and Athena and me, sitting in her living room with huge mugs of spicy-sweet hot chocolate that was more whipping cream than milk.

"So is this a good thing or a bad thing, that this power surge has unraveled the spell you wove around the girls?" I had to ask.

Angela pursed her lips and let out a sigh that sounded like a delicate snort, coming through her nose. "To clarify, I did not weave a spell, and what I did has not come unraveled, so much as it has …" She shrugged. For just a second I saw some of that weariness that had touched her (and scared me) when the otherness anchored in a house on the border of Darbyville and Neighborlee tried to take a bite out of her. "I built a wall to block memories. The bricks have worn thin, would be a more accurate description. "

"You took Lanie away from us," Athena muttered into her mug, and didn't look at either of us.

"Stephanie didn't want Bethany to be touched by her heritage. What would you rather we had done? Separated you?" I asked. "Yeah, great trade. You lose your almost-sister and keep me?"

Athena looked about as startled as I felt when those words came out of my mouth. Maybe I hadn't been part of blocking their memories, but I had agreed to being shuffled to the sidelines of their lives. I had been their favorite babysitter.

"The two of you are bound together," Angela said, "and when Stephanie died, Bethany needed you in ways I could only sense, not know for sure. We did what we thought was best at the time. Only a long look back, far in the future, will tell us if we made the right choice." She looked long into Athena's eyes until the impending storm in them calmed. "Besides, it would have just complicated things if we had tried to let you keep all your memories. Your bond with Bethany would have destroyed the barrier in her memories. Or allowed the blockage to affect you anyway. That could have led to complications."

"Something we need to consider," I said, thinking aloud. "Does distance have any effect on the bond between the girls? Will Bethany start remembering? Should we warn her?"

"I would rather not bring up the subject," Angela said slowly. "She may be totally unaffected by the changes here. The growing power could keep Athena's awakening memories from affecting her. Yet there is no telling, with the levels in fluctuation and so many changes within the town … well, no guessing what effect those changes are having on the outside world. We could be entirely invisible to potential enemies outside our borders, or we could be sending up signal flares, inviting them in. Without more time, without establishing some stability or pattern, I can only theorize the impact of our energy surges on residents of Neighborlee, living outside our borders."

"If she does remember, what do we do?" Athena asked.

"I don't suppose the boys would mind you taking some time off, would they?"

"From gaming or their computer lab?" I asked. I knew better than to ask if Angela meant time off from the growing relationship between Athena and Wallace, computer geek extraordinaire and potential GQ model. Athena was such a jeans-and-sweatshirt kind of girl, barefoot whenever possible, but she and Wallace just visibly clicked and belonged together.

"What exactly do you mean by time off?" Athena asked once she had taken another big gulp of hot chocolate.

"I think you should go keep Bethany company on location. Get away from whatever might be happening next, keep an eye on her, have a little bit of a vacation. Relax."

Athena liked the idea enough she didn't make even a token protest about school. That said a lot, because Athena, one of the most responsible girls I had ever had the delight to watch grow up, just didn't consider things like cutting a class, forget about weeks of school.

We should have moved a lot faster to make our plans and get Athena out of town. We were distracted with bigger concerns and temporarily forgot a fact of survival in Neighborlee: when Grandstones are deprived of what they consider their due rights or embarrass themselves, they strike at new targets. In our defense, they were so busy trying to convince the world they deserved some compensation for Sylvia's allegedly broken heart, we never imagined they would try for another dynastic marriage campaign at the same time.

Especially since they were still getting flack from Reggie Grandstone's failure last winter to convince the world that he and Doni Halliday were about to run off together to live happily ever after, with him devouring her enormous trust fund. Reggie was still getting jabbed by social media in the predator alert hotlines and podcasts, who felt it their duty to remind the world that a man in his early thirties had tried to marry a fourteen-year-old.

Doni had a lot of friends who were the next generation of the "We Loathe the Grandstones" club. They delighted in playing bodyguard, to ensure the Grandstones didn't manage to kidnap her as she went about her ordinary life in town, and brainwash her into submission.

Going even further back in history, the Grandstone clan had been trying to get their hands on Longfellow money and property since before Portia, Jinx and Lenore were born. The whole mess with FlopDrop last year had earned Athena, Wallace and Cosmo some national attention. Several companies had signed the triumvirate to design software for them. They had paid off all their college expenses and had established a scholarship for up-and-coming programming geniuses and madmen at Neighborlee High School. And they had money left over for fun. Wallace was into live-action role-playing, for starters.

We didn't expect a new target and a new player because we forgot one crucial detail. One Grandstone had been laying low for a few years, building up a good reputation as an architect, keeping his nose clean. A Grandstone who stayed out of trouble turned kind of invisible. We forgot about Freddie Grandstone.

That Monday, I was on the phone with Athena. She was a little giddy with excitement about how quickly things were coming together for her trip out to stay with Bethany. Despite her increasing involvement in the weird and wonderful aspects of living in Neighborleee, Athena sounded like a normal college girl planning a trip to hang out with her rising star best friend. I was at my desk at the newspaper and Athena was walking from her dorm to the closest cafeteria on campus.

"Hey, jerk!" she yelped, over the sudden grumble of an engine and what sounded suspiciously like deep slush splashing.

"What happened?"

"Some creep decided to step on the gas going through that huge crater at the -- Hey!"

I heard thuds and feet splashing and a clatter-bang. Athena shrieked that particular fury sound that reminded me of the self-defense classes Gordon had insisted on for our Star Trek club members. Yes, all members, male and female. He figured some of the guys were skinny enough geeks they would get picked on even more than the girls. Along with the self-defense lessons came a course in using volume to increase fierceness.

Athena was a good student.

I sat there, unable to help, because I didn't know where she was. The heck with the rule about not using my superhero powers in daylight. The heck with my inability to really fly since the power drain that had started before Stephanie died, and my broken back and ... *but wait, the power was coming back, wasn't it? Maybe the tingles in my legs meant I was healing?* I hadn't tried walking since I realized I was getting more feeling in my legs. *Maybe ...?*

Then I heard an unfamiliar baritone voice shouting through the scuffling and deep splashing of multiple feet in slush. At least I had a better idea where Athena was on the campus. There was only one place where slush was deep on the sidewalks, and where the sidewalks were next to deep craters in the road and --

Heck with it, I was going to help Athena. I got to my feet, braced against my desk, and took a deep breath to concentrate and try to remember what it felt like when I could kinda-sorta fly. I needed a running start, though, if I was going to fly without Kurt taking control. That meant I needed to get outside. *Oh, heck.* Well, at least my legs were steady. Could I get to the door without triggering heart attacks in whoever was still in the office?

By then, the shouting stopped, and I heard the rumbling of an engine gunning as a car raced away, and that baritone voice was asking if Athena was all right.

"Let me take you to the hospital? They hit you." Followed by some semi-mild expletives.

"Athena!" I shouted, and wished I had Kurt's ability to zap electronics and give them extra power. I was determined to make myself heard. "Athena, are you all right? Who's there? What happened to her? Who --"

"I'm okay," Athena shouted over my shouting.

Several of my co-workers came running up one ramp or down another, from different sections of the building. Not one of my more dignified moments, but I didn't care. Athena was as close as I was ever going to get to having a kid of my own, I figured.

"What happened? Someone said you were hurt?"

"The slimebags knocked me down, trying to take my computer. I'm okay. My clothes are wet, but I'm okay. They didn't get my computer." She laughed a little unsteadily.

"End of the world as we know it. Want me to call Ford? Or Charlotte?"

"Maybe you should." She sighed. "Campus police just showed up, and it's that ink-for-blood regulation-bound weasel at the wheel, which means reports in triplicate."

The baritone voice started arguing with someone in the background, insisting Athena needed to get checked by a doctor before she gave reports.

I grinned and about half my tension dropped off, because if Athena could say what she did about the one-and-only Julia Irving, head of campus security (voted most likely to bankrupt the college from too much paper-pushing), then she was all right. She might be wet, she might have fallen down, she might be upset about having to fight to protect her computer, but she wasn't hurt, and she wasn't scared.

"Who is that guy?" I had to ask, as the baritone voice got louder, drowning out Julia's whiny voice. She certainly sounded like the chittering of a weasel, and all the slinking, self-righteous little sidekicks of despots ever portrayed in movies.

"I'm not sure, but he does look familiar."

Within two hours, an outraged Ford Longfellow reported that Athena's knight errant was none other than Freddie Grandstone.

"It's a setup," Doni insisted an hour after that, when she and Cosmo and Wallace came by the newspaper office to have a conference with me.

"London contacted me to get to Athena," Wallace broke in, "because something was jamming the phone signals, so she couldn't get to her. I was on my way over, and London and Sherwood were both cutting into all the security cameras around campus. They got the plates, and the car was reported stolen three days ago. It was seen parked behind the Wypnash Building, and the drivers have been seen hanging with Freddie Grandstone multiple times."

He winced and his hand went to the Bluetooth link in his left ear. Wallace was one of the few guys I knew who wasn't entranced by Bluetooth. He only started wearing it recently, to have audio communication with our two AIs.

"Yeah, the two of them are going to town, gathering gobs of evidence. The four creeps in the car seem to be regular minions of

Monsieur Architect." He wrinkled up his nose.

If Reggie Grandstone was planning on taking the legal profession by storm (and saving the Grandstone clan hundreds of thousands of dollars every year by handling all their false claims and counterclaims) then Freddie was setting himself up to become a world-changing architect. Or so he claimed. The last any of us knew, he had managed to stay for two solid years at the fourth architectural firm he had joined since graduating from college. Rumors speculated that the Grandstones wanted to remake Neighborlee from the ground up. Freddie would be in charge of having the architectural plans and designs in place. Rumors spread by various members of his former architectural firms said the entire town had already been redesigned. Where the Grandstones were going to get the equipment to raze buildings and rebuild them quickly enough to suit their vindictive aspirations, most people didn't know.

After everything we had learned over the last few months, chances were good the Rivals probably had an entire fleet of construction equipment poised and ready to assist the Grandstones in their schemes. Maybe that was part of the plan to break through to Big Ugly and set him free from his interdimensional prison. Physically break through to whatever dark, slimy, glow-in-the-dark-growth-filled cavern Felicity and Kurt and I had glimpsed in our dreams. Or at least weaken the barrier between worlds enough to let our ancient enemy out of his prison.

The actual attack on Athena: According to the few witnesses and dozens of security cameras and cell phones conveniently hijacked by London and Sherwood, at the time of the attempted theft, Athena had paused and was talking on her cell phone. The girl was smart enough to know that walking-and-talking was just as dangerous as driving-and-talking. The car with the Grandstone minions passed her three times before they made their move. After studying the video from multiple angles, it appeared they didn't attack right away because they were waiting for Freddie to get into position. He came from a coffee shop two blocks down, and apparently he was having his daily snit over his order not being right. He had exacting tastes when it came to his ten-dollar cup of high-calorie coffee. Sherwood caught the image from four different angles when Freddie carefully put down his cup before leaping to allegedly rescue Athena.

The guy at least took enough self-defense classes to make it look real when he dove in and used a couple fancy flips and kicks and arm twists to send the four minions running. Yes, I said *look real*, meaning it was staged. In slowing down the video, London and Athena both caught a half-dozen places where the minions leaned *into* Freddie's swing or kick.

My phone had caught two voices during the tussle. One said, "Time's up," and the other, Freddie, said, "Careful, that's cashmere."

Now, standing in the office, the gang spilled their gleeful, scornful report of all they had found out. The evidence kept piling up even higher against Freddie Grandstone being the hero of the hour. As if there could have ever been any doubt? Wallace and Cosmo and Doni kept shoving their cell phones and tablets in front of me, showing what London and Sherwood had just dug up.

"Okay, it's hilarious, but why are you getting me involved? Athena knows about all this fakery, doesn't she?"

"Yeah, London finally broke the interference, which she figures came from that car, but get this," Doni said. "Grandad thinks she should play along and let Freddie play Prince Charming, until we can figure out what he wants."

"Like, duh," Wallace grumbled, lowering his voice and making it sound like he had a major head cold. "The guy wants a tame computer genius in his back pocket."

"Not from what I've heard about the Grandstones. They think the way to a girl's brain is --" Cosmo gulped and went bright red, glancing at Doni, then at me. "Well, through satin sheets."

Wallace went white and I swear steam came out of his ears. Then he went an even darker red than Cosmo. The difference between caveman-level defensive fury over the woman he loved and an innocent geek's embarrassment. Cosmo and Doni were an item, and everyone was pretty sure it was for life, but she was still in high school and he was the epitome of clumsy, adorable chivalry.

"Dang, are we going to have to have three weddings this year?" I blurted. Honestly, I didn't mean to say it. It just slipped out.

Wallace went white again. Then pink. He sank down into one of the visitor chairs lined up against the railing that divided my level of the office from the one lower down.

"Is anyone following up on that interference, that kept London from warning Athena? What was she going to warn her about?" I asked, in mercy for Wallace. I had never seen the guy at a loss for words before. I took it as a good sign of his feelings for Athena.

"Yeah, Sherwood thinks it was some kind of tracking program and something to control communications. Badly put together," Cosmo added. "Like they were trying to tap into her phone, like for GPS. Blocking anyone from getting through was a side effect."

"That sounds like something the police need to know about. Have you told Gordon? They found the car, have they caught the guys in the car?"

"It's abandoned," Doni reported. "Sherwood found it and let Gordon know, and they're following all the security footage around town to track where the creeps went. Right now, Freddie is raising unholy heck with campus security and threatening to sue Neighborlee PD that something like this could happen in broad daylight. Who is the slimebag trying to fool?"

"He obviously thinks he can fool Athena," Wallace said. Something about him struck me as very grim under the regained calm. "Overdoing the gallant knight routine."

"He's asked her to have dinner with him five times already," Doni reported, glancing at her cell phone, where London was most likely keeping her updated. "He's tried a dozen times to get his hands on her backpack with her computer in it. London detected some kind of electronics hidden in the sleeves of his coat. Maybe something to try to hack into her computer."

"Maybe Athena isn't the target," I offered, and felt very cold as the idea came to me. "What if it's London and Sherwood? What if the Grandstones figured out there's more to the whole FlopDrop incident? What if they know London and Sherwood are people?"

"Whatever equipment he's carrying," London said, coming onto my computer screen, "the signal is weak enough that he would need physical contact with Athena's computer to establish a connection. Fortunately, she's smart enough to have it triply shielded and encrypted. And since the link to our network was taken down a year ago, all the fancy hacking he and his cohorts might try to come up with for the next ten years won't do them a lick of good."

"Good to know. But that still doesn't do anything about the guy slobbering over her," Wallace said.

"Do you honestly think Athena would let the guy get close enough for that?" Doni sneered.

"Where is she now?"

"Granddad had way too much fun, blowing a gasket and hauling her home to keep her safe. The Grandstones were burning up the phone lines trying to find someone who could come to the house and act as intermediary, since their aunt blew it so bad last year, trying to help Reggie get at me." She snorted, very unladylike, and her eyes sparkled.

I wondered how long that ploy would work, keeping Athena safe as the newest Grandstone target. One thing I knew for certain: the guardians needed to have a meeting. London agreed, and took care of notifying everyone. The gang went back to their dorms and home and I tried to focus on my tasks for the rest of the afternoon. I did have a job to do.

~~~~~

By the time the team met at Divine's Emporium that night, Col. Hayward had joined us. That made me wonder just who was keeping watch on Athena for him, and if so, why they weren't close enough to intervene when she was pseudo-attacked. The entire Longfellow family and the computer gang joined us. The Colonel's connections had lots of juicy data to add to what Athena's team had dug up to use against Freddie Grandstone.

With anyone else as a target, it might have been a clever plot, using the hero-to-the-rescue tactic. And yes, Freddie Grandstone could be charming to the point of melting even a sensible girl's brains. The Grandstones probably went to summer camp to take charm lessons.

Sherwood produced hundreds of emails, from temporary email accounts dismantled just hours before the attempted kidnapping. That had been the original plan, according to the earliest emails: kidnap Athena and get access to her computer while she was being terrorized. Freddie had changed the plans at the last minute. He had just gotten his car detailed, so he didn't want to chase down slushy and muddy streets and through the Metroparks to the place where he would cut off the kidnappers' car and force them out for a faked showdown. His cashmere coat wouldn't stand up to the slush.

At the bottom of all the communication, the arguments and
~~~~~

changed details, the target was indeed access to the hidden nexus of FlopDrop and control of London and Sherwood. Fortunately, the unnamed puppet masters giving Freddie orders to recruit Athena "by any means" didn't believe they were real, thinking people, with souls germinated from Doni and Cosmo. Just incredibly complex computer programs. They wanted Athena to join their organization, so they could control London and Sherwood, and generate more like them to add to their arsenal.

The frightening part? If the puppet masters were the Rivals, maybe they knew Sherwood and London could monitor the power defending Neighborlee. And maybe try to control it.

As a side note, Freddie was to determine if Athena had created London and Sherwood on her own. If not, then he had to determine who the true geniuses were. Only geniuses were wanted, and Freddie was to cut them off from the useless members of the team.

"Hey, I think those guys insulted us," Wallace said.

He had been holding Athena's hand since before they came into Divine's and we all gathered in the front room. Now that I could see the winkies, I saw how they stretched the walls out to make the room bigger, and even brought extra furniture through dimensional slits in the walls, so we could all sit down. Fascinating, but a little frightening. What else could they do, without warning, and what would happen if they weren't paying attention, and people were sitting in furniture they removed?

"They insulted all of us," London said through the computer sitting on the counter, where we all could see her and Sherwood looking back at us. "Granted, none of you actually did any of the programming that created us, but …" She smirked.

I was relieved that most of us could laugh. Looking around at our gathered team, I felt a little satisfaction and some sense of security, at our numbers. More important, I could clearly see some fatherly concern from Hayward to Athena. He had been waiting when she walked in the door. He gripped her shoulders and looked into her eyes a long moment, when he asked if she was really all right. I think Athena liked it. Knowing he had been checking up on her all her life helped ease a little of the resentment any kid would feel toward a father who chose not to be in her life. I still wasn't sure what communication Athena and Portia had had since the big revelation, but my feelings toward the oldest Longfellow girl had certainly changed. I had to hope Athena and her mother got along better now.

Guardians were asked to make a lot of sacrifices, and as Athena slid more into her duties and responsibilities, she was coming to learn that. And accept it. I just hoped Wallace wouldn't be one of the sacrifices expected of her someday.

Far down in the report, Hayward reluctantly revealed the discovery of new activity on the Halliday front. They were back to trying to gain custody of Doni, and thereby drain her trust fund before she turned eighteen. His allies had already thwarted several efforts to paint the Longfellows as kidnappers and brainwashers, and to manufacture evidence that Doni's parents did want her to marry Reggie Grandstone.

"Unfortunately, they've managed to track down some judges and lawyers who are on their side. Misogynistic, patriarchal old fools who think foot binding and chastity belts are common sense. As a Halliday, you are their property, essentially. They're calling in all sorts of archaic legal precedents to back up the claim that the use of the paternal name bestows all sorts of authority on them." He shook his head and waved his hand in front of his face like he was trying to get rid of something that smelled awful.

"I'll give them a legal precedent," Doni growled.

"Give them a black eye in the public eye," Angela said, sounding and looking as smugly serene as always. "If carrying the Halliday name bestows any kind of authority, then let Doni get rid of the name altogether. The wrangling over that little step will embarrass the Hallidays badly enough, they could be distracted from other concerns."

"Especially if their claim to authority over her depends on her name." Charlotte had a growing sparkle of malice in her eyes.

"Please?" Doni clasped her hands under her chin and wriggled in her chair, earning some chuckles from the rest of us. "Please, can I change my name? Pretty please?"

Chapter Two

"Suits me," Ford said. "I think your dad would be the first one to vote yes. In fact, I have a couple of letters from him and your mom, when they were talking about changing his name to Longfellow, after his family did something especially nasty or embarrassing. I can probably dig those up and use them as documentation that they both would approve."

"What are you going to be?" Felicity asked.

"Doni Longfellow, of course. That's what I've been all this time, anyway." Doni grinned and gave one more wriggle for emphasis before settling back in her seat.

"For a while, anyway." Cosmo went bright red. "I mean, you'll change your last name when we --" He didn't so much fade out as sort of choke and visibly stop breathing.

I swear, I could see the waves of heat rising off his face. It was cute. Especially when Doni went very still and her eyes went wide and sparkled, and she blushed the prettiest matching shade of pink that ever could have been seen.

Ah, young love.

We discussed the arrangements for Athena to join Bethany. Now we had even more reason for her being out of town. For all we knew, the Rivals might target Bethany next. They knew enough about us to target me. Granted there was some question of their intelligence if they kept relying on the Grandstones to run errands. Still, the safe tactic was to assume our enemies were smarter than they had proven so far. What if they could figure out from past events that Stephanie Miller had died fighting an interdimensional invader? They might try to get their hands on Bethany. We needed to get the two best friends together. They always had been each other's defenders.

"And I'll have some of my people keeping a watch on both girls," Hayward said.

"Like always?" Ford asked, raising one eyebrow so high it threatened to skid right off the top of his bald head.

"Not me, entirely. Portia has some connections and talents of her own." He winked at Athena, who had gone very still when he said her mother's name.

"One of these days, Mom and I are going to have a really long talk," Athena said, after a few seconds when the air almost buzzed with the intensity of her thoughts.

"I'll alert NORAD," Hayward said. That got a snort and a grin from her.

After that light moment, we got down to serious business. We had to, because Freddie Grandstone called me while I was sitting there at Divine's, and he was looking for Athena. That was a little scary, that he knew enough about me and my relationship with the Longfellows to hope I would know where she was. He had been calling the whole family, but they had his number blocked on all their cell phones.

It was time to get Athena out of his reach, before a Grandstone minion struck again, or worse, the Rivals got involved.

By Wednesday morning, we had Athena's tickets. Multiple trips, leaving the country, heading for Canada and Mexico, and several cruise lines. London sounded the alarm as soon as Athena got onto an airline site to book her plane tickets to fly out to join up with Bethany. Someone was watching for her next move. What was interesting was that they hadn't tracked down her particular presence online, but had all sorts of trigger codes downloaded into the airline's website. A quick check by Sherwood revealed that every major airline that serviced the northern half of Ohio was being watched. Athena couldn't even drive to Akron-Canton Airport or Toledo to catch her flight and avoid the notice of the nasties and her erstwhile sweetheart.

Poor Freddie. Every call he tried to place to Athena was cut off before the phone started to ring. It didn't matter if it was her dormitory phone, her cell phone, the Longfellow house landline. Gotta love having really alert, wicked-sense-of-humor AI's as allies.

Athena left town by car, with Hayward. He drove her to JFK, where she caught the first of an even dozen flights, hopscotching around the country. Meanwhile, London and Sherwood were having fun playing with the video cameras and surveillance systems in every hub airport in the country, convincing the watchers that Athena was about to board airplanes going in contradictory directions. If we had wanted to implement a major attack on the Rivals, that would have been the day, because they were distracted, trying to find out which Athena was the real one, so they could track her.

To cap everything off, Hayward gave Athena her very first fake I.D., complete with dogears and fading so her driver's license and credit cards and insurance card all looked like they had been well used and were ready to be replaced.

Yes, someone could accuse him of trying to make up for all the years he couldn't be active in his daughter's life. Someone else could ask why he bothered, since he had only been a sperm donor, and he had nothing to feel guilty about. But that was the kind of honorable guy Col. Franklin Hayward was. I think he enjoyed being a dad at long last.

Bethany was preparing to help Athena change her look, thanks to her friends in the makeup team for the movie she was making. Not just hair and eyes, but skin tone and build and the way she walked and talked. The rest of us would settle back and watch how intensely the Grandstones scrambled to try to track down Athena. Maybe we would discover the strings being pulled, to follow them back to the evil spider puppet masters. Hopefully clipping those strings would cripple our enemies even more.

At least, that was the plan. Things got weird and distracted me, so I wasn't really involved in all the cyber-spy work, which Hayward and his allies and Athena handled quite well. I got to enjoy the slide show later, when Bethany came home for a visit and treated us to all the pictures and videos of her and Athena's semi-under-cover adventures.

Thanks to less power being sucked away and more power building up in Neighborlee for our defensive purposes, I was getting leg tremors and prickling at the most inconvenient times. Winkies swarmed me at the most inconvenient times. It was one thing to be the only one in the room who could see them. It sometimes got pretty dang difficult to sit in a meeting at work and not swat at or laugh at the sparkling bits of light creating images in the air around my co-workers' faces.

Along with the winkies, Fae came to visit. Not Will and Phil, who I had gotten used to during their infrequent visits when I was younger. These were people who sort of ghosted their way through town. Gliding through the crowds of shoppers and people taking advantage of unseasonably nice weather to get outside and socialize or just get their steps in for the day. I recognized them by the trails of winkies. If that didn't confirm their identity for me, their pointy ears did.

Funny thing. Most of the Fae, I saw at Miller's Diner. They didn't seem to be making any effort to connect with Ben Miller. Who, I might add, displayed definite points in his ears. I hadn't seen those points until our New Year's battle with Big Ugly solved the whole power-siphon problem. (And created some new ones. The fluctuations as energy levels struggled for a new normal made my legs twitchy. A few times, I needed to get out of my wheelchair and walk, to get rid of the feeling, before I started screaming. However, I couldn't really explain to people the whole power field problem and how I might finish healing after all these years, now could I?)

I ate a lot of meals at Miller's, and encouraged co-workers to have our lunch breaks at the diner, just so I could keep watch on the pointy-eared visitors. It wasn't exactly a Star Trek convention, or LOTR fandom gone amok. Ben Miller didn't seem to notice anything unusual about his new customers. Maybe the Fae came in and clouded the minds of the wait staff while they helped themselves to food. I caught a lot of them checking out the rogue's gallery, as Stephanie had called the photo display of Miller family history down the back hallway.

Some of those photos went missing after the influx of Fae calmed down. Angela theorized the spell that made it possible for descendants of Fae to be seen in public without their ear points being noticed might have been failing in those photos. She referred to it as the "don't see me" spell, and ... honestly, that couldn't be right, could it? I mean, no, I didn't expect fancy foreign words along the lines of Tolkein's Elvin languages, but still, something a little more dignified? We were dealing with magic here, right?

While we were on the subject of the Fae, Angela assured me that Bethany had always had a few Fae "observers" since she left Neighborlee to pursue her rising star. They were keeping watch on her. Angela had requested extra vigilance for Athena's sake, since any threat that found Athena would latch onto Bethany. After all, if our enemies figured out enough to identify guardians, past and present, they might have the sensitivity to detect her mixed blood heritage.

After things calmed down more, Angela determined the real draw for bringing Fae into town was Eden. Our community center sat over a huge clump of the collected magic that defended our town. Like, duh? We all knew that already. We figured that was the reason Big Ugly or the Oil Slick, if they weren't the same, had manifested at New Year's, caused time slips, and drained people.

The Fae were in town to conduct scientific studies of the shift in power flow and usage and analyze what had gone wrong over the years, to allow the enemy to siphon it away. If Big Ugly or some other enemy had been able to use the energy for their own nefarious ends, or if they had been draining it to make sure the guardians couldn't use it, no one was sure yet. It might take years of study. Then Angela gave me the disquieting news that the Fae experienced time differently than Humans did. Fae time wasn't along the lines of how God experienced time, while living outside of time, being a non-linear person. The Fae could spend years sequestered in their enclaves, living separated from Earth's time stream, and step through a portal to Earth and find out that only a few months had passed. Or they could go home for a weekend and return to Earth to find a century had passed. Sometimes Fae who had chosen to settle among Humans, or just to "vacation" among us for a few years, would get into serious trouble, send up a metaphorical signal flare for help, and none would come for weeks, months, or years. Then when help showed up, they would discover that the people back home had just gotten the SOS and had come as quickly as they could. There was that lovely time differential. So when the Fae said it could take years to decipher what had happened, what had gone wrong, how to prevent it happening in the future, Angela had no idea if it was years in Earth time, years in Fae enclave time, or any reliable translation between the two.

At least I knew why those people were skulking around town, and I decided to take it as a good sign when their numbers decreased to the point I wasn't seeing clouds of attendant winkies everywhere I turned.

Of course, maybe they were still there, but I didn't see them when I became seriously distracted with a new problem.

~~~~~

Thursday after we got Athena safely out of town, I went out at lunchtime. Deliberately. I was in a snarky mood and *wanted* to be
~~~~~

accosted by Freddie Grandstone, who was starting to look a little frantic as he wandered the streets of Neighborlee, looking for "his" sweet Athena. Seriously? The guy obviously never met Athena Longfellow. Yes, she was always a good girl. Smart. Funny. Loyal. Determined. Sassy. Innocent in many things. "Sweet"? Nope. Not the way Grandstones applied it. For them, sweet equaled stupid, gullible and malleable. Not my Athena!

My mission was frustrating him. I so much wanted to stare him down and tell him, in complete honesty, that I didn't know where Athena was. Because I didn't. She wasn't due at Bethany's shooting location for another five or six hours.

No Freddie appeared. Maybe the dweeb knew I was looking for him? Grandstones had to have some kind of defensive radar, to have lasted so long, despite all their failures. Maybe that showed how desperate the Rivals were that they hadn't wiped out the Grandstone clan as an unreliable weapon.

However, that was the day I ran into Jane Wilson, finalizing her paperwork to take over the Spindelmutter building and set up her spa, and fulfill the visions I had had long before Christmas. After our conversation, I remembered her and made my guess about her being the person I saw in my dream/vision, when I watched someone rescue Hayward, Steve and Toby.

I nearly had those thoughts driven out of my head when I got back to the office and listened to a message on my phone.

My past came back to haunt me, with a vengeance. The voicemail was from a classmate I barely remembered, from a class I wished I could forget, first semester of my senior year of college.

"Hey, Lynny, it's Harrison Kamel from the 'commercial psych practices' class at WBC. Long time no hear, huh?"

I couldn't remember the name right off, but the class, I did remember. Utter misery. I was glad I hadn't been there to take the call. I wanted to delete the message right there, but I had been working at the *Tattler* long enough to have a sense for phone messages that I needed to hear through to the end. The end always contained the dangerous portion. So I kept listening. Hopefully, the worst of the call would be to find out he was on his way in to visit me. Hopefully, I had time to go out another door.

"Commercial psych practices" was exactly what it sounded like. I took it only to fulfill requirements for my teaching certificate.

I got twice the credits for half the time spent in the classroom because it was an experimental class. Seriously, I should have taken warning from the "experiment" those poor professors had tried to carry off on the entire freshman class, my first year of college. Despite that, I took the class to get those credits and have more time for guardian duties. And yeah, there was this guy I started dating. That didn't end well, either. The class basically studied how to use psychology for commercial practices, such as advertising.

I still couldn't remember Harrison or his project.

"You were part of my testing group."

I was in a lot of testing groups. If we weren't theorizing and setting up experiments, then we earned our credits by being tested, usually by filling out reams of questionnaires or watching videos with electrodes attached to our heads.

"I think you'll be very interested to know that I parlayed my relationship analysis program --"

Oh, dang. Him. Mr. Computers-will-do-all-the-dirty-work-and-let-you-get-to-know-someone-twice-as-quickly-with-half-the-fuss.

" -- into a matchmaking program. I've been in business a couple years now, and doing very well, if I do say so myself." He gave the name of his company. Even though I had heard of it, serving the higher economic bracket of the East Side, I hadn't heard much of anything about the company, good or bad.

"Anyway," he continued after a short pause. Like maybe he expected me to pick up, all excited about his programming genius and financial success? Was this guy expecting me to be all gaga for him? (Maybe gag-gag.) "Just for grins and giggles --"

Yeah, I remembered him now. What a stupid line!

" --I still had your profile from that class project. Heck, I have everybody's profile. I put them all into the program, just to see what or who would pop out. Hey, Lanie, I found your perfect match. Now, as a favor to an old college pal, normally I'd charge two big ones for the basic level service."

I certainly hoped that when he said "big ones" he meant hundred, and not thousand. Because if he did, and if he expected to get paid for something I didn't ask for, I was going to break every vow of ethics controlling the superheroes in all those comic books I read growing up. I would sabotage all those computers he loved so much. And that was just for starters.

"But for you, it's free."

"Better believe it's free, considering he put your private information into his system without your permission," Conrad growled, from about five feet behind me.

Yes, I jumped about four inches straight up out of my chair. The guy had snuck up on me. Just how often did that happen? I usually could tell when someone was watching me, trying to eavesdrop on me, or just plain sneak up on me.

For those coming in late to my series of confessions about life as a semi-pseudo-superhero, Conrad was a school friend, my boss at the newspaper, the *Neighborlee Tattler*, and had managed to convince my college roommate to marry him during a brief period of insanity. Hers, not his. Marrying Clarice was probably the smartest and sanest thing he ever did in his life.

"Just give the word," Harrison continued. "I'll flip the switch and let your Romeo know you're there, and send you on over his vital stats. Hey, I'm a firm believer in women having the right to make the first move." His greasy chuckle brought up a handful of college memories I would rather had stayed lost in forgetfulness.

To be fair, Harrison wasn't really a greasy character. He wasn't really that unethical or manipulative, either. He was just kind of thoughtless, and when he got his sights focused on a prize, it was hard to stop him from going for it. He tripped over a lot of people and got his toes stomped on. I really had to feel sorry for the guy, because he meant well. He just couldn't figure out things like proper procedures and privacy and personal space.

"Pretend you never got the message," Conrad said, when I reached up to my phone and ended the playback.

After Harrison gave me his phone and email, and then a condensed version of his spiel, then the phone and email again. Like I could forget, with shivers of horror trickling down my back and ruining the really good lunch I had just eaten?

"What, blame the equipment?" I turned my chair around to face him. Conrad was slouched into one of the chairs the trio had used on Monday to report on Athena's faked attack.

"It's convenient. Which is why I keep saying no to the new owner, who wants to upgrade all our equipment." He shrugged and gave me a thin sort of smile. "If you call the guy back, even if it's to say no, you will never hear the last of him. He screwed up big-time, using your information, and he's scrambling to keep from getting in trouble. No," he hurried to say, when I reached for the button to open up the voicemail controls. "You want that message to use against him if things get out of hand."

"Like what?" I shook my head and waved my hand to stop him when he opened his mouth to respond. "Don't even say it. Saying it aloud makes it possible. I can think of a dozen awful things that could happen. I'll transfer the message to my email and send it home, then delete it from here."

~~~~~

I didn't have to try to get all those awful matchmaking possibilities and scenarios out of my head. Weirdness descended the next day and demanded all my attention.

Maybe this was proof that despite the huge strides we had made in beating back the Rivals and keeping them from contacting Big Ugly, sometimes the reverberations from trouble just continued for a while. Or more accurately, not reverberations but fallout, or collateral damage. That was why Col. Hayward and Rodney had been working since New Year's, trying to track down where Rodney and the Terrible Trio had been kept prisoner and trained for the war that Neighborlee had certainly never declared.

I mean, be honest, anyone who tries to come up against Angela and our duty to protect Neighborlee from the world and protect the world from the wonderful weirdness of Neighborlee, they've entered a war they're not going to win. In the long run, anyway.

The battle at New Year's had unsettled the power flow when it stopped the energy drain. The same energy drain had contributed to Stephanie Miller dying, and me not healing completely when I broke my back. And maybe contributed to Big Ugly influencing the Terrible Trio to do that totally stupid, suicidal Senior Prank Night stunt in the first place. The reverberations from waves of power spilling back against Neighborlee and meeting the buildup of energy where there hadn't been any or enough for years ... that had some long-term effects. Some of the defensive shields that kept most wackos away seemed to thin out. That Friday afternoon was case in point. I called him Snow Commando.

Conrad and I went out for lunch to talk about some changes he wanted to make in the schedule for paper production. With Sheridan Communications now running things, we had to get some steps of the process done sooner. A delay that only minimally
~~~~~

inconvenienced us in the past now could impact a dozen other newspapers. As copy editor, I was technically an assistant editor, so Conrad valued my opinion. We were talking about ideas for the usual Valentine's Day mush-and-gush-and-overspending promotions (Conrad's words) when we came into the office. I was laughing at a joke Conrad suggested to add to my routine, relating to Valentine's. I didn't see the guy sitting on the floor in front of Matilda's desk until I was already inside and tipping my chair to knock the snow off the wheels. Conrad was behind me, having held the door open. His laughter stopped short like it had been turned off with a switch. It reminded me a little too much of several people vanishing and reappearing at New Year's, so I turned to look for him and make sure he hadn't disappeared.

Then I realized what I had just seen. A big guy who looked like a poster for the Russian breeding program, in full camo snow gear—white and gray, with snow goggles perched up on top of his furry cap, the big ear flaps pulled up, boots, heavy gloves and knee-length coat, and a backpack next to him. He sat on the floor, legs sticking out in front of him, boots dripping sludge onto the tile floor. That melting snow meant he hadn't been indoors very long.

"Are you the boss?" The guy had a deep, crackling voice. I swear, the furniture in the waiting area moved a little, like he started an earthquake just by talking.

"That's me." Conrad didn't hold out his hand, and he didn't give his name. Sometimes his survival instincts overrode the good manners he maintained as part of his PR image for the paper. "Is there a problem?" He didn't look at Matilda as he spoke, but I knew he was asking for her side of the story.

"I gotta talk to Terry."

"There's no one named Terry here. I'm sure our receptionist told you that."

"Doesn't mean Terry isn't coming in here."

"We don't have any employees named Terry." Conrad grasped the handles of my wheelchair. He never did that except when he needed a good excuse to get out of a room before a bomb went off. Or some psycho decided to pull a sub-machine gun out of thin air.

Considering the size of that backpack sitting inside the curve of Snow Commando's arm, that was a very likely possibility. Even in Neighborlee.

"If you'll excuse me, I need to help —"

"Terry, who writes the advice column. I gotta talk to her. She's the only one I can trust."

"That's a column that comes from our parent company in the newspaper chain." Conrad squeezed my shoulder, probably a silent warning not to say anything.

Who, me? My momma didn't raise no blabbermouth fool!

"It's syndicated into a dozen papers. It's not written here," I added.

Technically, that was true. I wrote my *Terry* columns at home. Some lawyer would probably argue that since I lived in the same town as the newspaper office, even though I got my email with the advice requests from the main office, technically Conrad was lying when he said the *Terry* column wasn't written "here," meaning Neighborlee.

With any luck, we wouldn't have to involve lawyers in this little problem.

"Then call headquarters and tell Terry to come out here. It's important." Then this guy pulled handcuffs from one of the multiple utility pockets on his parka. He slapped one loop against his wrist, so the handcuff went around it and locked.

My first thought was that he was going to handcuff himself to one of us. Probably me, because gimps made the best helpless hostages, right? The pity factor.

"I'm not leaving until she talks to me." Then this guy leaned over, reached for the fence around the reception area, and slapped the other end of the handcuff against the top railing.

Correction: he *tried* to slap the other loop of the handcuffs on the railing. I gave a hard mental yank on the handcuff and he missed. For good measure, I pulled on the arm bracing him, so he went face-down on the wet tile, into a trail of boot melt. He lay stunned for all of three seconds. Conrad pushed me up the short ramp to my office level and shoved me supposedly out of the line of fire. Yeah, like being a couple yards away would do any good if the guy opened up with a machine gun, a grenade or a small, hand-held atomic bomb?

"Police," he whispered, and turned back to face the loony.

I reached for my cell phone in my purse, intending to dial, but my telekinesis required a lot of concentration. Meaning I couldn't simultaneously dial and yank the loony's hand away from the fence when he tried a second time. And a third time. Matilda vanished into the circulation office. I prayed she was calling the police instead of the common sense move of running for another door. We had lots of doors at our office. Over the years the newspaper had taken over several connecting units in our building. I was too busy building up a headache and watching this escapee from some bad military movie try to make like a 60s protestor.

I guess it never occurred to him that the little wrought iron fence was mostly decoration and wasn't anchored well — the posts just sat in holes drilled through the tile into the cement, slab-on-grade. It wasn't the sturdiest fence, either, thanks to dozens of previous loonies who had leaned on it and kicked it and tried to knock it over or pull it up. A few whacks with a hammer would knock the rail loose, so we could slide his handcuff off with ease, long before someone might show up with the key to unlock the handcuffs. Not that I was going to let him connect the handcuffs to begin with.

"Hold it!" Conrad raised his voice so it bounced off the ceiling. It was a good thing that renovation with acoustical tiles never got done, because his voice bounced nicely and covered up the sound of Matilda talking with someone on the phone. "What do you need to say to Terry? Can we just pass it on to her?"

"No. I can't trust you. You'd tell them." He hunched his shoulders and leaned over like he hid something against his chest.

"Who is 'them'?" I had to ask. Okay, bad grammar, but there seemed to be no way of phrasing that question correctly to please everybody. So sue me.

"You know." He glared at me for about three seconds, then bowed his head again. At least he had given up trying to handcuff himself to the fence. Which was a relief, because I had a headache. Lifting something big and moving it a few feet is a lot easier than the fine control of repeatedly maneuvering something as small as a handcuff from twenty feet away, believe me.

"If I knew, I wouldn't be asking you. If I don't know who you're talking about, then chances are good I wouldn't be able to tell 'them.' Ever think of that?"

Conrad glanced at me and gave me that wide-eyed, *What are you doing? Do you want to get us blown up?* look. Come to think of it, that was the same look he gave me when I interrupted the quiet dinner he was having with my college roommate, just before he proposed to her. In my defense, how was I supposed to know? It was a whirlwind romance, but Conrad had never struck me as a whirlwind kind of guy, so I thought a crackpot customer who had driven his pickup truck through the plate glass window of the office might be a higher priority than a dinner with Clarice. I admit, that time I was wrong. But at least they always had a good story to tell at their anniversary party.

I doubted this situation was similar to the truck-wreck-and-jaws-of-life-versus-proposal choice. That was Conrad, making a national security crisis out of something simple and easy.

"Yeah, you might be right." Snow Commando frowned, his single eyebrow drawing down so it nearly made his eyes vanish. I could almost smell the smoke as the gears burned up inside his head from all that thinking.

The door crashed open and Gordon bulled his way inside, stomping snow off his feet and making enough ruckus to shake the whole building. Let me point out: Gordon, for all his Grizzly bear size, could move with the grace of a ballet dancer and as silent as all those hokey Ninja movies. So Conrad and I were stunned.

Fortunately, so was the loony sitting on the floor at Conrad's feet. He stared at Gordon, who was red-faced and wearing some silly penguin earmuffs Mandy got him for Christmas on a dare. (I was the one who dared her.) It was hard to notice the police uniform parka when a guy topping 300 pounds of muscle bulldozed through the door with penguin heads on his ears.

"Hey, Lanie, gotta talk to you about the wedding." Gordon ignored Conrad and Snow Commando. "Mandy's folks are driving us nuts, and we haven't even picked out the date. How serious were you about us having a Trek-themed wedding?" He stomped his size nineteen boots and headed through the office toward my section.

All of which told me Gordon had gotten the call about the guy wanting to talk to Terry. He had the kind of alertness that would have noticed the tension in the air twenty feet before he walked through the door. He should have changed course, come in the back door, and ambushed the guy. So coming in the front door was part of his plan. I hoped.

"Hey," the loony in question sputtered, and got to his feet.

Maybe he was jealous, with all the attention yanked off him. Or maybe the way Gordon could step right over the decorative fence.

"Got a problem, son?" Gordon turned and came back to the fenced-in area. He held out a hand. "Hey, name's Gordon. What's yours?"

Gordon proved he was a true descendant of a Lost Kid. He had to have some kind of superpower, that enabled him to hold out his hand, smiling and giving off a totally harmless impression despite the uniform and well, just looking like Gordon. For a guy that big to look harmless and friendly when his Godzilla-with-a-shave face was red from the cold and he was wearing a uniform, that took superpowers. Maybe telepathic. Because I swear, he *willed* the loony to take the hand he held out to shake.

Gordon snagged the guy's hand.

Twisted him around.

Stepped over the fence.

Got hold of the wrist with the handcuff hanging off it.

Cuffed the guy with his own handcuffs.

In five seconds flat. Maybe less.

"Everybody okay here?" Gordon said, just as calm and friendly as he had been ten seconds ago.

"My hero," I gushed, holding my fists underneath my chin and fluttering my eyelashes at him. Gordon glared, fighting a grin. Conrad sighed and sank down on the edge of Matilda's desk. She came back into the room and sat down at her desk as if nothing had happened. So maybe that meant we had more than one crazy person in the room.

"If you want advice from Terry," Conrad said, as Gordon maneuvered the ashen-faced commando into a chair in the waiting area, "write her a letter like everybody else."

"But I don't want them to find out I'm asking for help," the loony said, and burst into tears.

Chapter Three

"Who?" I slid down the ramp and stopped a good eight feet away from him. Just in case he had a madman's strength and broke the handcuffs before lunging at me. "If Terry answers your letter, it gets printed in the paper, so everybody reads it."

That stopped him in mid-wrenching sob. He blinked away his tears, sniffed a few times, then looked up at Gordon, who managed to look sympathetic. Another superpower. Definitely.

"The commander." He shrugged, trying to gesture at his gear without using his hands. So this guy was genuine military? He hadn't just been on a shopping spree at the local Army-Navy surplus store? That was kind of frightening, considering guys like this were supposed to be trusted with rounds of ammo and explosives and nuclear weapons.

"Army, Navy, Air Force, Marines?" Conrad guessed. He groaned, frustrated, when the guy nodded to all his questions. "Why don't you want your commander to know you're looking for love advice?"

"Not love advice." He reverted to head bowed and shoulders hunched. "These guys from my unit, they got in trouble here."

"Toby Malone?" I guessed. Maybe not that much of a guess, because the only other military I knew was Col. Hayward, and he wasn't the kind of guy who got in trouble with higher-ups.

I hit paydirt, because the guy went white and nodded and his eyes filled up with tears again.

"I'm the one they were hunting. Whatever they were after, it doesn't exist," I said, hoping and praying this wasn't another guy sent to bring me back for a mad scientist's dissection project.

Speaking of Hayward, I needed to make a call to him ASAP. This was useful new data on the Rivals and their reach and powers of infiltration. If this guy was genuine military, then the Rivals had roots or tentacles everywhere. Which made me pause for half a second and wonder how this guy got away to try to warn us.

Unless he was another nasty trick of the Rivals, following up on the Terrible Trio, to find out where they were? Or just testing us to see how much we knew. Or if the capture had been a total fluke.

My head hurt and I really wished I had indulged in that hot peanut butter fudge sundae at lunch.

"Did they hurt you?" Snow Commando asked, his voice breaking a little. His eyes widened as he looked me over and nodded at my wheelchair. Like it was the first time he noticed it.

What did that say about the state of our military, that he hadn't seen my wheelchair until then? Hopefully, this guy wasn't legitimate military, but a dupe of the Rivals.

I really needed to call Hayward.

"Lanie was hurt before that trio got here," Gordon said. "Let me get him back to the station, and we'll call the same folks who were planning on helping Toby." He hauled the guy to his feet, and when he let go, the commando slid down to the ground again, trembling like a gelatin dessert about to split down the middle.

My cell phone rang right then, with Kurt's name displayed. I had to take it. Besides, I was tired of the floor show.

Kurt was on his way over to Eden to talk with the folks doing follow-up on the testing for toxic substances. Of course, outsiders wanted to blame the odd events at New Year's on drugs in the food. Or tampering with the ventilation system. Or fumes building up in the soil and toxic substances filtering through the water and whatever. Since Kurt had been trying to fix the malfunctions that had been reported before New Year's Eve, the people doing the testing and sampling wanted to talk to him. There were rumors some doctors wanted to take test samples of the people who spent the most time in the building. Such as Kurt, Gina, the maintenance staff, the people who had helped set up for the party. Joy.

I told him what had happened, and he agreed, Hayward needed to hear about this. I promised him I'd call Angela in the meantime.

While I was talking with Kurt, Gordon's backup showed up and hauled away Snow Commando. Gordon stayed behind to check through the backpack. It looked like the guy had planned on staying in our office until Terry showed up to talk to him. Gordon unloaded a sleeping bag, military-issue ration packets, a mess kit, some heating tabs, some chemical light rods. At the bottom of the backpack, where it wouldn't have done him any good if he needed it (fortunately), was a nasty-looking pistol. And lots of cartridges.

"I think I'll go call Mandy," Gordon said, after putting everything back in the backpack. "Right now, eloping sounds a lot safer for both of us."

"For the record," I had to say, "I wasn't the one pushing for the Trek-themed wedding. It was that girl who was dating Riley, before he went over the edge and started coercing money out of kids."

"Come again?" Conrad grinned as he stepped closer. "This is a story I haven't heard."

"And there's a good reason," I retorted.

Conrad leaned on my desk. If he thought he was intimidating me, he should have had second thoughts. And third. Still, I couldn't resist that grin of his. I needed some silliness after what we had just gone through. Gordon helped me tell the story of Riley, who wanted to build a life-size model of the *Enterprise*. On the ground. Seriously? Just what kind of support structure would that need, since only the engineering section would be touching the ground? He had talked gullible kids into giving him money, until we had to cut him off from the club to avoid legal repercussions.

"This is not for public consumption, you understand," I said when we finished.

"Who, me?"

"I have been accused of hiding bodies where they can never be found," Gordon said, with a perfectly straight face.

That toned down Conrad's smile by about seventy-five percent. He still chuckled a few times as he walked back to his office. Gordon just shook his head and walked away.

My phone pinged an hour later. Hayward texted me, wanting to know if I was all right. Snow Commando was not genuine military, but he thought he was. One of Hayward's allies had been tailing him since he broke away from a temporary Rivals base more than two months ago, and thanks to Gordon and some paperwork prepared weeks ago, they now had him in custody.

No, he didn't tell me all that in the texts. I found out all that information the next day, when we had another guardians meeting. What mattered was that Hayward knew what had happened and he was concerned about me. I told him I was all right and he suggested I go to Angela's, and maybe bring my brothers, to stay with her until we could be sure the Rivals hadn't followed Snow Commando's trail to Neighborlee and to me.

Gee, I was all right until he texted that.

He was right, though.

Angela was waiting when we got to Divine's. Hayward warned her. The house expanded the guest room down the side hall from her apartment. That didn't freak me out as much as it should have. Maybe I was becoming immune to how Divine's was much bigger inside than outside. Or maybe since the guest room shouldn't have been there at all, because it "budded" off the house, it didn't bother me more when the guest room turned into two, with a shared bathroom. One room had a bunkbed for my brothers, and the other had a bed built into the wall. The view, when I slid aside the thick drapery, was a moonlit meadow in some other time or place. Maybe it looked into the same world as the garden that I had glimpsed through the wallpaper on the second floor landing.

We made pizza, Felicity and Kurt came over, and we talked late into the night. We discussed the questions of Jane Wilson and what Hayward would tell us when he joined us the next day. Then there were the implications of Snow Commando coming to check on me. A trick of the Rivals? Signs of them losing power or control over their puppets? Would Snow Commando turn out to be another Lost Kid, who had lost his mind thanks to Rivals conditioning? And where exactly did Jane fit into this whole thing, and the mysterious organization that had raised her, Hoax, Inc.? I kind of liked their name, but it bothered me a little that they seemed to be focused on doing what my own parents did: investigating the weird and wonderful and debunking most of it.

Were they protecting the true magic in the world, and protecting the world from the dangerous magical things, like Mum and Pop had done since before I met them? If so ... how come Hoax hadn't made contact and formed an alliance with Angela and the guardians? Did that note left with Hayward, when he was returned after being rescued from the Rivals, mean Hoax was reaching out to us at long last?

And just what did that portend for us? Was it a good development, or a sign that we, the guardians and all we protected ... were in trouble?

~~~~~

Rodney came with Hayward for the meeting on Saturday. He looked about four hundred percent better than on New Year's Eve.
~~~~~

Being essentially a battery for members of the Rivals to do their dirty work had to be a bum deal for him. What kind of semi-pseudo-superhero power was that to have? Yes, he could start fires, and that could come in handy. But not the part where others drained him until he resembled a concentration camp survivor. Rodney's freedom and regained health alone made me kind of glad we went through all that mess at New Year's.

We learned that Snow Commando's real name was Henry O'Shay. He was not a Lost Kid. In fact, he had a humongous family, and they were all very proud that he was on a long-term secret mission for a national security agency that could not be named. That was the story Hayward came up with. Henry had been in Jay Parker's unit and saw too much, so the Rivals grabbed him when they confiscated Jay. Well didn't that just suck, being observant and intelligent enough to question and know something was wrong?

Henry resisted a lot of the mind training the Rivals put him and the trio through. Not all of it, but enough to make him interesting to them. And yes, to us. We could use someone like him on our side. Rodney had met him while Jay and the others were being trained for the investigatory assault on me. So when Rodney vouched for Hayward, Henry trusted him. Which made it a lot easier to handle Henry, because the guy had major commando skills. Another reason for the Rivals to snag him and try to turn him into a brainless, devoted foot soldier.

Henry also had the mental strength, despite the anguish the Rivals put him through, to remember where he had been and what he had seen. That made him valuable in tracking down at least one Rivals storage depot, for records and equipment. He was more than willing to help take down the bad guys.

So that left us to deal with Jane Wilson. Since she was going to need someone to handle renovations inside her shop and turn it into that spa I so desperately needed (not just for me, but as bride gifts for Mandy and Felicity), we agreed that Kurt would sign on as her handyman. That way he could study her close up and determine just what she was and whose side she was on. And figure out what semi-pseudo-superhero gifts she had, to earn the moniker of Ghost, back in Fendersburg.

~~~~~

When things happen too easily, operations run too smoothly,
~~~~~

common sense and experience tell us to be doubly careful and downright skeptical.

So when Hayward's team got into the Rivals storage depot on Sunday night without any problem, we all were waiting for a bomb to go off somewhere else. Or maybe the depot would go up with the only truly trained military personnel on "our side." And wasn't it awful that we were consciously thinking about "sides" and all the ugliness of a war being declared without our knowledge or permission or cooperation?

Monday evening, though, we got word that nothing had happened to anyone who went in. They were still exploring the underground complex and hauling out boxes and crates of files. Apparently, the Rivals didn't store anything electronically or share it over the Internet. Which explained the paucity of information London and Sherwood had been able to scare up. If it wasn't accessible through the electronic world, they couldn't touch it.

Hayward called to report on their progress, and to warn me to keep my distance from Daniel Sheridan, whenever he returned to town. There were entire rooms of files on Sheridan family members and Sheridan Communications activities.

"Even if he and his family are totally innocent, it might be wise to maintain as much distance from them as possible," he said.

"Even *if?*" I hated how my mind snagged on that. It conveyed so much he hadn't said. Considering how careful Hayward usually was with his words, I had to wonder if he had said that deliberately to get my imagination churning with horrified possibilities.

Dang, I guess I really did like Daniel Sheridan and consider him a friend. And not just because I desperately needed to keep him as Communications Officer for my Star Trek club.

"I'm sorry, Lanie. Our preferred theory is that these people did such an intensive study of the entire clan because they knew they were descendants of Lost Boys, and because they wanted to recruit them and their communications empire. Maybe this was all to help Sylvia Grandstone snag him and drag him to the altar."

"What, like blackmail?" I felt a little queasy, and I wished he hadn't called so soon after dinner.

"I'm sorry. Again. You deserve a heads up, in case we uncover something … inconvenient, once we dig through what is turning out to be several tons of paperwork and photos and …" He sighed, and I envisioned him raking a hand through his stubbly gray hair.

They also serve who run interference.

~~~~~

Tuesday was mercifully quiet. That wasn't much comfort, because Hayward would probably wait until I got home from work to have a phone call report. Or ask me to go to Divine's, to have a conference.

Instead, when I pulled into the driveway, Felicity and Jake were waiting, looking pretty excited. For a few seconds, I was confused. Then I had to drag my brain off the Rivals-are-ready-to-drop-a-bomb-on-us mental track. If they had gotten news before me -- highly unlikely -- they wouldn't look excited. Even if it was good news.

Then I knew, and my stomach dropped and my blood started to freeze over in horror: Felicity had picked out bridesmaid dresses, or she wanted to show me something frilly and fussy she had picked out for the wedding. But… Jake wouldn't be needed for that. If she had convinced him he had to be involved in every silly little detail of the wedding, he wouldn't be grinning like that. My next thought was: *Please, Lord, let them tell us they just eloped and they're about to go off on their honeymoon?*

Their news was that the Willoughby House had become available. This was one humongous old mansion desperately in need of renovations, sitting on a high point overlooking the Metroparks. It was about twice the size of Divine's Emporium, and part of the back yard had fallen down into the Metroparks during a flood that eroded part of the cliff face. It was probably the oldest building in Neighborlee; brick and sandstone, when everything else in its time period had been built of wood and either rotted from neglect or got torn down for renovations and modernization or burned down.

Yes, the oldest geezers and the historical society still talked about the great Neighborlee Fire. Not to be confused with the Chicago Fire by any means, but a big enough catastrophe when the entire downtown area had been turned to charred rubble. Like Rome, there were a good number of people who suspected that the biggest land baron of those days (a Grandstone, of course) had set fire to the entire downtown area to force people to sell their now-worthless property to him. He vanished during the fire, so he
~~~~~

wasn't there to face charges or get lynched.

The Willoughby House had been brooding over the Metroparks all our lives. Kurt and Felicity and I had investigated it a few times in our high school years. I remembered now what I had seen then, so I couldn't understand now how Felicity could be so excited about gutting and renovating the place. Humongous and drafty and dirty and signs of animals nesting in it and probably twenty miles of drywall that had to be replaced and another twenty miles of carpet that had to be pulled up. This was one of those situations where I was glad I was in a wheelchair and couldn't help with any grunt work or renovations.

Half the big old house would be Jake's offices and staging area for his security company. The other half would be their home and an animal sanctuary. I did understand Felicity's excitement about being that close to the Metroparks. There was a steep, natural stairway of sandstone going down into the park, and I just bet they would easily get permission from the city to excavate and create a driveway going down, or maybe build a switchback stairway for easier access. Felicity's dogs would have the biggest back yard in the world to roam in. As long as they stayed away from the Parr course and other areas where people would normally hike, who cared where they left their piles and how late into the night or early morning hours they barked and howled?

Kurt pulled into my driveway about then and joined us. Felicity and Jake had called him and asked him to come over. They wanted his input on something, but wouldn't say what. They started over in their explanation as soon as Kurt got out of his truck. We looked at each other and rolled our eyes and smiled as Felicity and Jake took turns gushing about the purchase and their plans and showed us their floor plans. They already had long lists of things they were going to do, and the order in which they had to be done. Priority was getting a price estimate and approval from City Council and all the various boards that had to grant approvals. They forgot about the historical society, of course.

"You realize, somebody is going to raise the roof about you changing anything. It's the oldest house in town and they're going to scream bloody murder if you don't preserve something to show what pre-Civil War Neighborlee was like," I said.

"Hadn't thought about that," Jake said, nodding, that

thoughtful look in his eyes. I shouldn't have been fooled. "Do your folks have any friends on the society's board of directors? Anybody you can talk to? Come on, they basically took their hands off the place years ago. If they want us to preserve the place, they have to fork over some money to help with the restoration."

"There's gotta be a statute of limitations or something," Felicity added.

"I can talk to Mrs. Colworthy," I said, thinking out loud. "She's the most reasonable one. Meaning she's willing to consider expenses and weigh them against how much they want history to be preserved."

Yeah – unlike some of the hardliners, who demand that history be preserved, down to using the same brand of varnish and nails the founding fathers used, whether those brands even existed anymore, and yet refuse to give one penny to help with the work.

"You're the best!" Felicity gushed.

I realized then I had been royally set up. Kurt grinned at me, but he had the decency not to say anything.

Considering I didn't have to look at bridesmaid dresses or get roped into a discussion of colors and decorations, I got off pretty easily, all told.

When we split up for the night, we had our assignments. I was going to sweet-talk the historical society into easing up on possible demands that the Willoughby House be preserved as a historical monument, instead of a residence and business. I knew I could ask for Angela's help in that regard. It turned out she had pointed out to Jake and Felicity that the abandoned mansion was perfect for their needs. If I had known that, I wouldn't have worried at all.

~~~~~

Wednesday, I met up with Mandy for dinner before going to church. Lucky me, I was asked to speak about newspaper writing, for the youth group. Once a month, instead of playing in the gym or youth band practice after Wednesday night Bible study, the youth leaders had career night. With only twelve chances out of the year, I would have thought I would have escaped for a little longer.

Anyway, Mandy asked me to meet her at Miller's Diner. As soon as I scooted my wheelchair up to the table in the back corner, Mandy let loose.

"Were you joking when you talked to Gordon about the Trek-
~~~~~

themed wedding?"

"Uh yeah … kind of. Why?" I didn't have to touch her to get a strong wave of frustration and the sense she was holding back either a scream or a gusher of tears. Mandy in tears could not be a pretty sight. In fact, I had the feeling it could be downright frightening. "The family? Gordon let something slip, but I didn't know if it was his family or yours --"

"Both of them. My mother is already nuts, and she's going to drive me nuts. She keeps changing her mind about the décor and I swear, I thought Gordon's mother was her best friend in the world, but she keeps making these sideways, snarky remarks about how she wouldn't know that shade of blue if it punched her in the eye and …" Mandy shook her head, then kind of slumped forward and rested her face in her palms, with her elbows on the table.

"Is eloping an option?"

"Only if we never return to Neighborlee," she said, her voice muffled in her hands.

"So are you opting for the Trek theme because …"

"Because both families have already sworn if we do that, they won't help and they won't come, and that's the only way we're going to be able to enjoy our wedding day. Because it's *ours*, not theirs, but everybody has forgotten that!" she said, finally raising her head from her hands.

"So … you want me to be your wedding planner?"

"No." Mandy gave me the *well, duh!* look, or maybe it was the *Have you checked your medication levels lately?* look. Either way, she used them both quite often when dealing with the fun insanity of our club meetings. Then she grinned and about 500 pounds of tension shredded and dropped off her, and she slumped back in her chair.

"I swear, Gordon's mother is having too much fun being the sweet, reasonable one. She's always agreeable and asking for work to do to take the burden off my mom, and willing to change details. The really insane part is that we haven't chosen a date yet, and Mom keeps choosing and changing for us, and I swear, her number is going to be blocked on the phone of every party center and photographer and florist within fifty miles."

"Have the wedding at Put-in-Bay. They rent the gazebo in the center of town. As soon as you say, 'I do,' you and Gordon make a run for a convenient speed boat and head for Canada."

"I wish!"

"Would they really refuse to come if you go Trek?"

Mandy sat up, rested her elbows on the table, and got thoughtful. Her eyes narrowed a little and she tipped her head to one side. Then a tiny smile caught up the corners of her mouth.

"You know, it started as a joke, to shut them up when the first argument broke out. Never doing duo-family dinners ever again. But I wouldn't mind doing Trek. It'd be fun."

"It would be totally embarrassing, something to blackmail your kids and grandkids with, far in the future. Any time you want to shut them up, threaten to bring out the wedding album or post photos on whatever remains of social media and the Internet, on your anniversary."

"Yeah, well, that's what getting old is for. To embarrass your kids and grandkids. And this is the first time I've been able to think about having kids and making my mother a grandmother, without wanting to throw up and have my tubes tied." That last part dropped to a hissed whisper, while Tansy Bowman, our waitress, stepped up to the table with water. She put down a three-part bowl of guac, French onion dip and cheese sauce, and a huge basket of the veggie chips Ben Miller was trying out. He liked to experiment on his regular customers. Free food was fine with me.

"Your mother is already a grandmother."

"Yeah, but my brother's kids don't count. It's like some unwritten law that the daughter's kids belong to her side of the family more than to the son-in-law's side."

"Remind me not to get married or have kids." I shuddered.

Many snorted, scooped up some guac with green chips and chewed thoughtfully for a few moments. I wasn't sure I wanted to know what vegetable they were made from. I also didn't want to know what thoughts were putting that sparkle in her eyes. She swallowed, took a sip of water, then leaned forward and spoke in a much softer voice.

"I'm sure Daniel will be very disappointed to hear that."

"Daniel who?" slipped out before I remembered that Mandy had known Daniel Sheridan before he came to Neighborlee.

She laughed, shook her head, and reached for more chips.

Fortunately (for her), she left me alone on the subject of the Evil

Overlord while we went to town on those chips and brainstormed survival tactics for the next eight or nine months. Until her and Gordon's family killed each other off in the battle for dominion over the wedding. Or the two of them built up the courage to choose a date and put their feet down. Or took the cowardly, much wiser course of action and eloped.

I had an idea brewing at the back of my mind and held onto it while we came up with some semi-nasty tricks to play on her relatives to get them to back off. In my opinion, the best one was to reserve the small gym at Eden for the wedding and reception combined, set the wedding date between Christmas and New Year's, and declare it would be Trek-themed. At the very least, it would earn her and Gordon a few months of the silent treatment from both their families. Meanwhile, they could pick the real date and start making their own plans, pick their own colors and decorations and food on their own schedule.

With that settled, I told her about Jane and the spa coming to town, and asked what she thought about a spa day for Felicity as a wedding gift. Maybe an outing for the entire bridal party.

Mandy's eyes lit up. She was nearly drooling as she asked questions so fast, I nearly couldn't get in a word edgewise to answer her. Oh, yeah, she wanted one herself. Which meant I had the perfect birthday and wedding present for her. Provided Jane got her spa put together and open for business before Mandy's birthday. Or before she and Gordon eloped.

Winner!

Chapter Four

Friday, I checked in with Angela during my lunch break, just to see if she had heard anything from Athena or Hayward. Bethany had emailed to report that the two of them were having a good time and Athena was on the verge of being asked to stay and work for the production company. She had been in the right place at the right time to solve some computer problems for the special effects team. Then when Bethany "just happened" to let it drop that her best friend was one of the geniuses behind FlopDrop, the staff writers nearly started a bidding war for an option on exclusive rights to the entire story.

I was still getting over the oddness of hearing Angela talking about getting email. I knew she used a computer Athena had set up for her to handle inventory, and London and Sherwood regularly talked to Angela through it. I just couldn't see Angela as someone who lived that much in the twenty-first century.

Then she dropped an interesting piece of information on me. Jane Wilson had stopped in yesterday, officially reporting in and confirming that yes, she was settling into the building and renovating her living quarters and getting to know the town. Angela approved of Jane, the more she saw of her, and said she would put Kurt at the top of the list of people she turned to for renovations to the shop. Then before I left, she announced she was coming to my gig at the comedy club that evening.

Kurt came with me. Not that I needed a roadie, but there was always a chance the parking lot wouldn't be shoveled and the ramp into the club might be sabotaged. My brothers were busy and couldn't come with me. Kurt admitted he didn't like the thought of me going anywhere alone outside the borders of Neighborlee until we could be absolutely sure the Rivals weren't watching.

He had a point. He also mentioned he had seen Jane walking back to her spa, when I told him what Angela had said.

It turned out to be a good thing he came with me. And no, the Rivals did not make an appearance. The snow was coming down heavy by the time we got to the club in Independence. The maintenance guys there had a reputation for forgetting that snow turned into ice, and ice on the delivery ramp at the back of the club was not a good thing for people in wheelchairs. I could fight the ice using my telekinesis, getting myself up the ramp and inside on time, and risk a headache before the performance. Or Kurt could give me a push. He glared (with no results) at the maintenance guys who were sitting by the back door, enjoying coffee and cigars when they should have been outside shoveling and sanding the parking lot. And what were they doing smoking when Ohio had a no-smoking-in-public-places ban in effect?

Was it really my fault when both of them lost their grip on their cigars and both cigars conveniently did somersaults through the air to land in buckets of dirty mop water?

You betcha!

We got there early enough for Kurt to check the ramp management had installed for me to get up on the stage. He gave his approval: wide enough for my wheelchair, sturdy enough, and not too steep. I could have told him that three weeks ago, when I first started using it, but his approval did make me feel a little better. I still felt a little twitchy after the whole mess with the Terrible Trio, starting well before Christmas.

Kurt was late getting out front to sit with Angela, because he wanted to study the auxiliary controls for the lighting system, hung on the wall behind the curtain. It really was a chintzy set-up behind stage, but the ownership was making improvements. Gradually. In another couple of months, they might just have a real sound system, instead of a cannibalized microphone-and-cord-and-portable-speakers system they had probably bought from a school district when they upgraded. They might get maintenance guys who could make the connection between snow and ice and ramps and wheelchairs without needing flashcards or someone explaining it to them in words of one syllable.

Hugo, the owner, stepped behind the curtain and gave me the high sign. He was about to go out and announce the start of my routine. Kurt ducked out the side door. Hugo stepped out, bypassed the ramp, and leaped up onto the stage with an enviable lightness for a guy of his size. Did all big men take ballet or something, to help them move so gracefully?

A few seconds later, I wheeled out, gave myself a little mental push to get up some momentum, zipped up onto the stage and came to a semi-screeching halt. Then I tipped my front wheels back to make it seem like I had narrowly avoided going off the front of the stage -- right into the lap of a guy who already looked like too much of the evening had been spent in the bottom of his glass. How come I always had one like him at nearly every performance? Well, that was what I got for performing at a place that sold drinks as its livelihood. *Please, Lord, let him be a happy, sleepy drunk and not a nasty one? Please?*

Since Valentine's Day was fast approaching, of course I had to start out slamming that very expensive and painful holiday. It's only a fun holiday if you're in love, and the object of your affections is focused on you in turn.

I paid attention to the reactions I got to new material, to help me refine it. A few uneasy looks, some laughter, some thoughtful expressions. Hey, who ever said laughter should be brainless? The best humor, Pop always said, was the kind that made people think and maybe stretched brain cells in a new direction.

The people who looked confused laughed the loudest. Either that, or the bar was already doing a bang-up business.

Was my humor driving people to drink? Frightening thought.

I ranted a little while about people who didn't belong together and made a mistake getting married. I finished with something I actually heard someone say about a couple who got married their sophomore year of college and divorced before they graduated.

"I would not say their marriage was bad, but they sued their matchmaking service… and won. No, really, and I am not being disloyal by saying it was the wife's fault. She was the type of woman who would have made Adam say he wanted his rib back!"

That got some shrieks of laughter. Always a good thing.

I got the high sign from Hugo, so it was time to start wrapping up the routine. A few more one-liners and zingers, and then I spun my chair around and zipped down the ramp, to applause that shook a couple more layers of dust and grime from the rafters.

Normally, I didn't hang around after I performed. While the other comedians in the Cleveland scene were good, a lot of them relied too heavily on filth to be funny. I didn't think I was a prude, but I tried to hold to the "think on these things" principle. Yeah, and the garbage-in-garbage-out principle, for those who didn't know those verses from the Bible. Tonight, though, I went the long way around from the stage and went into the seating area. I had a guest tonight, and it just wasn't smart to leave Angela waiting.

It turned out that she had brought Jane.

We had time between sets to chat a little, about progress with setting up the spa, the ideas she wanted to pursue next. I was pleased that she wanted to take my idea of the tea shop and run with it. There was plenty of room on the second floor for a few two-seater couches and comfy cushioned chairs for people to relax and read or chat. Our plan for Kurt to get close to her was making progress, which might have been why Angela brought Jane to the show, to meet him. He would go over to the Spindelmutter building in the morning, to start looking things over and consider if he would handle Jane's renovations. Not that he really needed to check out the place. Kurt had helped with renovations to the building over the years. He probably knew it better than the current owner and landlord.

We only stayed through three more sets. It was getting late for me, and the guy who was finishing out the night was just a little too potty-mouth. He followed the principle that vulgar equaled funny, and sexist vulgarity was the height of intellectual humor. I tried to be discrete when I said I was leaving, but how many ways can you say, "I'll need to soak my brain and my ears in disinfectant and bleach when we get home. Listen at your own risk," without sounding like a self-righteous little twit?

Some of the people around us must have heard, because as I backed away from our table and maneuvered around to leave, I counted at least eight getting up to leave. They could have been going to the bathroom, but usually guys and girls don't leave to use the bathroom in public at the same time. Angela and Jane left with me and Kurt.

Funny, but despite me being the only person in a wheelchair at the club that night, nobody seemed to recognize me from the stage. Ah, my wounded ego.

Kurt was quiet as we made our farewells from Angela and Jane and headed to my Jeep. I was worried that he had sensed something, some fluctuations of energy. Or maybe Angela had given him bad news. I kept watch on the car that Angela and Jane got into. Jane was driving, of course. Funny, but I hadn't thought about how Angela was getting to the club until then, because I knew she didn't have a car.

Kurt took care of folding up my chair and stowing it in the back seat, so I could get in the Jeep right away. That was nice, because the air felt particularly misty-chilly. I didn't start the engine, but waited for him to get into the passenger seat and close the door.

"What's wrong?"

"Not wrong." He frowned at some spot in the air between his nose and the glove compartment. "Jane hums."

"Uh huh." I couldn't help smiling. That was pretty much the first thing Kurt said to me, when we met as children. Granted, I was practicing my kinda-sorta flying at the time. "What was she doing? Turning invisible?"

"I think she was tense. Makes sense, unfamiliar place, on the alert for trouble or danger, if what we're guessing about Hoax and the Rivals and all that is true."

"What did you think of her?"

"It's going to be interesting, working with her, figuring her out."

I started the engine then, and Kurt spent most of the drive back to my place going through his observations of her. Our plan was proceeding for him to get close to Jane, observe her, and figure out whose side she was on and what she was doing in Neighborlee.

Jake was at Felicity's, getting ready to leave when we pulled into the driveway. We ended up having an impromptu meeting in Felicity's doorway, discussing the evening, meeting up with Jane at the comedy club and our impressions of her. Angela seemed to like her, and that said a lot for her. The fact that it was Angela's idea to bring Jane to see me perform … well, Felicity and Kurt thought it meant something, but they couldn't quite decide what. Until we knew for certain Jane had been the Ghost, we couldn't exactly invite her to join our little gang to protect Neighborlee, could we?

"I'm starting to think Angela brought her specifically to meet me," Kurt said, shrugging. "It was the perfect opening to link us up so I could do her renovations. Angela told her I was the best one around for checking out her store and bringing things up to code, and handling the renovations, things like building shelves, fixing the elevator – "

"What elevator?" Felicity interrupted. She looked at me. I

shook my head.

"I didn't know there was an elevator in the Spindelmutter building," I said.

"Yeah, it's been broken so long, nobody uses it. People have been using it as a storage room. The last I saw it, it was full of crates and other junk the last tenants left there. Somebody painted over the old controls so many times …" He shook his head in disgust at the abuse of electronics. Especially old-fashioned electronics. Antique machinery was Kurt's passion, the way other guys got passionate about baseball cards or fly fishing.

"So you're in the perfect position to keep watch on her and check if she really does have any powers," Jake said slowly.

Felicity gave me a cat-in-the-cream smile. Well, I didn't blame her. Jake had certainly adapted to the existence of our mutant-or-alien powers a lot faster and easier than Gordon and Mandy had. Of course, Jake spent a lot more time reading comic books as a kid than Gordon or Mandy. They were more the TV-and-movie SF fans. There was a difference in mentality, though it'd take a couple hours of talking our brains into knots before we could really define what that difference was.

We agreed on some tactics. Felicity and Jake would wait a while before introducing themselves to Jane, maybe wait until the spa opened. Then they would volunteer to help her get settled into the town proper, introducing her to the various store owners and community activities. Kurt would keep watch on her, right underneath her nose. The first time she activated her Ghost talents, whatever they were, he would know and he would borrow them and figure out what they were.

This was going to be interesting.

~~~~~

Sunday, I ran into Jane at church. She was coming in for the first service while I was heading to my Sunday school classroom. She seemed interested in learning I was a teacher, and laughed in just the right way when I admitted I only got access to those pliable little demented minds when the other teachers were out on emergencies. She commented that she had heard I played basketball. I invited her to the next Ezekiel's Wheels game.

All in all, I got good vibrations from her. And not just because she came to church without anyone dragging her or threatening her
~~~~~

or drowning her with holy water and clubbing her semi-conscious to get her through the doors. Yes, I'd seen that tactic, or heard about it being used on others. And people who use those tactics actually wonder why people *don't* want to come to their church? Give me a break!

Like a friend from the hospital would say: Which vertebrae?

~~~~~

That following week, Kurt gave us short reports every night on what Jane had done or said while they were working together, the errands she ran, and any conversations he overheard. There wasn't much. I had the feeling that irritated him, but the feeling was so iffy I couldn't call him on it.

We were officially into Valentine's Day countdown now that January had finally turned the corner into February. Tuesday, I learned Harrison Kamel did not understand that when someone did not respond *at all* to his offer of free matchmaking services, that equated to not just a solid "No," but a pretty hefty "Leave me alone."

Not that Harrison contacted me to follow up, either with emails or more phone calls.

His Romeo did.

On my personal email.

Just how much searching did that entail, to find it? My work email, sure, anybody could contact me there. It was printed in every edition of the *Neighborlee Tattler*, just like everyone else on the staff. Why my *personal* email? How?

I considered tracking down Harrison and laying some tire tracks up his back. Too much effort. Maybe if I ignored Romeo and left Harrison alone, the first would believe it was a wrong address, and the second would think he had made a mistake, and I didn't get his phone call.

Such reasoning made my head hurt. Just like the email:

Dear Elaine:

Either Harrison was officially an idiot or Romeo assumed too much. The only place I was ever recorded as Elaine was in the naming documents when they found me on Old Mill Road. I've seen them. *Elaine* was struck through with red pen and changed to
~~~~~

Lanie.

I look forward to the day we meet face2face.

Another strike against him. I despise people who use shorthand like that in letters. Texting, fine, but not letters!

Harry has told me so much about you, I know already we are destined for a life of perfect harmony.

Really? Harry? Either this guy took liberties, or Harrison had changed. When we were in college, he insisted on being called Harrison. He had no idea who Harrison Ford was, so he didn't insist on being called Harrison because he was man-crushing. And really? Harrison could tell Romeo "so much" about me? I was pretty sure Harrison knew more about my test scores than about me, the person.

I can't wait for spring to come, when we can take long hikes together. I too am an athlete. We have so much in common. I can't wait to take you dancing in the moonlight and watch your long hair float on the breeze as we spin across the outdoor dance floor at Wintertop Winery.

Yeah, definitely Harrison didn't know anything about me. Certainly not about my wheelchair, or the fact I had cut my hair short since high school, because while long hair streaming behind you as you race to the finish line sounds poetic and beautiful, when it's sweaty and clumping together and slapping your sunburned back, it's downright uncomfortable. And dancing? I have been allergic to dancing since I was traumatized by square dancing in gym in class in fifth grade.

Yours always, and very soon,
Carlo Carnova

Seriously? This could not be his real name. Although yes, I had heard of parents being so cruel they would give their children names that would get them beat up at school. When I first read it, my heart nearly stopped, because for a second I thought his name was Casanova. Bleah! And what was with this "Yours always, and very soon"? Was that supposed to be mystical or philosophical? Did this guy ransack the romance section at the library and glean phrases he thought would enchant me? Should I feel sorry for him?

Or should I invest in holy water and garlic and other defensive items?

Wintertop Winery gave me a launching point to try to find out about Romeo, his stomping grounds, the things he was interested, first by determining just how far away he was and maybe help me find out something about him. The most important thing was looking for clues if I would need police protection. Because seriously, either Harrison or Romeo had a problem with boundaries and protocol, and understanding that silence either means I never got the first message, or I wanted nothing to do with the whole whackadoodle matchmaking scheme.

Ambush and pushiness are never romantic tactics. Yes, many women want to be pursued, but not when they feel the need for pepper spray and a tazer.

I found Wintertop Winery, on the far side of Summit County. Not far enough away from Neighborlee, for my shudders.

Next consideration: Call in Gordon, ask him to run a character search on this guy, or ask Athena? It might give her a distraction from her current romantic woes. Freddie Grandstone was sending her several texts and emails every day, expressing his frantic concerns for her safety and promising all sorts of extravagant adventures together for their first date. What part of, "Uh, no thanks, not ever," didn't he understand? And I'm not joking, that was her response to him, multiple times, through her grandparents and Uncle Jinx, then via emails.

If I gave the investigation job to Gordon, it would distract him a little from wedding planning woes. Maybe I should bypass both him and Athena and ask London directly? And while I was at it, I could ask her to pry through all sorts of personal information and investigate another matter that would bring happiness to all the guardians.

Within an hour, London sent back my answers. Yes, Romeo's real, given-at-birth name was Charlie Carnovolio. I kind of winced and didn't blame him, a little bit, for changing it. His mother made her living writing romance novels that dripped purple ink, and he was seriously infected or influenced by the language and what passed for storylines. He ran a gym for bodybuilders, wrestlers, and boxers. Why was I not surprised? Sometimes bruisers had the most purple-tinted imaginations when it came to romance. Maybe it was a result of getting whacked in the brain pan so often.

I had an awful vision of this guy volunteering to carry me around on dates, rather than letting me ride along in my wheelchair.

Which made me send up a quick, fervent prayer that our theories about the increasing energy returning to Neighborlee would eventually lead to full healing for my broken back, giving me my legs back, letting me escape the wheelchair once and for all. I bet with Charlie (I refused to think of him as Carlo) on my heels, I could get back into blue ribbon track star condition really fast.

Then London sent me a picture of Charlie.

Life was so, so, so unfair.

He was muscle-bound enough to be able to sweep me out of my wheelchair with one arm and set me on one exceedingly large and bumpy shoulder. The guy had no neck. I wondered how he could turn his head, because it seemed to just emerge from his shoulders, with little hills of muscles threatening to reach up and swat at his earlobes.

Let's just simplify things: he was a vision out of all my hormonal adolescent dreams, all smooshed together and sculpted with just the right sharp angles, all my Marvel superheroes combined in one package.

Ever had one of those moments where you lose your breath, swept up to the heights of, "Oh, yeah, that's what I'm talking about!" and then two seconds later, plummeted down to the nauseous certainty that trouble is around the corner? Yeah, that was how I felt, looking into Charlie's face, beaming with the innocent delight of a cute little boy with chocolate smeared on one sunburned cheek and his hair messed up by the wind. Charlie, not the kid.

I just knew this was too good to be true. Because experience said when dreams came true like this, with no explanation or expectations, that was usually a sign the enemy was getting ready to slam me with the Terminal Tower, so hard there wouldn't even be a grease spot on the pavement where I used to be.

Because just a few seconds to step back, metaphorically, and think sent up a red flag. Why was a guy this incredible resorting to a matchmaking service? He should have an entire caravan of salivating women following him everywhere he went -- but he was trusting Harrison to make a match for him using data that was over fifteen years old? People change as they get older and go through the strange and weird and wonderful of life. Especially in Neighborlee.

Bottom line: A package that gorgeous meant there was either junk, or nothing whatsoever, inside. Or maybe worse than that, he was a nice guy, but he was a dupe of the enemy.

I kind of felt better when I thought of that. I asked London to investigate him, see if there were any traces or links to anything or anyone related to the Rivals, or at least suspected of being related to the Rivals.

Then I did the sensible thing. I sent a copy of the letter and the picture to Conrad, since he knew about the matchmaking scheme. I asked him to set up an alert system, so if Romeo came through the door or called the office looking for me, the first step would be to warn me so I could run for the hills. Then call the police. And then I asked about the policy that had been discussed from time to time in the past, of issuing tasers to everyone to keep in their desks, and a giant economy-size pepper spray cannister for Matilda's desk. Just in case.

Then, to clear my mind and calm me down, and yes, let me work off some tension with the anticipation of releasing my inner snark queen, I pulled up a batch of Talk to Terry letters that Daniel had forwarded me. I had the house to myself, since the boys were busy with friends from church.

No surprise, the letters were Valentines' Day-related. Some of the letters to Terry were stupid. Guys in a quandary over Valentine's Day coming up. Ready to bail because they knew they'd mess up, or not wanting to stick a crowbar in their wallets. Griping about the expensive holiday and all the emotional blackmail attached to the price tag. Girls who were pretty sure their guys were going to break up with them just to avoid the whole romance-required hassle or having to spend anything on them. Should they take the guys back a week or so after Valentine's was over, when they showed up with candy and other trinkets still showing the half-off sales stickers?

Seriously? They needed my help to figure out the simple answer? Two choices. First, make the guy suffer and spend five times as much on her as he would have if he had just bitten the bullet and endured Valentine's Day. Or second, never take him back and post his name on a bulletin board listing cheapskate losers in the romance department. And if there wasn't such a list somewhere, some smart girl should start one this year.

One stood out. And not just because Daniel had marked it for special attention and put it at the top of the queue.

After reading the letter, I wasn't sure if I should get angry or try to read something into the whole "coincidence," or accuse him of a set-up. Seriously? Why was this letter coming now?

Dear Terry:

I've always thought people who wrote to advice columnists were kind of pitiful. Well, that's me now. maybe I deserve this. But you seem to talk a lot of sense while blasting idiots who can't figure stuff out for themselves, so here goes ...

I just got a Dear John letter -- with a twist. My girl is in the military, and I'm home. A pal of hers in the unit got a Dear John letter, and she was comforting him and as she says, it "just happened." I can hear you saying right now, "Yeah, right!" But what if she's not conning me?

Maybe I was expecting it all along? I'm a teacher, in a wheelchair, and every once in a while I kind of slam my brakes on and wonder how the heck I got a girl like her to like me. And I don't know if this sick falling feeling is relief, like I've been waiting for it to happen. I'm trying to be forgiving and understanding, because yeah, they have a lot more in common than my ex-girl and I ever did, and danger creates bridges, but I really thought she loved me. You know?

Help me figure out how to start getting over her? Because even though it hurts, I'm not so pitiful that I'm going to let losing her totally destroy my world. Life goes on. Just not like I planned. Advice? Please?

Chapter Five

The letter wasn't signed. Daniel hadn't even made up a name for the jilted Romeo. I slapped a sticky note on it and wrote *Four-Wheel-Drive Heartache* on it, but doubted that name would end up being printed.

What kind of advice could I offer the guy? My last romance had been with the slimebag who wanted to use me to get at either my kids in school or my Sunday school class. If I ever ran into the perv predator, he wouldn't open his eyes until a month later, and he would still have tire tracks all over his face. And that was just for starters.

Dear 4WD Romeo (note to self: working tag only)

Congratulations on trying to have common sense and not let this ruin your life. Because even if it feels ruined now, it isn't. It's okay to be hurt, to feel betrayed and abandoned.

Sometimes the best way to survive hurt like this is to offer all that love to people who you know can't pay it back.

You say you're a teacher. I know lots of teachers. I know how much they pour into their students. Even if they might not say it or show it, I bet a lot of your students think you're the greatest. Pour into them. That kind of love is the best kind, the purest kind, and it'll help you heal.

I know a lot of people in wheelchairs. They all face a decision to either sit in a corner and feel pitiful and rejected over something that probably wasn't their fault, or they can get out into the world and blow people's minds with their awesomeness despite the barriers and difficulties. I've got a friend in a wheelchair who pulled her life back out of the gutter. As in gutter balls in bowling. As in getting caught in the mechanism at the back of the lane. She was a schoolteacher too.

While I'm thinking of it, I hope you aren't blaming your chair for the breakup. I'm all for cross-socializing and against the really limiting mindset that forces people to only date within their own "kind." What are you supposed to do to be romantic? Lock wheels? Oh, shiny chrome, be still my heart! I'm totally against in-breeding, so don't limit yourself to dating chicks in wheelchairs. Be adventurous.

The only limits are the ones you put on yourself, what you can do and be. Don't let the stupidity and fears of others limit you. Honestly, I've run into people who think there really are gimp germs, and if they start hanging with the folks with natural four-wheel-drive, their legs will go numb and they'll talk funny. (They should be so lucky!)

For now, go ahead and wallow. You deserve it. Indulge in a nice dive into the candy box or whatever socially safe but definitely not totally healthy means of comfort suits you. Whatever you do, don't answer the girl. She's not your girl anymore, you have no obligation to her, and if she wants to stay in contact, don't! She's just trying to make herself feel better at your expense. If you have to answer her back, burn the letter before you send it. You'll feel better.

Whatever you do, don't beg, don't whine, don't try to make her feel guilty, don't chew her out -- and don't tie yourself into knots to make her feel better. If she feels guilty, let her stay that way. Silence will leave her wondering. If there's no sense of guilt, if she goes on with life perfectly happy, you don't really want to know that, do you?

Of course not. Because you're a sensible guy.

Roll on, hero.

~~~~~

Wednesday, Charlie emailed me again. This time at work. Now I was irritated. And worried. He knew how to find me, and where, day and night. Bad enough he had my personal email address. This was getting too close. With a little judicious masking and detouring on the electronic pathways, London could make sure the guy could never get another email to me.

The playing field changed when he knew my location details. Short of interfering with traffic signals and posting totally false police reports to get the guy tackled and tasered if he came within a mile of the office or my house, there really wasn't anything she could do now that he knew where I worked. I was really hoping he hadn't connected me with my job. That hope was now dashed.

I was grateful I didn't have a byline on the *Talk to Terry* column.
~~~~~

That would just be too embarrassing, and might give Romeo ideas. Of the wrong sort.

So he had found me. What could I do?

"Well, duh," Clarice said, when I told her about the puzzle.

She had stopped in to have lunch with Conrad. Yeah, they were that kind of married couple who tried to have lunch together a few days a week. Being old college roommates, she stopped to chat on her way to his office, and she just happened to see me scowling at my computer screen, with the freshly read email on it. She knew about Charlie and Harrison and the whole matchmaking problem, because, see the statements above, she and Conrad were that kind of married couple and we were college roommates.

"Meaning?" I said, after a few seconds of giving her a dirty look that didn't set her on fire immediately.

"Contact the bozo who started the whole mess. Threaten him with a harassment suit and the expense of restraining orders if he doesn't get the guy off your back."

"Not gonna let him get close enough to be on my back to get him off," I snarked back. And made a mental note to find a comedy routine to put that into. It was pretty good for off-the-cuff, if I did say so myself.

Clarice just groaned and rolled her eyes, slapped my shoulder, and sauntered away to find Conrad. I turned back to my computer and got to work finding Harrison's matchmaking service, physical address, email address, while mentally composing a "cease and desist -- and make Romeo cease and desist, or else" letter.

I went out for lunch, despite the drizzly-icy weather. I needed the workout and the cool-down. That let me take the long way around, so I could do a roll-by of Jane's spa and check out her progress. I caught a glimpse of Kurt hard at work on something near the back of the main room, but no sign of Jane. How was he going to keep an eye on her and study her if she wasn't there? That was his problem. For all I knew, he had worked out the bugs on his version of "bugs" to follow people, so he could let her run around town without losing contact with her. It cheered me a little, thinking of Jane's fury when she found out about it. At least, I thought she would be furious, hoped she would be. We didn't need a wimp to add to the roster of the guardians of Neighborlee, if she was everything we hoped. If she was the Jane we remembered from

Neighborlee Children's Home days. Angela reminded us of a few times when Jane stood up to bullies at the orphanage and in school, defending other, younger kids. That made her one of us already.

After my less-than-satisfactory roll-by, I went up to Stanzer's office to check with him about Charlie and my options. I gave him the printouts of what I had found out about him and Harrison. Unfortunately, while Stanzer was fully on my side, he did point out something I hadn't considered. If I had signed a release form when I participated in the (required) class project, then Harrison could do what he wanted with my information. Did I still have a copy of that form, to determine whether or not I had given permission for him to hand my personal information over to other people? The question he had to look into was whether that permission, if it was ever granted, could be applied to new information, more than a decade later, after we had both left school. Stanzer seemed to like the challenge, and promised he knew a couple people who could help him tie Harrison and Charlie in legal knots if they got beyond the irritating stage.

I asked how he was doing with his search for other members of the Hunt, the children who had been sent from another dimension to find refuge on Earth. Stanzer's smile faded.

"There are pieces to the puzzle I'm missing. I've been finding geographic features that match my memories of home. I can't help feeling the Hounds brought us here, specifically, for a specific reason and ... the rest of the Hunt should be within those boundaries."

"You told us one time a little bit about how you got here. Wouldn't the others have arrived the same way?"

"Well, you'd think that thirty-some children arriving in a wild storm where the sky splits open, all with fresh-burned scars on their wrists, from where the Hounds took hold of us to drag us through the dimensions ... that would stand out, wouldn't it?"

Right about then, with the fresh aching in his eyes, I was sorry I had asked. Sorry, but that was how my folks raised me, to always try to switch some of the attention off myself and show concern for other people's problems. Finding the other refugees from a galactic despot was a big concern for Stanzer. I knew what that was like, feeling like I was alone in the universe. A freak of nature. Even though I wasn't, with Kurt and Felicity and the other guardians around. It had to be ten times worse for Stanzer, because he really was alone. What made it worse was that he knew the names of most members of the Hunt. They were friends, cousins, even a girl he was expected to marry when they grew up.

I had to wonder if this girl had given up on finding the rest of the Hunt, and she had settled down and gotten on with her life. Career, marriage, maybe even kids by now. Stanzer said she was only four years younger than him. That thought had to hurt. At least I had sense enough not to mention her and remind him.

"Have you asked London or Sherwood to do a search? Maybe get into the weather bureau or agency or whatever it's called, where all the weather patterns from around the country, maybe around the world, are collected. If they are collected? I mean, what if this geographical feature you're focusing on doesn't match up, and it's the storms you should be focusing on?"

"That ... would be ... a big ... help," he said, nodding, while his gaze seemed to be somewhere a thousand miles away. Stanzar's smile returned, but only half the strength. Like he couldn't figure out if my idea was a help or made things worse.

Yeah, I seemed to be doing a lot of that lately.

"Could you ask them? It seems to take some effort for them to get through the electromagnetic field or whatever the Hounds give off." He shrugged. "We don't talk much. The Hounds have been more protective lately since all the fireworks at Eden."

"I don't blame them. Sure, I'll ask."

The Hounds and interdimensional visitors and energy and other things like that were on my mind as I made my way back down increasingly slushy sidewalks to the newspaper office. I stopped at Hunky & Dory's for one of their killer sandwiches, the kind that gave me an aching jaw from opening my mouth so wide. I spotted some winkies hanging around Bridget, who supplied the most decadent desserts imaginable for several restaurants in town. That made sense, because I could swear sometimes I saw points on her ears. Only someone with some Fae blood, or magical heritage of some kind, could create such incredible treats. The question, though, was if she was aware of her heritage. Now was not the time to ask her. I had to get back to work.

A floppy kind of dog sidled up next to me when I rolled out of the door of Hunky & Dory's. He was one of those beige-gold-chocolate-streaked, incredibly fuzzy dogs that probably would drive those DNA tracer sites crazy with all the bloodlines he carried. I couldn't have guessed what his dominant breed was if I had a Kennel Club guide and a couple weeks to study it. He grinned at me, tongue hanging out on the other side of his mouth, and trotted along beside my chair. Like he belonged there.

Dang if I didn't see a few winkie sparks clinging to his coat, which was becoming more draggled and heavy-looking as the sleet in the air thickened. He didn't seem to feel any discomfort. Maybe he even liked the sloppy-wet-cold.

I kind of liked having company for the couple of blocks I had to travel to get back to the office. And I was grinning despite the sleet coating my face and making me glad I didn't wear makeup. The suspicion that Felicity was waiting for me at the office didn't pull down my mood. In the past, she had sent not just her own mutts to look after me, but had sent the dogs that roamed the back streets and shadows of town to find me or Kurt or spy on people from time to time, as we were growing up.

Come to think of it, though, she hadn't done that with a stray dog for a few years now. Maybe the encounter with the Oil Slick Monster at New Year's hadn't just snapped something into place in her head, giving her control over her EM burst talent, but let her do more in-depth spying through the eyes and ears of dogs.

"Testing, testing, one, two, three," I said, keeping my voice down and my head turned so the people in the offices we passed wouldn't see me talking to the dog. "Can you hear me?"

The dog's ears pricked up, but there was no indication that someone was there behind his eyes and ears except him. I turned the corner to cross the parking lot at the *Tattler* building, and didn't see Felicity's car. I didn't see Jake's SUV either. So I was wrong, and she wasn't waiting to ambush me with more wedding details.

"You don't have a message for me, do you?" I said, sliding to a stop at the base of the wheelchair ramp.

The dog cocked his head to one side and his tongue lolled out even more, but not to the point that it looked ridiculously and maybe even freakishly long. He had to be miserable, with the sleet collecting and turning to ice in his coat, and making it clump up like dreadlocks.

I held out my hand without really thinking, because if this dog was sent by Felicity, there would be a little bit of programming to carry over. It wasn't like I was dealing with an entirely stray, wild, no-owner dog. At least, I hoped not. He tipped his head to the other side, and then took two steps closer to me, so I could touch his neck. I was looking for a collar among all that thick, wet fur. Which turned out not to be that wet beyond the outer layer. It was warm, which meant it had to be dry, when I got my gloved fingers down through maybe two inches of astonishingly clean fur. Weird, but nice. And no collar. Not even a string with a message clipped to it.

"So ... just making friends?" I had the oddest urge to bring him into the office so he could sit and dry off and warm up. Not that he needed to, with all that warm fur.

He barked once, and I swear it sounded like those hokey Lassie episodes, where the people ask questions and Lassie barks and it's supposed to sound like a conversation, with the people making educated guesses.

Yeah, my blood sugar was low and I was getting cold, now that I was sitting still and not generating heat by wheeling myself around. Time to get to my desk and inhale my sandwich.

"Thanks for walking me back." I grabbed my wheels and tipped myself enough to pivot and head up the ramp. Then I had an idea. "Hold still," I said.

Like I expected him to really understand me? I wasn't his Human, so that made no sense. I pulled out my phone and snapped a couple pictures of him. He kind of jumped a half-step back, like that startled him. The phone made soft clicks, but it wasn't like there was a flash, so what was going on?

"Thanks, but I have to get back to work."

The dog barked again, and his tail wagged like he was perfectly happy being left behind. He waited until I got to the top of the ramp and reached for the door, then he trotted off, across the parking lot, back the way we came.

I saw a few more winkies sparkle in his fur, blue and green and pink, before he turned the corner and vanished from sight. That was a little weird.

The weird increased when I got to my desk and checked my phone, and the pictures I had just taken weren't there. The weird increased even more when I called Felicity and described the dog to her, and yes, verified she hadn't been spying on me through the dog's eyes.

"Although that's a good idea," she admitted. Then when I described the dog to her as best I could, she said there was no dog matching that description in town. I knew better than to ask her if she was sure. Felicity was more familiar with the strays all around town than she was with a lot of people.

"There were winkies in its fur," I admitted, when all the other explanations had been crossed off the list.

"That should mean it's on our side. Right?"

"You're the dog expert, not me."

Felicity laughed a little at that. "Maybe the winkies found a new stray in the park and made it come check on you. Maybe they sensed trouble lurking. Like that bozo is spying on you."

"Which one? There are so many who hate me, starting with sports parents and …" I sighed, knowing who she meant. But I had filled my quota of words on that subject for the day. "Yeah, that would make more sense than a magical dog that deleted photos from my phone."

"Since when does anything make sense in this town?"

We laughed together about that very real truth, and then I had to get off the phone because after all, I was at work. A twice-weekly paper didn't mean as much work as a daily, but we had a smaller staff, kept busy, and were always working against some deadline.

I looked for the dog when I left the office that evening, but he was nowhere in sight. I was both relieved and disappointed. I looked for him, and tried not to, when I had to wheel around town for anything, and half-expected him to be waiting on the doorstep when I left the house in the morning. Felicity's dogs never made a sound during the night, warning and complaining about an intruder, but then I couldn't be sure they would protest the appearance of a dog touched with magic. For all I knew, they were oblivious to the presence of winkies.

~~~~~

Thursday I was caught up in new questions for the *Talk to Terry* column, and the fun of the grand re-opening of Eden. So I didn't even think of mentioning the dog and the winkies to Angela, when I ran into her at the festivities. Not that any answer she gave me would have changed anything, when Romeo showed up on Friday.

Harrison Kamel was in such serious trouble. When I got hold
~~~~~

of him, if I ever found the weasel, he would regret his great-grandparents being born, forget about him regretting having a birthday.

Romeo/Charlie/Carlo swooped down on me as I was preparing to leave the office, with chocolate and roses and the deluxe dinner package from Mancuso's Pizza: cheesy garlic bread, antipasto, Florentine pizza, and tiramisu. And a triple dose of Andes mints to deal with the garlic bread overload, because hey, it was their Valentine's special deluxe dinner package. Forget that there was still more than a week until the day. They wanted to be prepared and celebrate the entire month. (That was a quote from their latest ad running in the *Tattler*.)

I was most definitely not in a celebrating mood. And don't ever make the mistake of thinking I was going to kiss a guy the day I met him, just because he seemed to read my mind and know what I was craving after a really, really hard day at the newspaper office.

Maybe *because* the guy seemed to read my mind, actually. I had had enough bad experiences where unplanned, brief physical contact had put me inside someone's head. I did not want that to become a regular occurrence with anyone. Especially a stranger who waltzed into the newspaper office with a stack of heavenly smelling boxes and announced that he was sweeping me off my feet. And looked muscle-bound enough to be able to do just that, sweep me out of my wheelchair with one arm while balancing all that food on the other arm.

On top of being a conglomeration of all my favorite movie heart-flutters, he had a rumbly kind of voice that made my chest sort of vibrate from the moment I heard him talking. *Before* I heard him say my name. His face just glowed with delight, the amperage tripling the moment our eyes met.

Yeah. Like I said before, because it bears repeating and remembering: *When dreams come true all at once, with no explanation or expectations, that's usually a sign the enemy is getting ready to slam you with the Terminal Tower, so hard there's not even a grease spot on the pavement where you used to be.*

"Sweetheart," Charlie said, and put that stack emitting all those incredible odors down on the corner of Matilda's desk. Then he rubbed his hands together in anticipation -- bad move! -- and took a step toward me.

"No." That was all I could get out of my throat. It wasn't that I was scared. More like stunned. But there were a thousand other words and emotions creating a logjam in my throat and my brain.

He blinked. He didn't take a step back, but at least he stopped. "I don't understand."

"You shouldn't be here."

"But baby --"

"I am not your baby, I am not your sweetheart. I am not yours! We shouldn't even be having this conversation. Harrison Kamel is on his way to every courtroom I can find and being sued on every count I can think of!" My voice echoed off the tiles in the lobby and Matilda's desk and the ceiling tiles. Not bad.

"But -- but --"

"He matched us without my permission. He gave you my personal information, without my permission. You are here despite my refusing to contact you. Which if you had more than a single-digit IQ, you would have realized meant I didn't *want* any contact with you."

"But honey --"

"Get out!"

Then I gave him a mental shove, knocking him backwards so hard and fast his feet shot out in front of him on the wet tile floor and he went down with a crash. That drew all the attention that my shouts hadn't. Everybody in the office came running.

"But he said --"

"You aren't listening!" I rolled down the ramp and slid to a stop only an inch away from running over his feet. Of course, considering how big they were, the toes of his glossy black cowboy boots pointing straight up at the ceiling, I probably couldn't have gotten over them without tipping my chair back.

"Get him out of here," Conrad said, gesturing to the circulation guys. "Matilda, call the police."

Chapter Six

"No, please don't!" Charlie blurted. He held up his hands as if to protect himself from being beat on.

Note: the circulation guys stopped about three feet away from him. Charlie looked like a bodybuilder, after all, and they were probably afraid he'd beat up on them. So what was he suddenly afraid of?

"Mr. Kamel told me you were shy, and you wanted to be swept off your feet, and you were looking for someone to look after you, and I found out your favorite place and everything and I just want our first date to be perfect!"

So help me, the big, musclebound guy's bottom lip quivered and I thought he was going to burst into tears any second.

"Mr. Kamel is a liar and playing you, and you can probably sue him for malicious intent with his advice." Conrad stepped up so he was standing over Charlie, who was sitting up now but not trying to move. He towered over him, which was quite a feat, considering how tall Charlie was, even sitting on the wet tile floor. "I'm Lanie's boss, and I can guarantee she is not shy. She does not need anybody looking out for her, and she most definitely does not want to be swept off her feet."

So help me, I almost interrupted and corrected him on that. Yeah, I was knocked off balance. It was just the cussedness in me, as Pop would say, and laugh. I kept my mouth shut.

The circulation guys helped Charlie get to his feet and they kind of acted as an escort, standing between him and me as they herded him to the door and out.

The moment the door opened, that dog from Tuesday came tearing into the office, growling. He ran around Charlie three times, snarling, weaving in and out among the circulation guys' legs. Then he darted over to my chair and sat down and looked up at me, kind of quivering and whimpering and sniffing at me. Maybe I didn't speak TV dog, or Lassie mode or whatever it should be called, but I knew he was clearly asking if I was all right.

"I'm okay. Thanks for asking," I said, and held my hand out.

The dog sniffed at my fingers, then his tail started wagging hard enough to create a breeze.

By that time, the circulation guys had herded Charlie outside and down the ramp. The door was still open, so the dog darted away and out the door. I wheeled after him, but doggone if I could find him when I got to the door and looked across the parking lot just a few seconds later.

That was the wrong move, because Charlie looked back, heading for his big monster truck with all the fancy swirling silver paint on black. His face lit up and he turned around and started reaching for me. I backed out of the doorway fast and gave that heavy metal panel a mental slam-shove.

Not a good move. My head throbbed and I let out a yelp and pressed my fists to my throbbing temples. Matilda and Conrad got to me fast and waved away everyone else who was still in the office. I let them fuss over me while I fought down the nausea from the strain. They got me into the lunchroom and dug through the office first aid kit for aspirin and got a cold can of ginger ale. Good for nausea. When the circulation guys came back in the office, they verified Charlie was gone. We sort of sat there in the lobby and decompressed a little. I opened up the boxes from Mancuso's then and read the receipt and found out what Romeo had brought for our first date.

shudder

Ain't never gonna happen. That's just too heavy-handed.

I offered to split it up among my rescuers. There was no way I was going to take it home and eat it, not even to save on having to cook that night, which was my turn. They took it, joking about the chances of Romeo having put drugs in it to make me cooperative. Yeah, it had to be a joke, because as much as the circulation guys were moochers, they weren't stupid enough to eat any of that food if they had any doubts about its safety.

Meanwhile, Conrad had retreated to his office. He came out when I was heading for the door, again, assuring Matilda yet again that I was fine. He asked me to hold on for a second. Then he walked over to the big printer the size of the space shuttle that served all the different departments of the office, and got a few sheets that had just printed.

"This is a copy of the email Harrison Kamel sent to that

wannabe Cassanova. Either the guy is lying, and had his lies prepared in advance, to cover his sorry backside ..." Conrad shook his head and handed me the sheets. "Or someone's playing some nasty tricks on you."

The unspoken "again" seemed to ring through the office.

The email, which certainly had all the markings of being taken from the "sent" folder in Harrison's email program, warned Charlie to stay away from me. He took full responsibility for "overstepping" and said he was looking into how Charlie had gotten my contact information. He claimed he hadn't even given my name to him, much less my emails. Harrison clearly stated that both he and Charlie were legally obligated to respect my wishes. He agreed that any contact without my permission and cooperation could be considered not just a violation of privacy, but harassment.

"I wonder, if this is true, maybe someone sent Romeo emails from me, encouraging him to come by," I said, after reading through everything and thinking, and handing the printouts back to Conrad.

"You really want to risk encouraging the guy by contacting him and asking?" Matilda said.

"No. But I have options. I went to Stanzer about the problem the other day."

That seemed to satisfy them. I didn't mention that I would ask London and Sherwood to dig into Charlie's email and get me copies of everything. We needed to figure out who was lying and who was delusional and who was out to get me.

The floppy dog wasn't there when I came out and crossed the parking lot. That was disappointing and encouraging at the same time. I had no doubt that if Romeo had been lying in wait, the dog would have been there to protect me. Maybe the dog was why he *wasn't* there?

<div align="center">~~~~~</div>

I decided after that strain and weirdness, I deserved some pampering. However, the spa was just opening up for business the next morning, Saturday, and I hadn't signed up for massages yet. Survival instincts said for me to hurry over near the end of the day to get my name in the appointment book. Fortunately for me, Jane seemed amused by my showing up like I did, rather than irritated. Or maybe frightened, or suspicious. I knew we were going to be great friends. Eventually.

I ended up staying for dinner with Jane and Kurt, talking about the spa mostly, just getting to know her. I liked her. Kurt had little to say about her, withholding his judgment until he had spent more time with her. Which, looking back, I found a little odd. On a positive note to end the evening, I found out that one of the girls from the children's home, Penny, had been sent over by Angela to work for Jane. That said a lot about Angela's assessment of Jane, to trust one of the NCH kids with her.

I had high hopes for our future friendship and partnership. And yeah, learning just what she did to earn the name of Ghost from the people of Fendersburg.

~~~~~

Sunday, I glimpsed Jane in church again. I didn't dare hang around and try to meet up with her, because I also glimpsed Charlie wandering the halls. He looked a little forlorn, but I wasn't about to trust or pity him. If he claimed he was a nice, old-fashioned, church-going boy who loved his mama … I might just blow a gasket. Better to avoid him seeing me and just get out of there.

When I got home, Sherwood had left a present in my computer: copies of all Charlie's emails for the last two months. Just like I had feared, he never got Harrison's emails telling him to stay away from me, and the legal repercussions for unwanted romantic contact. More to the point, there were faked emails from Harrison, encouraging Charlie and even giving him details of my life: the things I liked to eat, my schedule, my favorite activities. All sorts of things calculated to help a guy sweep a girl off her feet, even if she wasn't in a wheelchair.

Fortunately, and much to my relief, there were no fake emails from me, encouraging or welcoming him. That would have been too much.

Sherwood added that he had created a simple warning system with several dozen trigger words. Next time Charlie wrote or called someone or they contacted him, and the subject was me or the matchmaking business, we would get a warning. Hopefully, it would be fast enough that Sherwood or London could then follow the signal to its source and find out who was interfering.

In the meantime, he suggested that I find a neutral spot, with witnesses, where I could have a reasonable conversation with
~~~~~

Romeo and get the whole problem out in the open. Drain the wound, so to speak.

Who was he, little more than a year old, to offer me relationship advice? And where did he come up with those metaphors?

Still, I couldn't help being grateful, and smiling a little at all the help he and London were offering.

That didn't mean for the next week I went out for lunch and ran the risk of running into Charlie. Or answered any calls from unfamiliar numbers, or opened up my email without some trepidation.

Staying in the office and taking no side trips between home and work also meant I didn't see the dog. That kind of disappointed me, because he intrigued me. And not just because he was a dog Felicity didn't know.

~~~~~

No word came from Hayward and Rodney about all those documents they had hauled out of the Rivals' depot. No update on deprogramming Snow Commando, either. Yes, I knew his real name now, but I kind of liked calling him Snow Commando. I was kind of touched that he was concerned enough to try to do something about the Troublesome Trio, and worried about me.

Of course, what did that say about me that only wackos were interested?

Kurt reported to us on Thursday that he hadn't felt any flickers of energy at work at the spa. Of course, since the spa was open for business, there weren't as many opportunities to be around Jane, watching her, waiting for hints of her Ghost talent. Maybe we were wrong?

"It's time to push her," Kurt told us, after tossing the options around for maybe half an hour.

The funny part was that Felicity's heart really wasn't into the discussion. Jake was getting off work around 10, and she wanted to meet up with him for a late night tour of the Willoughby house, checking out things the first of several inspectors had marked for either repairs, upgrades, updates, or "requested items for preservation by the local historical authorities."

"What do you mean by push?" I had to ask.

"Make things uncomfortable."
~~~~~

"No," Felicity said. "She was nice and she looked out for the little kids, back before these Hoax people took her. I haven't been able to meet her yet, but ... just don't, okay?"

Kurt rolled his eyes, but he agreed to be nice.

Somehow, I didn't believe him. Or at least, his idea of nice wasn't going to match Felicity's and my idea of nice. I just hoped we weren't going to find out the negatives of what Jane/the Ghost could do, when she was pushed hard, to her limits. Kind of like Felicity when she was infuriated and scared at the same time, and let go of an EM burst that killed small appliances and even some cars within a 100-yard radius.

~~~~~

Friday. Valentine's Day Eve. Yes, I know there's no such thing, officially. Considering the waves of panic spilling through Neighborlee and all the guys frantically racing around, buying up the last white and red roses and boxes of chocolate, it had the intensity of panicked last-minute Christmas shopping.

Daniel Sheridan finally showed his face in the *Tattler* office. And he came bearing gifts.

Unfortunately, most of them were for me.

Not from him, fortunately, because on first sight I had a few seconds of panic myself. Four of the six packages were big, heart-shaped boxes of candy. From Terry's admirers.

Doubly unfortunately, my personal lunatic Romeo followed Daniel into the office. He stepped up to the ramp to my section of the office in time to see Daniel grin evilly and put those heart-shaped boxes down on my desk, one after another. An anguished wail echoed through the office.

I had maybe three seconds to enjoy the white-faced confusion and terror that swept over Daniel. Not nearly enough time to thoroughly enjoy having the tables turned -- because those "tables" were turning so fast I got clocked by a couple corners, metaphorically speaking.

Charlie launched himself up the ramp, reaching for me with those huge, calloused weightlifter hands. Tears filled his eyes.

"Why? Why? What did I do wrong? Give me a cha-a-a-ance!"

Something underneath his coat glowed into life. At the same time, winkies shrieked into the building, coming from all directions -- the ceiling, the wall, and even up through the floor.
~~~~~

Ya think they were warning me?

My most basic survival instincts kicked in. I shoved with my mind as hard as I could, to the point of giving myself a nosebleed. Charlie slammed backwards, his feet about two feet off the ground. They caught on that stupid wrought iron railing that certainly didn't do a lick of good, keeping troublesome visitors contained in the lobby. His feet caught hard enough he dragged the railing with him as he flew into the chairs on the other side of the lobby and hit the conveniently placed half-wall there.

I saw stars. More accurately, I saw those streaks of light lancing out from my head from the effort.

Daniel took a step back, clutching the last candy box to his chest. He stared at me like he knew exactly what I had done. I saw his eyes move, following the winkies as they spun around my head. I swear, I heard some of them whimper and kind of make cooing sounds, like they were trying to soothe me. He took a deep breath, then turned as the last few people remaining in the office came running. With a glance at me, he tossed down the box on my desk and hurried down the ramp into the lobby to check on my lunatic Romeo.

I didn't knock him out, but I did stun him. He just curled up, whimpering softly.

Daniel came to my rescue and came up with the cover story so I didn't have to, with my aching head. He said Charlie had come racing up the ramp and slipped on some wet streaks, where the rubberized strips had worn or torn off. Kind of convenient that the day had been another ugly, sloppy wet one, and there had been a lot of traffic into the editorial department, making that ramp wet and slick. Did I say convenient? I'll fight anyone who disagrees with me that this was a sign of God's mercy and providence. Pre-planning, if you want to call it that.

The winkies swirled around me, and their cooing turned to a soft, soothing kind of song. A lot of them brushed against my face, and there was a cool kind of tingle that eased away the ache in my sinuses, where I sometimes got headaches from using my telekinesis too much. Trying too hard to lift something or push something I shouldn't have tackled. Then they faded away.

I would have given anything to grab my coat and backpack and make a run for it. Well, not a run, of course, but a mad dash at

Warp Ten, if I could manage it. And maybe get through the door without opening it. However, with all my co-workers gathering in the lobby, there was no way I could sneak out. So I settled in at my desk where I had a front row seat to watch Daniel and Conrad overseeing the guys who took care of Charlie. They got him sitting up and someone ran for ice in a towel to put on the back of his head.

Someone called for EMTs, and then the police and Gordon showed up, making it even more difficult for me to sneak out. The crowd of onlookers kept growing instead of shrinking. So I stayed there. Not that I minded, because despite my need to get out, get away, put the whole weird scene behind me, my head hurt. I needed to sit still. Besides, I was shaky and afraid to discover I couldn't stand up enough to get from my wheelchair into the driver's seat of my Jeep, when I finally got out to the parking lot. So I stayed.

One good thing about staying at my desk? All that freshly delivered chocolate, just sitting there. Daniel had said it was mine, just before the explosion. I needed that chocolate. I didn't consider the chance that maybe the Rivals might try to poison me, in the guise of gifts sent to Terry. That paranoid thought didn't occur to me until after a major therapeutic pig-out. The chocolates were really good quality. Cleveland's own Malley's Chocolates, high quality stuff. I ate all the Malley O's (chocolate-covered Oreos) and the buckeyes by the time the EMTs had hauled away a very quiet, and oddly deflated Charlie.

Not just subdued and emotionally deflated, but the guy actually looked *physically* deflated. Like he had shrunk somehow, in all dimensions. Weird.

Somewhere during all that, the winkies must have decided I was all right, or at least I didn't need their sparkly protection or oversight or whatever they were there for. They faded through the walls and ceiling, I was grateful. My eyes sort of hurt, so the lack of all that sparkle was sort of soothing. At least, until the interrogation started.

"You okay?" Conrad asked, heading up the ramp with Daniel right behind him. Everyone else was making their slightly delayed departure at the end of the day and week.

"I'm poised on that fine line between being loopy from too much sugar and sleepy from too much fat and ready to get disgustingly sick," I said after a couple seconds of thought. That announcement didn't stop me from reaching for one more buckeye before I picked up the half-emptied box to offer to him and Daniel.

"Lanie --"

"How come the wackos are coming out of the woodwork and they're all aimed at me?"

"What other wackos are you talking about?" Daniel asked, as he settled down in a chair against the far wall.

Conrad brought him up to speed on Snow Commando and the whole matchmaker service fiasco and the very clear signs that someone had been interfering in Harrison's efforts to control the situation.

"Gee, that sounds like something I should know about, as owner of the corporation that runs this paper now." He said it sort of lightly, sort of casual, sort of … I wasn't sure what feeling he was trying for, but it failed. I could almost hear the ringing of mounting tension radiating from him. "And don't give me the line about Neighborlee taking care of their own. I've heard it far too many times lately, and I swear that's half the problem."

Still, in that light tone.

Yet something cold curled up inside my chest.

Conrad really had nothing more to tell Daniel, because he had gone through everything he knew about Snow Commando and Harrison's inadequate attempts at disaster management. Daniel didn't really look at me, but I had this sensation of all his other senses being focused on me while the two of them talked.

Not a fun experience.

I had had just about enough. While they were agreeing on what steps the paper would take to deal with Charlie, since Daniel felt the incident occurring on the *Tattler's* premises made it a company concern, I put on my coat and wrote notes to put on the candy to leave in the lunchroom. Let everyone else eat themselves sick. Although yeah, it hurt to leave the second box of buckeyes behind. Someone knew me very well, knew my tastes, what could tempt me …

Maybe that wasn't a good sign?

My hands shook just a little as I tore up the notes and dug through the bottom drawer of my desk to find a shopping bag to put all the candy in. I knew exactly what I had to do next, and fast.

Take everything to Angela. Have her dose me with one of her teas that would counteract any poison or mind-controlling drugs I may have ingested. Leave the remainder of the candy with her to hand over to Col. Hayward, to have him test it. Or maybe if this came from the Rivals, Angela should test it? Like, maybe there was some nasty, interdimensional whammy involved?

"What are you doing?" Daniel rested a hand on my shoulder.

I yelped and my legs stiffened at just the right angle I nearly pushed my chair over backwards.

The fluctuating pins-and-needles sensation in my legs chose that moment to surge up so bad, I shoved back my wheelchair and got up, bracing myself on the desk. A glance around showed he and Conrad must have finished talking and Conrad had left.

"Lanie?" He gripped my arm, with real concern on his face.

"It's okay. The half-dead nerves try to play Lazarus once in a while, and when they do, it kind of hurts." I tried to smile, as sweat beaded on my face.

No way I could tell him that with the slowly replenishing levels of the defensive energy filling Neighborlee, I might just be getting my legs back. That would take too much explaining.

"You're sure?"

I gave him one of my "don't mess with me" looks, left over from teaching days. No, I couldn't see my own face, but I knew what it felt like when I wore the look. He grinned and gingerly released me and took a step back. Breathing got a little easier.

"Can we talk?" He gestured at the ramp and the gap in the decorative fencing where Charlie's flight had knocked it down. "About what happened?"

"I really have to run some important errands." I dropped back down into my seat.

And halfway there realized I had shoved my wheelchair back, away from my desk. Another thoughtless mind-yank to get my chair into position meant another throb in my temples, followed by the sensation of a spiked ball dropping into my stomach. That surge of nausea combined badly with all the candy already down there. I really wished the winkies would come swirling back into the office, because I needed more of that soothing they had done. If I was feeling so lousy now, how would I be feeling if they hadn't done some soothing earlier? Scary thought.

Another widening of Daniel's eyes, with a flicker that somehow made me think he could see what I had just done. Like he could follow the streamer of energy from my head, snagging the wheelchair and dragging it back under my butt before I dropped too far and hit the floor? Like Gordon had been able to see at New Year's?

Oh … heck …

Yet it kind of made sense. Daniel's grandfather was a Lost Kid. Had he inherited some sensitivity, like Athena and Doni?

"I really think we need to talk," he said, and gave me a little, helpless shrug.

"Hey, Lanie?" Somehow Gordon got into the office without either of us hearing or reacting to the door opening. He stomped up the ramp. "You're coming with me. Urgent."

"Can it wait?" Daniel said.

"I have to run over to Divine's," I said at the same time. "Angela is expecting me."

All right, that was a lie, but considering what had just happened, Angela might have felt the disturbance. Besides, I planned on calling her when I got into my Jeep. So then she would definitely be expecting me.

Gordon blinked, looked at Daniel, then at me. "I have strict orders from the highest authority." He winked, and suddenly I knew he was talking about Mandy, not Chief Tanner. "But yeah, we can make a detour to Divine's. I don't know if you've been around long enough to pick up on it, but nobody with any brains disobeys Angela."

"I'm picking up on that," Daniel said, nodding. He gave me a determined look. "We need to have that talk."

"Yeah, let me catch my breath, okay?"

He nodded and stepped out of the way so I could shove my wheelchair, with my hands and not my head this time, and glided toward the ramp. Gordon followed me out to the parking lot. I told him about the candy and my suspicions. That protective fire touched his eyes.

"You want me to drive you?"

"I am not coming back here to get my car. Besides …" I took a deep breath. "When I shoved that guy away, Daniel saw something. Maybe it was like for you, at Eden, at New Year's."

"Is that a good thing, or trouble?" he said after thinking for a few seconds.

I really, truly did love Gordon, so much common sense and calm, handling all the Neighborlee weirdness without flinching.

"I don't know. First step is getting this to Angela, having her check me for poison or anything else. Then ..." I shrugged. "I really don't want to talk to him just yet."

"Then don't." He grinned. "Mandy is demanding your presence as possible maid of honor."

"Oh ... heck." I really did need to learn some Klingon to cover moments like this. Plain old English wouldn't stretch to deal with what I was feeling, and I didn't want to have to wash my mouth out with bleach or something gritty-caustic and disinfecting afterwards.

Chapter Seven

Gordon left me in suspense all during the drive over to Divine's. He followed me, and got my chair out of my car for me. Honestly, I felt like I didn't need my chair to get into the shop. With so much tingling and energy flowing through my legs, I could have walked. The problem, and what brought me to the decision to rely on my chair all these years, was that the tingling and energy and sense of control could die at any moment, leaving me stranded. Or falling down at the worst possible time in the worst possible place. Besides, I kind of liked my handicap access card and premier parking spots when I had to go shopping.

Angela didn't demand an explanation when I started with my biggest concern: the candy being drugged or poisoned in some way. She held up a hand, gesturing for us to wait, and hurried upstairs to her apartment. That was when Gordon explained what Mandy had planned.

They were going to a bridal fair in Sandusky this weekend, leaving in two hours, and after hearing what had happened to me, Mandy insisted I come with them. While Gordon had been sent to kidnap me, Mandy was adjusting their hotel reservations, and including Felicity and Jake. We would have connecting rooms. The girls in one room, the guys in another, and when we weren't touring two bridal shows on Saturday and one on Sunday afternoon, we would be relaxing in the hotel's extensive spa facilities.

"If they've got a hot tub and massage therapist, I'm all in," I said.

"That sounds like the perfect prescription," Angela said, coming back far too soon for that mug that smelled of pungent herbs to be steaming. Yet there it was in her hands. For all I knew, she had the water boiling while Gordon and I were on our way, and she just needed to throw the different herbs together into the infuser once she heard what I needed. Sometimes I had the feeling that at least one of the locked doors on the third and fourth floors were actually time travel doorways, allowing her to roll back the clock just enough to have things ready at the moment of need.

I drank down the tea. Slightly gritty despite the fine weave of the infuser, shaped like a phoenix with its wings folded. Knowing Angela, the infuser itself had as much to do with the healing and protective properties of the tea as the herbs themselves did. By the time I related the whole weird incident at work from the beginning, the tea had done its job. The sick feeling, the ache in my temples, and the sugar-and-fat overload, all wiped away. She said Hayward and Rodney were coming to town, probably by late Sunday, and wanted to have a meeting with the guardians. Then she cheered us both by reporting that Freddie Grandstone had tried to come into the shop every day this week, looking for Athena. Obviously, he didn't believe the college when they said Athena had taken a break from classes. Doni had just reported on the progress of officially changing her name, and she said Freddie and his aunt had both come by the Longfellow house twice the past week, looking for Athena. The funny part was that after the Monday visit, whenever Freddie came to Divine's, he parked right in front of the gate, got out of his sports car, and then wandered up and down the sidewalk, looking very lost and confused. He even resorted to checking his phone, probably for his GPS. Somehow, when he got out of his car, he couldn't find Divine's Emporium, even though he stood on the sidewalk with only a wrought iron gate between him and the shop.

Angela credited the swarms of winkies that filled the air inside the barrier of the wrought iron fence that surrounded Divine's.

That was what I called a cloaking field. I could have used something like that for my wheelchair a couple dozen times, the last few years. Too many wackos approaching me after comedy performances, trying to get me to hire them as my writers. Why would I need writers when my own warped mind provided enough insanity and to spare? Or they were the people who saw wheelchair and immediately equated it with limited intelligence and seriously flawed senses. Usually hearing. They always doubled their volume, and wanted to know what group home I lived in. Seriously?

Gordon and I had a good laugh before we left. I headed home to throw some clothes and toiletries into an overnight bag and call my fellow Sunday school teachers, to let them know I wouldn't be there to ride herd on our juvenile-delinquents-in-training. Fortunately, the rest of our team were all planning to be in class. I couldn't decide which of my swimsuits were in better condition, so I packed both, and seriously considered buying a new one at the resort/spa area of the hotel. If they were a decent price. Maybe there would be bathing suits for sale at one of the bridal shows? The question was if a bathing suit intended for a honeymoon would be suitable for someone who was visibly in decent shape, but had some scars she didn't want exposed to public view.

Daniel called while I was tossing items into my toiletries bag. He wanted to come over on Saturday to talk about what had happened that afternoon.

"Sorry, but I'm going out of town in about half an hour, and won't be back until Sunday night. Monday? Meet for lunch?"

"It'll have to be Tuesday. I'm in meetings all day Monday, and I know by the end of the day I won't be in any condition, brain-wise, for the talk we need to have." He chuckled, but it sounded a little strained to me.

Yeah, I could understand what he had to be thinking.

Normally, I would have told him to come over, and asked Gordon and Mandy and the others to delay our drive up to Sandusky for an hour or so. Maybe more, if we had to end up going to Divine's for him to have one of "those" talks with Angela.

However, Hayward had asked me to keep my distance from Daniel until he and his people could go through all those files the Rivals had on the Sheridan family, and figure out just what the links were between them.

I liked Daniel. Even if he was the Evil Overlord and the Evil Empire had changed my writing career. Bottom line, though: the safety of Neighborlee and all it protected came first. That included my physical life. So friendship … that was a minor loss.

At least, I hoped it would be a minor loss, if it came to that.

"Tuesday lunch," he said, his words barely penetrating the buzzing of my thoughts.

I felt kind of overheated when I hung up, so I headed outside with my duffle to wait for Gordon and Mandy to show up. Jake's truck was parked behind Felicity's garage apartment, so I knew he was inside and probably teasing her while she finished packing.

A soft padding on the shoveled driveway got my attention, and I turned to see the dog coming up from the backyard. Felicity's dogs were outside, just lying there, and didn't react to his presence.

Either I was hallucinating or this dog had powers of control over Felicity's mutts that were even stronger than hers ... or this wasn't exactly a dog.

Then it passed through probably the only clear streak of moonlight and I caught my breath as all that shaggy, soft fur vanished, revealing a sleek, streamlined, silver-and-gold shape. In those few seconds before he left the moonlight, he reminded me of those hunting hounds painted on the walls of Egyptian tombs. Royal dogs that accompanied the pharaohs or the gods. Then he left the moonlight and he was a shaggy shape wrapped in thick, soft fur again. He came up to me and went up on his hind legs just a little, to put his paws on my knees, and we were almost eye-to-eye.

"You're more than a dog, aren't you?"

I swore he smiled at me, and not a doggy kind of smile that's just an open mouth and tongue lolling out.

"Have you cleared things with Angela, got her permission to hang around our town?"

Dang, but he kind of shrugged and looked away for a second. If a dog could look sheepish, that one did. Well, it was kind of easy, with all that fur in his face.

"If you're going to hang around here ... look, I'm grateful for what you did today, and if you want to look out for me, if you're joining the guardians, that's cool with me. But you need to go see Angela first. She's the boss. Understand?"

He tipped his head to the right, then to the left, and under all that soft, thick fur his ears seemed to perk up and swivel like radar dishes. He bowed his head and bobbed it up and down twice. Then he took his paw off my knee and backed up and went down on all fours again.

"Are you Fae?" I had to ask, as he turned to trot down the sidewalk toward the street.

His mouth dropped open and a rasping kind of sound that I swear was a weird kind of laughter escaped. Then he trotted away, into the darkness, vanishing way too soon for all that pale fur that should have picked up street light and moonlight.

Felicity's dogs still didn't make a sound or even move. I had to wonder if maybe I had imagined all that. But then I looked down at my knee, and a few strands of that fuzzy fur had been left behind, clinging to my jeans.

Felicity and Jake came out then. She went through the process of setting up the doggy door at the back of the garage-turned-apartment. The dogs only had free access to go in and out when she wasn't going to be there for a day or two. Inside, all the gates had been put in place and the timer/sensor dog waterer-and-feeder Kurt had created for her had been filled and turned on. The weather forecast promised unusually warm weather for Valentine's Day weekend, so the dogs would spend most of their time outdoors in the fenced-in area. Meaning Felicity's place faced less chance of some disaster when her Houdini-inclined dogs got past the barriers.

Gordon and Mandy arrived in the huge, three-row SUV he had found somewhere. Plenty of cargo room for my chair and our luggage. I had the middle seat, with the cooler of snacks, and Felicity and Jake had the back seat. I played with a couple of snarky remarks about being a fifth wheel, which was ironic considering I was the only one with built-in wheels, but I kept them to myself. I had more pressing concerns on my mind once we got onto the highway and heading north-northwest.

"There are plenty of bridal fairs in Cuyahoga County, why Sandusky?"

Mandy laughed. "To get away from our families. I was a witness to what some cousins went through, so I know what disasters can strike if anyone in my family comes to a bridal fair with me. It's worse than *My Big Fat Greek Wedding*. Before the day is half over, we'll be signed up for the cake and invitations and dance band with at least three different places. And the same problem with the reception hall and our honeymoon. Because everybody who came with us would have their own ideas of what was perfect, without asking us, or working together. And then the most horrific fighting between them, and putting guilt trips on us. Plus the problem with non-refundable deposits put down everywhere, for everything. Did I mention some of my cousins have this incredible talent for snooping, to get the credit card numbers and bank account numbers of the bride and groom, so all that money comes out of our pockets when reservations are canceled? Not theirs.

"Plus there's the whole mess when they pick out our colors for us. Which are never our favorite colors, even though the people who grew up with us know what our favorite colors are. Then there's always at least five different places where they order the bridesmaid gowns and tuxes. In the most horrendous colors imaginable. Without knowing who our attendants will be, or their measurements.

"And, after that happened with two weddings, the big interfering dummies learned a new trick. They assigned spies to follow the other teams planning the wedding through the whole bridal fair, to come up behind them at each vendor and cancel orders almost as soon as they were placed. Resulting in even worse family feuds. And then we have to deal with the games everyone plays, the guilt trips they put on us, while every single one of them plays innocent and all hurt feelings and 'What, don't you appreciate all the stress we're handling for you?' and totally oblivious to what we want. And the fact that they're the ones *causing* the stress. Why do relatives always think that their dream wedding is your dream wedding?"

"Probably because we really haven't decided on anything yet?" Felicity called from the back seat.

All five of us laughed at that.

~~~~~

For future note: a bridal fair being held on Valentine's Day weekend means over-the-top goodies and freebies being handed out everywhere. I scored so much chocolate and other heart-shaped sweets, and heart-shaped bottles of massage oil and scented hand cream and flower-scented hand sanitizer and scented candles and on and on. Anything that could have a heart slapped on it was there for the taking.

We got back to the hotel exhausted on Saturday night and played what Kurt had long ago dubbed appetizer roulette. Everyone ordered double-size plates of their favorite appetizers. Without telling the others what we were ordering. Then we sat around a table in the pool area and shared. I slowly steamed myself into total relaxation in the hot tub. The leg tingling had faded about half an hour after we left Neighborlee. So I had been pretty comfortable Friday night and all day Saturday, but this was bliss.

The bliss didn't last long, because I finally gave in to duty and set up a group call with Kurt. We needed to find out what he was doing, watching and figuring things out with Jane, and tell him
~~~~~

about the incident with Romeo and Daniel seeing something, and my upcoming talk with him. Kurt didn't want to talk very long. He didn't want to talk about Jane, either. Mandy and Felicity both widened their eyes and waggled their eyebrows, and for a few seconds I was just as lost as Gordon and Jake.

No. It wasn't possible. Jane was so not the kind of girl Kurt had been looking for all his life. Yes, he wanted a semi-pseudo-superhero girl, but we had always teased him that he wanted a girl like in the comic books. The ones who were top-heavy, so you wondered how they could fly, much less punch out the bad guys. Jane was athletically slim. Besides, the few times I had run into her, the short time I had spent talking with her, she seemed much too commonsense and independent to put up with Kurt's occasional straying into he-man mentality.

~~~~~

We all had an incredibly good, relaxing time. Maybe being surrounded by all the over-the-top glitz and glamour of the wedding industry ignited our sense of the ridiculous. Nobody signed up for a single thing at any of the three bridal fairs we attended. Not even the all-expense-paid honeymoon drawings. Seriously? There had to be a catch among all that fine print none of us could read. Gordon didn't have to tell us that making something difficult to decipher was a sure sign of a boobytrap. Like maybe the winning couple would have to undergo complete makeovers (not paid for), with their names and faces used in advertisements. They would be followed around on their honeymoon, with no privacy, and enough stress and posing and glamour shots to shatter their marriage before it really got started.

We did the tourist thing on the way back from Sandusky, stopping at every attraction along the highway that was still open on a Sunday night. We talked about plans for both weddings, starting with dates and décor. Felicity and Jake were going for simple, inexpensive, and small, late summer at the gazebo in town. Gordon and Mandy were talking a winter wedding, just to frustrate their families by waiting so long. They also wanted it simple and inexpensive, at our church. They were considering no attendants whatsoever just because so many cousins were already fighting over maid of honor and the pecking order. Mandy tried to laugh when she said she should have seen the trouble coming from years
~~~~~

away, when she agreed to be in so many cousins' weddings in the past. Now they expected her to reciprocate.

By the time they dropped me and Felicity and Jake off at my place, I was thinking about my folks -- as if I didn't think about them at least once a day, and pray they were all right? This time, though, I was thinking about how I would handle it if, against all odds, I got married. Mum wouldn't be there to drive me crazy with details, and Pop wouldn't walk or roll me down the aisle.

Then I saw the dark shape huddled up in the corner of the ramp next to my door, and all other thoughts fled my head. I said goodnight to Mandy and Gordon and watched them drive away. Felicity and Jake went into her place for a more private goodbye, and that left me alone with the dog.

"So did you clear things with Angela?" I asked, pitching my voice low, because it was nearly midnight, after all.

The dog raised his head and I shuddered a little, seeing the double exposure of big, fluffy mop, and underneath, the sleek hunting hound with long, pointed muzzle and tall, pointed ears. He sat up, waiting for me when I got to the top of the ramp. As I reached for my backpack to get my keys, he raised one big paw, somehow grasped the doorknob, turned it, and opened the door.

I was too tired to ask or be worried if the dog had opened the door with magic, or my brothers had gone to bed with the house unlocked. Not that any strangers or troublemakers would dare try to sneak in. Our enemies knew better, even the crazy ones. The dog moved aside. I wheeled into the house. He stayed outside, with just his long muzzle crossing the threshold.

"Are you waiting to be invited?" I was also too tired to debate whether this was a trick. As far as I was concerned, the dog had been warned not to mess with us because Angela would deal with him if he did. "You can come in, but maybe you shouldn't let my brothers see you. Or is it that only I can see you? Forget I asked that. They saw you at the office the other day ..."

I waited until he stepped in and passed the kitchen table, then I shut and locked the door. We navigated through the shadows, down the hall to my bedroom.

I had to use the bathroom. After I had washed my face and came out, I found the dog had pulled a small throw rug from the hall closet and put it in the corner of the hallway by my door.

Conveniently placed so no one would step over him when a brother-type person came stumbling out of his bedroom with one eye closed, on his way to the kitchen for breakfast.

"Okay, if you're going to stay here," I said, as I wheeled past him to my bedroom door, "I need a name for you. You're not wearing a collar, so I have the feeling a collar and license would be an insult."

The dog's ears flicked and his mouth dropped open in that not-quite-doggy grin.

"So I can't find out your name. Should I give you one, or wait until Angela tells me your name?"

His ears flicked, and I had the feeling he was laughing at me. Forget that -- it wasn't a feeling, I could almost hear the laughter.

"Okay, smart-guy," I said, and wheeled into my bedroom. I turned around and looked out at him again. "Keep it up, and I'll stick you with a name you'll hate. How about something from mythology?"

More ear flicks. My head was getting fuzzier by the second, and I really wanted to go to bed. Being me, I didn't want to let this issue rest. The guy was irritating me. I couldn't call up many dog names from mythology and legend. Definitely not Old Yeller or Lassie or Rin-Tin-Tin or even Petey, from the Little Rascals. Fluffy, Hagrid's dog from the Harry Potter books? No, too cute.

Then I had it.

"You're here as my bodyguard, aren't you? The powers-that-be or whoever is allied with us, watching what's going on, they're worried, they know I'm being targeted maybe?" I waited, and the dog slowly sat up and nodded his head twice. That put a shudder in my gut and a chill down my back. "There's a whole lot more to you than even I can see ... you're kind of a reverse of Cerberus, maybe? Protecting us from the underworld and Big Ugly?"

The dog's ears swiveled forward and seemed to point at me. He closed his mouth and gave me a very somber look.

"Okay, until you let me know otherwise, we'll go with Cerberus, okay?" Then my sleepy brain threw in some whimsy. "Cerb, for short?"

Cerb's mouth dropped open in a grin and he settled down on the rug in the hall, where he could see down the hall and see my bedroom door at the same time.

"Good night, Cerb. I hope we have some leftovers you like, for breakfast, until I can get you some dogfood you'll like. Or is that an insult, too?"

Cerb just gave me a level look, neither insulted or amused. Fine, we would deal with that question in the morning.

My last thought before sleep pulled me down in a dizzy, darkening whirlpool, was to wonder whether it was wrong, even dangerous, to feed a Fae dog ordinary dogfood.

~~~~~

Cerb was there in the morning, so I didn't hallucinate him in my exhaustion. Neither of my brothers noticed him until both had eaten breakfast and washed up and gotten dressed for the day. By then, I was dressed for work, and Cerb and I were having breakfast. I decided to play it safe and fed him the same thing I made for myself: sausage and scrambled eggs with cheesy home fries left over from the cooking the boys did over the weekend.

"Huh, I kind of wondered." Harry paused in the doorway from the hall, to look down at Cerb, who was eating from the glass mixing bowl, set on a throw rug by the coat tree bench.

"Wondered what?" I asked, nearly choking on my last swallow of green tea.

"He was hanging around all weekend, and Felicity's dogs acted like he wasn't there, and I heard about the dog that got into the office and ..." He shrugged. "Got yourself a new friend?"

"You could say that."

Leave it to Harry to take new weirdness in stride. Pete, however, was more normal in his reaction.

"Yes, we finally got a dog!" He made a wide berth around Cerb as he headed for the door. "Where'd you get him? What's his name? Hey, buddy, are we gonna be friends?" He eased in, hand outstretched, very careful as he touched Cerb for the first time.

Cerb's tail turned into a cyclone as Pete patted and stroked him for a couple minutes. Then Pete had to leave for school and Harry had to head out for his first deliveries of the day, and it was time for me to go to work. Cerb followed me out the door like it was our ordinary pattern, established for years.

"So what are you going to do all day? Ride with me to work? Check out the town?"

Cerb tipped his head to the right, then the left, then his tail
~~~~~

slowly wagging, he trotted down the ramp and around the corner of the house. I didn't see him as I got into my Jeep, and I didn't see him on my drive to the paper. He showed up to walk with me when I headed out at lunchtime, and seemed to enjoy the deluxe extra-meat steak burrito I bought him for lunch. He vanished on the short trip back to the office, and was there at the end of the day, waiting next to my Jeep, to ride with me to Angela's for the meeting of the guardians.

He sat in the front seat and I had to fight down the urge to put the seatbelt on him. That could have turned out awkward. I debated for about two seconds if I would have to put down the window for him, but it was too dang cold out with nightfall fast approaching, and I just wasn't going to have that argument with him. Cerb looked straight ahead and didn't seem to need to have his head hanging out, so maybe that wouldn't have been a problem. When we got to Divine's, I fully expected to disembark in reverse order from how we got into the car -- I would maneuver my chair out of the back seat, settle into it, then Cerb would climb out the driver's side and I would close the door. However, when I sat down, there he was, already standing on the snow-covered grass, waiting for me to bump my chair up over the curb and head for the gate. I figured he had opened the door latch with his mouth.

"There better not be dog spit all over my door handle."

Cerb snorted at me and sauntered down the flagstone path ahead of me to the front door. There was a definitely saucy swagger to his backside and tail.

Angela came to the door before either of us reached the porch. Cerb went into puppy mode, frisking around her skirts, and then darted past her through the open door.

"So, is it okay he's hanging around?" I asked, pivoting to wheel up the short ramp that only seemed to be visible when I needed it.

"I honestly doubt that 'okay' could ever be applied when that one makes an appearance." Angela gestured for me to go into the shop ahead of her.

"I got the feeling he's here to deflect trouble?"

"Trouble draws him, threats, and he's another sign that the energy levels are rising higher than they've been in years." Angela sighed and for a moment, she looked tired. She gave a pensive glance toward the main room. "Maybe decades."

"Decades?"

I turned into the main room, to find Ford Longfellow on one knee, giving a good, vigorous scratching to Cerb. That entirely doggie look of ecstasy in his eyes hinted he was ready to melt into a puddle on the floor. His back leg was thumping in counterpoint to his tail, which didn't seem right, to me.

"Haven't seen this guy since I was ..." Ford sighed and his smile dimmed. "Since I was at NCH. Bad sign that he's back?" His gaze landed on me and then flicked to Cerb. "Uh huh. Someone's targeting you, Lanie. Hate to tell you, but you need to be warned." He maneuvered up off his knee and slid into the chair behind him.

"I kind of figured out when the bodyguard showed up. So he was around when you were a kid?" I guessed.

"Him," Angela said, "or another one wearing the same costume."

Cerb snorted and settled down at Ford's feet, tongue lolling out and looking entirely self-satisfied.

"Costume? So like ... what, he's a probe sent from another planet or universe or something? What is he, or what is the being or mind or whatever inside the body?" I had to ask.

"The easiest explanation is that he is an overgrown winkie." Angela wrinkled up her nose at Cerb, who sneezed this time, and stepped around the counter. "I was pleased that you sent him over here to clear things with me before you fully accepted his presence."

"So any word on who or what is targeting me, and what I can expect?"

"Unfortunately, there is only a sense of malevolence, a sense of purpose and of energy gathering to make a strike. Instead of the general attack on the barrier, you are the focal point. Enough of a focus that our allies in other dimensions sensed it and felt it worth the energy expenditure and risk to send help." She gestured at Cerb.

Chapter Eight

The door opened, letting in a gust of cold air strong enough to get down the short hall to us. Kurt, Felicity, and Jake came in together. Angela set out hot drinks for all of us and in the fuss of pulling up more chairs to accommodate everyone, I didn't realize Cerb had left until he just wasn't there. I gestured down at Ford's feet. He looked, shrugged, and shook his head. I guessed Cerb would be waiting for me when I left. Maybe he felt it necessary to walk patrol while the guardians were indoors, meeting. Maybe he didn't want to risk getting stepped on.

Gordon and Mandy didn't join us. Neither did Charlotte, but Doni, Wallace and Cosmo came. When Col. Hayward made his appearance, I learned he had left Rodney behind at their headquarters, wherever that was, to keep working on the boxes and crates and reams of records they had liberated from the Rivals' records warehouse. What was with bad guys that they generated even more paperwork than allegedly law-abiding bureaucracy?

Doni updated us briefly on the progress of her application to legally change her name. Her father's side of the family had no legal right to know, but that didn't mean some schmoozer wouldn't alert them, in the hopes of currying favor. The Longfellows were braced for a last-ditch effort to sweet-talk Doni or even try to kidnap and brainwash her into being a true Halliday.

Finally, we got down to the real business that brought us there. Hayward reported on what he and Rodney had been digging out of the records taken from the Rivals. First off, they had proved that the people acting as caretakers for the property didn't know what they were guarding, for a fake corporation.

The records dump was extensive. As in three sub-basements the caretakers didn't even know were there. Different sections of the complex were assigned to different factions or divisions within the Rivals. From what Rodney and Hayward's team had uncovered so far, each faction had accumulated evidence to use against the others, if anything in their operations went south and they fell into a fatal power struggle. That was good for our side.

"Maybe," Hayward said, when Ford verbalized that thought. "It's pretty contradictory, when you read far enough. For all we know, we'll find out everything we dug up is planted, or it's part of a failed plot, or something they set up as a failsafe. In fact, that's what Rodney fears. A failsafe, just like all the false stories about ..." He paused and nodded to me. "About the Sheridans."

I got this uneasy shiver across my back and over the top of my scalp, with a twisting kind of nauseated feeling. Just for a second.

"The rumors the Grandstones spread, that there was something going on between Sylvia and Daniel?" Felicity offered.

"We found multiple versions of every event. It was like a clearinghouse for a massive PR campaign. Instead of deleting the files when something didn't work, they kept it." Hayward shook his head. "It's going to take months of reading, going through files, backtracking records, separating truth from lies. If there is any truth. It would be hopeless without London and Sherwood to speed through and organize and compare for us."

"Multiple histories? Like someone is practicing quantum physics?" Doni offered. She grinned when Cosmo's mouth dropped open. "You didn't think I was listening, did you?"

"What branch of quantum physics is that?" I asked, only vaguely remembering something I had overheard the kids discussing months ago.

"Basically, the theory that reality can be rewritten by the power of belief," Wallace said. "Yeah, it kind of makes sense. Or maybe they're just pack rats and they held onto the fake stories in case they came in handy in the future. For blackmail, maybe? What's the worst part of it? Some of the stories blame multiple people for the same crimes?"

"That's it in a nutshell." Hayward gave him a little nod and smile. "We have evidence of Grandstone activities on behalf of the Rivals. Enough to get them thrown into prison in multiple countries around the world. The same evidence paints the Sheridans as the guilty parties in the same activities. Then there is evidence naming the Grandstones as the ones trying to lay the blame on the Sheridan clan, then the flip side, with the same evidence saying the Sheridans are trying to frame the Grandstones. Then, another division uses that evidence to portray both families as partners in multiple activities and businesses. Evidence sitting on shelves only an aisle away proves that neither family has ever done business with, much less heard of the other."

"The Rivals are utter loonies," Kurt muttered.

"And then there are the records in another section, studying the damage done to the Rivals by an organization they are unable to identify. Bits of data picked up over decades, especially when they are beaten in the race to identify and snatch a talented child from Neighborlee Children's Home, when gifts manifest."

"Hoax?" Jake said.

"The people we're sure Jane works for?" Felicity added.

"If that's true, if Hoax is completely opposed to these people …" Ford glanced at Hayward, who gave him a slow, definite nod. "People, we have been hobbling and blinding ourselves for years, fighting people who should have been our allies. Hoax has been snatching children away to protect them from the Rivals, and we've been fighting both sides. Franklin, it's time we got together with these fellows at Hoax."

"That's a given." Hayward glanced at Angela. "But I think the more important task right now is to determine if the Sheridans are innocent, if they're being framed, or if they've been the masterminds all these years, using the Grandstones to take the fall as the visible face of the effort."

"Simply because we have befriended the heir to the throne." Angela nodded. "Lanie, I'm sorry, but perhaps you should put more distance between yourself and Daniel. For the time being."

"That's going to be hard," I said, with a shrug. "After what happened Friday … Daniel saw something. I'm sure of it. And he wants to talk. But if he's got guardian-level talents, inherited from his grandfather, and they're working with the Rivals … maybe this is what Cerb is here to protect me from? Is Daniel preparing to make a move on me? Maybe that was the whole purpose for the company buying the *Tattler*, to get at me?"

"Who's Cerb?" Kurt said.

"The dog I was telling you about last week. He's not really a dog."

"Oh, great." He gestured with a jerk of his chin at Felicity. "Isn't that your territory? Aren't you falling down on the job?"

"Like she said, he's not really a dog," Felicity shot back. She wrinkled up her nose. The light moment didn't last long.

"I'm afraid Lanie's theory might be right," Hayward said. "One of the Rivals' storylines says Sheridan Communications coming back to Ohio, digging in roots here, will support the long-range plan to establish a new base of operations right under our noses. It could be the reason for sending Sylvia after Daniel, to trap him into a relationship and give them an opening to take over the corporation. Or, if half their stories are true, the Sheridans have been part of the planning all along.

"Maybe they're ramping up for a repeat of their effort at New Year's, to open the doorway and make contact with the power or being on the other side of the barrier."

"Oh, goody," Kurt muttered. "The Oil Slick Returns. The Oil Slick Monster Strikes Back. Dawn of the Oil Slick. Bride of the Oil Slick. How many sequels can they make to the same badly written movie?" He slouched on his chair, grumping, with a hint of mischief in his eyes.

I really loved Kurt, my pseudo-big-brother. He always knew when a bit of snark helped lighten the mood.

Hayward snorted, and one corner of his mouth quirked up. "In most of the storylines, they firmly believe that power will be their tool. They have some delusion that it's more an amorphous energy, semi-aware power, rather than a sentient being with an agenda of its own. Therefore, they believe they will have no trouble bending that power to their will and goals."

"That either means they have had no direct contact with Big Ugly, or they have, and it has completely fooled them, to manipulate them. Most likely to sacrifice them in the effort to open the barrier," Angela said. "My greatest fear is that they have been able to connect events and activities, to identify the guardians. Now they can strike at us individually, not just in a general effort to do some damage."

"So my accident was a lucky strike for them, but now they know at least I'm a guardian, and they're connecting the rest of you to me?" I hated to vocalize it, but what good would it do anyone hiding the theories and possible truth?

"I fear so. They have been observing us for generations now, picking up patterns, putting the pieces together after the fact, making feints and drawing back. Gaining ground and moving slowly. They suffered a huge loss at New Year's. Perhaps because they expected a major victory and put a great deal on the line. Or perhaps that was a testing feint, and they were willing to suffer losses to deceive us, make us relax, while their true weapon got into place. Close to us." She sighed. "Under our noses. Accepted as a friend and ally."

"Daniel. Sorry," Kurt said. "I thought the guy was pretty decent. Maybe even somebody we could work with. I mean, since the grandfather was a Lost Kid. Makes sense, if you think about it. The Grandstones have screwed up so badly, it's time to move out the second string losers and bring in the ringer."

"So what do I tell Daniel when we meet for lunch tomorrow?" I said. "He saw something. I'm positive. And he seemed kind of immune to things at New Year's. He saw the Oil Slick. He didn't get his time sense rearranged and he remembered things that happened, that other people temporarily forgot."

"Play dumb?" Wallace held up his hands, like he expected to be hit. "No, I mean like pretend that you're just making it up as you go along. No guardians, no alliances, no warriors defending the town. Solo acts."

"That's kind of hard, because he was there when we joined up and stood against that thing, and he knows we were working with Angela," Kurt said.

"Maybe go the other direction?" Doni said. "You know, play hard ball. Tell him you like him, he's a nice guy, but he has to prove himself before you can tell him anything?"

"If I tell you the truth, I'll have to kill you," Jake muttered. He grinned when Felicity sighed and slapped his arm.

"That might just work," Hayward said. "Test him, make him prove himself, put his neck on the line, maybe introduce you to his contacts."

"A sting operation," Cosmo said. "Cool." He smirked at Doni. "Major cool."

She groaned and leaned over, bumping him. *Major cool* was her pet phrase. Gee, it was cute seeing kids in love, teasing each other.

"Reveal enough to make him hungry," Kurt said. "Or drive him nuts, if it's like we hope and the Sheridans are just targets. Maybe coming back to Neighborlee, connecting with the power, that's made him able to see things he couldn't see before. Could drive him away if he sees enough. And like a lot of people, he'll be so freaked he'll make himself forget."

"Yeah, great, wonderful plan," I muttered.

"Hey, speaking of contacts," Felicity said, turning to Kurt. "How's it going with Jane, getting close to her? When are we going to meet the big bosses of Hoax?"

"It's … complicated." He shrugged and looked down at his clasped hands.

That was just different enough from the usual confident, determined Kurt I had grown up with, I had the feeling something weird was going on with him and Jane.

Or maybe that was it? Something was going on with him and Jane, relationship-wise, and it was getting in the way of his investigation?

Hoo boy …

I mentioned my suspicion to Angela, after the meeting had broken up and everyone else had gone home. I was delaying, waiting for Cerb to show up. He hadn't yet.

"Hmm, yes. I'm detecting some negative vibrations, so to speak, around the shop. Some tension between the two of them that wasn't there last week …." Angela tapped her index finger on her bottom lip. "It might be time for some intervention. Or give Kurt a good hard kick to his backside."

"How about upside his head, kick his brain into gear again?" I offered.

She laughed at that.

Cerb was waiting, sitting on the hood of my Jeep when I got outside.

"So, overgrown winkie?" I said. He sneezed at me and got up to jump down and walk around to the driver's side door. "Do you want to help me pick out your food? If this is just a borrowed costume, we need to take care of it."

He tipped his head to one side, and his eyes narrowed just a little while he considered that. Funny, but it didn't really freak me out to be having a conversation with him, as one-sided as it was. Maybe I would be worried if there were other people around, witnessing it. Cerb ended up coming into the grocery store with me. No one seemed to notice him, or else they figured dog plus woman in a wheelchair equaled service dog, so they couldn't throw him out. Cerb led me to the pet food aisle. He walked up and down a few times, sniffing at the bags of dry, nosing the boxes of treats. Finally, he nosed a few cans of wet, a bag of dry, and some bacon-based treats. Well, it wasn't the most expensive stuff, but it wasn't the economy, pseudo-meat-flavored stuff, either. I pulled out the net bag I kept in the front pocket of my backpack and hung it off the pegs on the side of my chair, put the cans and box in that, slid the bag onto my lap, and we headed to the cash register.

On the way, Cerb led me on a detour to the day-old rack, where they were just loading up all the bakery goodies that hadn't sold that day and had been marked down. I checked my watch. It was after eleven, so technically that made it day-old? Cerb got up on his hind legs and nosed the long boxes of donuts, a dozen to a box, all of them with pink icing and all sorts of silly Valentine's-themed sugar sprinkles. I bought three boxes. Hey, I love a good sugar-fat-fried-dough-rush once in a while.

Cerb ate five donuts on the way home. I ate two. It was kind of nice knowing we had that addiction in common.

The boys had put together a dog bed for him and rigged one of those self-feeding water dishes. The kind with an upside down two-liter bottle that kept the water bowl filled. Cerb's tail wagged a little faster when he saw that. I offered him another donut before I went to my room, and he surprised me by refusing. It was kind of nice knowing my bodyguard had some self-restraint.

Most of my prayers when I went to bed were for guidance in handling Daniel when we met for lunch the next day. Snapping out the snark, playing games with people's minds, is very different from walking a mental tightrope and deliberately lying to someone you're starting to consider a friend. I wasn't sure I could do it.

~~~~~

Okay, can I say I'm living proof that God answers prayers? And it's great when He does so in ways we didn't ask?

Daniel called about 10:30, cancelling our lunch meeting. Another crisis to deal with, related to the problems the Grandstones were making for the PR department. I sent a quick message to the AI's, asking if they had caught anything, legal filings, press releases. Sherwood got back to me about 12:30, when I was coming back from a lunchtime roll around town with Cerb. We shared one of the super-deluxe corned beef sandwiches from Hunky & Dory's. Those sandwiches were enough for three people to share. Cerb did
~~~~~

not want the pickle or the horseradish coleslaw. Sherwood sent me a string of files, showing Grandstone activity in Paris and then Frankfurt, placing false press releases about Sylvia's activities. Specifically, a massive shopping trip, putting together her wedding trousseau. Seriously? They were trying to convince people in other countries that Sylvia and Daniel were getting married? What would they do when the bride didn't show up at the altar? I read on, half-expecting to find a press release or hidden camera footage revealing a Frankenstein creation Sylvia, re-animated, tottering around and wailing for "my Danny" to come help her.

Any way of shredding those press releases and sending out evidence it's all fake and she wasn't there? Maybe show she hasn't been seen since New Year's anywhere? I typed in response to those articles. Amazing I was that coherent, since I was wearing gloves and tapping on the tiny screen keyboard on my phone.

Sherwood responded with a string of smiley faces.

~~~~~

The Jane-and-Kurt situation hit the fan that evening. The big goofus finally confessed to us later that he had been kind of nasty to Jane. Playing tricks on her. Using his Handyman talent to borrow her Ghost powers and use them against her. Trying to irritate her into considering leaving Neighborlee. Pushing her, to prove what side she was on. That had been going on for just a few days, until Angela showed up, metaphorically slapped their faces, and told them to talk and play nice.

Before they had that talk, a spoiled rich kid named Evan got nasty with Penny, the orphanage girl who was working for Jane. Something or someone, we weren't sure who, intervened and nearly sent Evan's expensive sports car over the edge into the quarries. He and Penny shouldn't have been at the quarries that late in the evening, but that was part of Evan's ploy to get Penny to break the purity pledge she had made in our church youth group. Jane and Kurt were there, and they worked together to prevent disaster. Then, they continued working together, trying to track down the source of the energy that slapped the snotty rich boy. Another emerging semi-pseudo-superhero?

Over the next few days, they tried to find out what was going on. Kurt became worried for Jane, because suddenly she was drained and eating three times as much as usual.
~~~~~

I worried when I didn't see Jane in church that Sunday. Kurt was spending lots of time with her, or hanging around the spa, trying to decipher what he could only describe as fluctuating energy fields that he didn't think were coming from Jane.

And all this time, Daniel was busy dealing with fallout from the Grandstones trying to practice their own brand of quantum physics, rewriting reality with the power of belief, excessive volume, and venom. Someone hacked security recordings at the exclusive shops where Sylvia had allegedly been shopping and proved she hadn't been there. Now, the Grandstones were getting nasty and the press was having a field day, commiserating with Daniel or else labeling him the runaway groom. Which kept him away from the *Tattler* office, with trips to Sheridan Communications headquarters to deal with the PR storm.

Maybe I prayed too hard?

On a different level, all this trouble for the Grandstones was theoretically draining more of their resources, claiming more of their attention, and making them less useful to the Rivals establishing a foothold or base camp or whatever in Neighborlee.

If the Grandstones were their only allies in Neighborlee.

If the Sheridan clan weren't the Rivals' true ace in the hole.

If.

Ever consider a two-letter word worse than a four-letter word?

Monday, Kurt emailed me and Felicity and asked us to include Ford, Angela, and Hayward. Something that Jane referred to as "the Voice" had made contact and was asking for help. He or it or they claimed to be trapped in another dimension (*gee, that didn't sound familiar*) and to have information on the truth of Jane's origins, maybe all the Lost Kids. Kurt didn't trust it, because every time Jane had contact with it, she was drained, pale and disoriented. Worse, sometimes he sensed a discord of energy, and other times he couldn't sense Jane's presence at all if he was nearby. He had been able to sense when Big Ugly/Oil Slick was on the move leading up to New Year's Eve, but he couldn't sense the Voice. That worried him. What worried him more was that thanks to how he had originally approached her, pushing her and testing her, he was afraid she didn't quite trust him. He was afraid maybe she trusted the Voice more than him.

Well, duh, I didn't blame her.

So it was no wonder that the dreams came back that night. The ones Felicity and I had before the extra weirdness started tangling around Eden. Dreams about something with lots of sharp teeth, chewing on the roots of the houses in town. Deep below Neighborlee, I had a glimpse of something big kind of rolling over in its sleep, like it was having a bad dream. Grumbling and cranky. Swatting at a fly buzzing around its head. Yeah, and if this stuff we were facing came from it when it was asleep, please, don't ever wake it up, because we would be in deep doodoo trouble when it finally woke up on the wrong side of the bed.

I got up early the next morning, about 5am. Felicity must have gotten out of bed about the same time, because the water had just started dripping into the coffee pot for Pop's special brew tea when there was a knock on the door. Cerb went over to the door, but before he could get up on his hind legs and grasp the handle with both paws, the door opened, and Felicity came in. When the dreams had started bothering us around Christmas, I had taken to leaving the door unlocked so she could walk in whenever she needed. I hadn't taken to locking up again. I mean, why bother? Especially now that Cerb was here. We were in Neighborlee, we were the guardians, and if something really wanted to hurt us, a locked door wasn't going to do a whole heck of a lot of good.

Felicity was kind of funny looking, with her big emerald green robe and her hair sticking up in all directions and neon orange boots on her bare legs. She kicked her boots off and curled up in a chair at the end of the table with her legs tucked up inside her robe. Cerb whined and went over to her and rested his head on her thigh. She smiled a little and leaned down to hug him and give him a brisk rub. Loving on dogs was always good for Felicity's mood.

"The dream is back," she said, after she finished and Cerb came back to his rug, and we looked at each other, waiting for the other one to speak.

Or in my case, trying to wake up all the way so I could manage coherent thought. It's a terrible thing when you know you could fall back to sleep if you just closed your eyes, but you're afraid of what you'll see when you go back into dreamland again.

"Think we should go talk to Angela again?" I said.

"Oh, yeah. If the dreams came just before that interdimensional whammy started running around Eden, maybe these dreams are a sign it's starting again. I want to head this thing off at the pass."

"I'm thinking, if Jane came to town because of the ruckus at Eden, maybe we should include her."

"What are the chances she'll trust us if she knows we're a team with Kurt?"

I flinched when the coffee maker let out that loud gurgle that meant it was nearly at the bottom of the reservoir. I rolled over to the refrigerator to put some ice in our mugs, from the ice dispenser in the door. Otherwise it would be too hot to drink right away.

"This is one of those times when men need to be saved from themselves," Felicity said, once we had our mugs filled and were adding lots of cream. "Yeah, I can see him doing the cave man routine to protect us, but … Jane is one of us. Angela likes her. I say that's an automatic positive vote."

"True." I took a testing sip of my tea, then a long drink. "I say we get Angela as reinforcement and get things straightened out. There are way too many questions as it is. If we're looking at an attack from the Rivals, we need to make sure Jane is on our side, and her bosses at Hoax."

We planned to go to Angela after I got off work that afternoon, of course. We didn't get to be the age we were, with only one major setback in our superhero careers, without learning some caution and commonsense maneuvers. Felicity was right. If Angela liked Jane and sent Penny to work for her, then Jane was on the right side of the equation.

~~~~~

Felicity and Cerb and I hurried into Divine's that night, dripping gobs of melting snow and ice. The reprieve in the weather had definitely ended, and we were paying for the warm snap with a vengeance. Diane was just finishing up her stint at the register and called out a farewell to Angela as we wiped the crusty ice off my wheels and hung up our coats. She grimaced as she looked past us, out the door.

"I'm half-tempted to spend the night. Looks miserable out there. But I have a test in the morning and I haven't studied yet and my books are at home," she added, as she pulled her scarf from around her neck and wrapped it around her head, muffling her last few words as she covered her mouth.

"Good luck. If you get lost, give me a call and I'll send out my
~~~~~

dogs," Felicity offered.

"Those slobber machines? I'd rather freeze, thanks," Diane said, chuckling. She nodded to us and headed out into the threatened whiteout.

"You two must have something very serious to talk about," Angela said, beckoning for us to come to the main room.

Of course, our drinks were waiting at the little bistro table in the corner.

"It's Jane," Felicity said, while I was still maneuvering my chair up to the table.

That hot chai latte with whipped cream and cinnamon sprinkles was calling my name. It had been a rough day at the paper, with two truly moronic Terry letters to answer and another lunatic fan who called every single paper in the conglomerate, trying to track down where Terry worked.

"I think it's time to stop letting Kurt be point man, and confront her," I said. "We both had those Big Ugly-type dreams again last night. We're pretty sure Jane is tied into whatever is making our freak-o-meters go off again, and while Kurt is telling some of what's going on, he isn't telling it all. We think he messed up."

"Ah." Angela nodded and sat very still, hands folded in her lap. She never lost her usual serene, slightly amused expression, but there was a new depth to her eyes that made me think she saw very, very far away, beyond the shop. "I am flattered, and yet discouraged, that you two think I am somehow the fountainhead of all answers."

"But if you don't know, then we're stuck. Right?" Felicity asked.

Chapter Nine

"There are times when it is best if we operate on faith," Angela said slowly, "unsure of either the extent of our abilities or our limitations, or the abilities and limitations of our enemies. Too much confidence can be as bad for us, in our duties as guardians, as the fear that we are incapable. I think sometimes the greatest miracles come when we don't know we are defeated, and we keep trying."

"Meaning?" Felicity turned to glare at me. "You just thought of something, didn't you?"

I didn't realize I had made any sound or reacted, but she was right, something had popped up at the back of my mind. Not quite solid as a thought yet.

"Not really just thought, but ..." I shrugged. "Okay, say Jane is the same Jane who got yanked out of NCH just when we were starting to think another Lost Kid was starting to emerge. And yes, she and Kurt are sensing another Lost Kid about to bloom. And that's what brought her here, not the mess at New Year's."

"So she's back to grab more kids who are ready to emerge?"

"No," Angela said. "Jane has come home. She is seeking answers, not students or minions. I am inclined to believe she is the next step, following up after that letter left with Franklin, when he and the boys were rescued from the Rivals."

"And Kurt messed up things, going all hormonal-hyper-protective, pushing her when we told him not to. Great," I muttered, more thinking aloud than really talking to them.

Angela reached out to take my hand. "I have firmly believed that as the enemy tries harder and the stakes grow higher, the numbers of the guardians will increase, and our allies will emerge. Or return, as the case may be." She tipped her head to one side and smiled just a little more. "How often have the three of you gnawed on the question of why you were left behind, not taken by the Rivals or by Hoax? You weren't left because you were unimportant, but because seeing eyes were made blind. You are the ones with the hardest duty of all: waiting."

"They also serve who do laundry," I whispered. Felicity sighed, but a moment later she laughed. She caught the reference, to a Star Trek fanzine story about a lowly crewmember who worked in the laundry room on the *Enterprise* and never got anywhere near the bridge and the command crew.

"Okay, so we've been whining," she said. "Are we making the right move, trusting Jane before we've really got any answers? Big Ugly is on the move again? Is that what our dreams mean?"

"I believe so," Angela said, nodding. "It might be that if you confront it and attack it before it can return to its pattern, you can halt it even more strongly, do it more damage, make it wait and rest and lick its wounds even longer."

"But not stop it?" She looked as disappointed as I felt.

"I'm sorry. The more crucial the timing and the choices that we make, the less clearly I can see and sense. Often, I can only trust that when the time is right, I will see clearly. If I do not have clear answers for you, then I must take it as a sign that you are more than capable of handling this test. And so must you."

"Yeah, well, Lanie is the expert on faith," Felicity said, hooking her thumb in my direction. She looked a little more glum than her tone implied, and she focused on her mocha espresso.

I heard the wind howling beyond the deep windows of the shop. I did not look forward to going out into that slush and ice and the ruts that had likely formed from my trip between the Jeep and the front door. I supposed I should have brought four pairs of gloves with me today, instead of my usual two -- one pair to dry out while I wore the other. Fur-lined chain mail gloves wouldn't be a bad invention right about now, and actual chains to go over my wheelchair tires, or maybe even snow spikes. Unfortunately, despite all the wonders and quirky, unbelievable things that could be found at Divine's, I doubted even Angela's magical talent for finding the unfindable could produce wheelchair tire chains. So I didn't even let myself hope, much less ask.

When Felicity and I finished our drinks, Angela took the tray away, and came to the door with a long, hooded cloak she flung around her shoulders while we were getting our coats on. We both gave her surprised looks, but she just looked at us, her serene smile quirked with mischief.

"Are we going somewhere?" Felicity finally asked.

"I thought we agreed it was time to stop waiting for Kurt to finish licking his male ego wounds, and confront Jane directly."

"Fine," I said.

What I really wanted to say was something along the lines of: *You already know the answers, but you're not going to tell us, are you?*

Because I knew the answer to that was yes, and while I loved Angela dearly, sometimes I just couldn't stand to see her smirk. That would hack me off enough to do or say something stupid.

So off the three of us went in my Jeep. Without Cerb. As soon as we stepped out the door, he ran off into the blowing sleety-slushy snow. I knew better than to worry about him. He might even beat us to Jane's, and I knew he would be waiting when I got home.

We were able to park alongside Jane's spa just as she came to the door to turn the sign around so it read *closed*, and pull the shade down in front of the big display window. Angela climbed out of my Jeep and Jane came to the door.

"And here I thought this storm would drive away all my customers, and I could close up early, have a movie and a big bowl of popcorn."

All I got from her was a grin when I used my telekinesis to push my chair up over the curb and threshold and down into the shop. Okay, so she expected some special stuff from us. That made me curious just how much Jane and Kurt had been talking, and why exactly he hadn't reported much of anything to us.

Honestly, the whole encounter went far too smoothly, considering how much inadvertent sabotage Kurt had done against an alliance between Jane's team and ours. She welcomed us in and didn't pause very long when Felicity confronted her with our knowing she was the Ghost. Soon, we were all comfortably seated in Jane's loft apartment upstairs. Just like Kurt had described to us, it was very nice. Jane believed in open space, low couches and floor pillows, and lots of books. Not much in the way of knickknacks or decorations. She served us some simple refreshments on clunky, simple plates and mugs in dark blue, dark green and white. I liked her style. Simple, useful. Her dishes reminded me of the heavy, durable ones at the summer camp our church sent the kids to on Kelly's Island.

We talked about our training in being semi-pseudo-superheroes, on both sides, learning from comic books and some of the things Jane had learned from her teachers, whom she referred to as the Old Poops. Angela just sat there, quietly sipping her drink, watching us with that serene, slightly amused, thoughtful smile.

Jane became my hero by upgrading the cheese and crackers and other snacks to two big gourmet, self-rising pizzas. When they were ready to come out of the oven, Felicity got up to help her.

"You're doing fine," Angela murmured, as we watched the two of them pull out dishes and the pizzas and set things up with all the ease of people who had worked together a long time.

"It's too easy. I like her, and I trust your judgment. So I know we're doing the right thing, taking the right approach, but that still doesn't make it feel right for it to be this easy," I said, just as quietly.

"You've earned some easiness," she said with a reassuring flash of mischief in her eyes. "Trust yourself.

"Okay, where were we?" Jane said, as she came back over to the seating area and deposited the pizzas, which smelled heavenly, onto the low round table within everyone's easy reach. Just because we were among friends, I showed off a little by mentally lifting two pieces onto a plate and lifting the plate to my lap. Jane grinned, watching me.

"What do you see when she does that?" Felicity asked. "Do you see any energy at work? When we fought the Oil Slick, with all the warping of fields and dimensions and whatever, Gordon could see the power going out of Lanie when she slammed a bunch of chairs into it."

"Yeah, streamers of energy going out from her head, and ghost arms reaching and lifting the pizza and the dish." Jane's smile faded into something thoughtful. "And I definitely need more details than the little Kurt told me, about New Year's and the fight right afterward. Not that I'm going to tell Demetrius and Beau squat until I get some more answers from them." She nodded decisively.

From there, we learned how Demetrius and Beau, the Old Poops, identified which Lost Kids needed watching, and how they swept in and faked the right paperwork to let them make their new students vanish to safety. I felt a little better, realizing Kurt, Felicity and I had been just different enough, low-key enough, we fell through the cracks. That was a good thing, because the Rivals didn't notice us either. After hearing how Rodney had been raised, I wouldn't have wanted to go through that, either.

We had a light moment when we realized that Jane and everyone at Hoax also referred to the Rivals as the Rivals. That made sense, since Col. Hayward got the name from Demetrius and Beau when they were rescuing him and the other boy the Rivals had tried to snatch.

We learned Jane had been acting as Fendersburg's Ghost as a trap. She wanted to get the attention of the Rivals and hopefully get them to step out of the shadows, so they could be identified, to help Hoax in its efforts to dismantle them and free other prisoners. She was intrigued to learn we had rescued Rodney during the whole mess at New Year's and were learning quite a bit from him. We laughed to learn how Jane had received permission from her teachers to abandon Fendersburg and leave the residents to learn how to take care of themselves again. They had grown too dependent on the Ghost to rescue them from their own carelessness and laziness. Besides, the Rivals weren't watching Fendersburg anymore.

"Either they figured the Ghost was bait and they weren't biting, or they turned their focus elsewhere." Jane spread her hands. "Here?"

"That makes too much sense," I said. "With all the ruckus at New Year's, sending in Sylvia, trying to make contact with Big Ugly, break through the dimensional gate, yeah, they're focusing on Neighborlee. Both our enemies have pulled back and are licking their wounds, gathering their strength for the next attempt. We're a long way from winning."

"Consider that this alliance Jane's teachers are offering could be the turning point in the war," Angela said.

"Which brings us to this new guy or thing or whatever you met," Felicity said. "New player, or new tactic?"

"What if the Voice is telling the truth?" Jane blurted.

"It's a tricky combination. Asking you to help him, and sucking you dry worse than all of Buffy's vampires," I said. "Kurt thinks it's Big Ugly trying a new tactic, but it's too soon to tell. I do agree that we shouldn't make the mistake of taking him at his word, that he's friendly."

"I need to know more about your previous encounters with Big Ugly." Jane took a big bite of her pizza.

My pizza got cold by the time Felicity and I finished sharing everything we remembered from those crazy few days. The power fluctuations at Eden, items and then people vanishing and reappearing, and the temporary amnesia that essentially made people shrug off what should have been frightening incidents. Jane agreed with our theory that the disappearance of my parents near the Bermuda Triangle might be tied into all the other weirdness going on, putting a lot of blame on the Rivals.

"What are the chances Big Ugly or the doorway it's fixated on is located specifically underneath Eden?" Jane asked. "I can analyze better with my Ghost field turned on, but you can't exactly go invisible in the middle of a crowd."

I checked my watch. "Maybe we should see how well we work together, and do something about the vortex or event horizon... Are we ever going to come up with a name for that thing?"

"Probably when it's closed up for good or we can get control of it," Jane said. She put her now-empty plate down on the table and jumped to her feet. "How late is Eden open?"

Felicity and I exchanged satisfied looks. Jane already thought the way we did, as if she had belonged to our partnership for years. We were going to work really well together. I hoped that whatever happened, however soon we got to the bottom of the events at Eden, she would be able to stay permanently in Neighborlee. I liked her. I especially liked how quickly and easily she started saying "we" and "us."

Angela opted out of the trip to Eden, so we dropped her off at Divine's before heading over there. Felicity had called Kurt, and he caught up with us when we were a block away from Eden, all three of us riding in my Jeep. The big grins and nods he and Jane exchanged when we got out in the parking lot at Eden intrigued me. I made a note to grill Kurt later. Maybe he was just fascinated with her Ghost field, as Jane referred to it. Kurt did love to play with my ability to fly, and Jane's "wings" had a lot more bells and whistles than mine did.

At this time of night, with less than an hour left until Eden closed down, there was enough traffic to keep Gina and her assistants from noticing us and coming out to see what we wanted or needed. Honestly, with the weather so lousy, what was anyone doing there at that time of night? We walked Jane through the building, giving her the behind-the-scenes tour. Through the main gym, the room where Murder had been set up, the locker rooms and bathrooms where various people had been found, even going into the furnace room, so Kurt could point out the control panel of the HVAC that had vanished and reappeared.

"Yeah, some echoes of warping." Jane gestured at the HVAC unit.

"Got it. It's like the molecules haven't quite shifted back to where they were before, and they don't like it. They're disturbed because they can't finish settling back where they belong." Kurt caught me and Felicity staring at him. "Oh, sorry. The Ghost field. I'm riding the slipstream, so to speak."

"Uh huh." Felicity raised an eyebrow at me. We were definitely going to have to get together later, when Kurt and Jane were gone, and compare notes.

I really wanted to know what had happened during those encounters he hadn't really told us about in any detail.

Then I had other things to think about. The Oil Slick monster appeared when we returned to the lobby. Jane sensed it coming first. I wondered if anyone ever told her that her blue-green eyes got misty gray when she used her talent. Kurt knew how to use Jane's Ghost field. He made us invisible to the last few people in the building while Jane studied the power and defended us from whatever was about to emerge from the opening dimensional gate.

I didn't care how fascinating Kurt found it, I didn't like the sensation of the Ghost field wrapped around me. My skin felt itchy and ... shifty is about the best word. Like it wanted to slide sideways and peel off my muscles. The air around us turned hazy, kind of like bad TV reception when the cable was dead and we had to hook up an old antenna, before things went digital. Gina hurried through the lobby, looking all around, and obviously not seeing us. I flinched when she walked right through Kurt's arm and didn't react. He gave me a queasy grin. It was kind of reassuring to know he wasn't quite used to all the aspects of borrowing Jane's power.

About two seconds after Gina went into her office and picked up a ringing phone, the swirling oil slick appeared in the open area of the lobby, almost exactly where we had fought it before. Only this time it was full of colors, in direct contrast to the haziness that filled the air around us.

So this was what it was like to be shifted half a step sideways, being out of phase with everything else. Not fun.

Felicity zapped it good this time. Of course, it took a lot of energy out of her. The encounter with Big Ugly took something out of all of us. Since my place was closest, we ended up there to snack and recover. Harry was out of town on an overnight delivery run, and Pete was involved in something at church, so we had the house to ourselves. I pulled out my stash of dark chocolate-dipped cookies and triple chocolate hot cocoa mix, remembering Jane's comment about needing lots of chocolate to get through that night's revelations. We three girls laughed when Kurt made his usual comment about just not understanding what it was with girls and chocolate.

"It's just another proof that men are a completely different species, that's all." Jane slouched a little in her chair at the table and cradling the big, clunky, cobalt blue mug filled with hot chocolate and whipped cream. It was nice to know we had the same technique for making hot chocolate. Something else we had in common. Jane was going to fit in just fine with us.

"An inferior species. Yeah, yeah, I've heard all that before," Kurt grumbled. Then he winked at Jane.

And she blushed.

Felicity and I exchanged wide-eyed looks. She nodded to me. We didn't need telepathy to know we were thinking the same thing: Kurt had definitely found the superhero girlfriend he was looking for, and Jane wasn't immune to him.

As Felicity and I had said many times before, only someone who hadn't grown up with Kurt could fall in love with him. He had told Jane we were more like brother and sisters, and that was fine with us. She was going to be our sister now. We weren't exactly the Fantastic Four, but that was fine, because no way was I going to even hint that Kurt could be Mr. Fantastic.

Snicker. Snort. Wink. Grin.

The meeting broke up shortly after Pete got home from church. By then, we had a little bit of a game plan. Jane would give only an abbreviated report of what we did and learned and talked about to her teachers, Demetrius and Beauregard. We agreed not to ask anyone's advice or share information until we got a better idea of what we were facing. Felicity had given Big Ugly a stronger jolt than she had given it at New Year's. If it wasn't permanently disabled, it would stay shut down longer. If the Voice didn't make contact again with Jane, that would be confirmation it was indeed Big Ugly.

~~~~~

Maybe I spoke too soon?

I was out at lunch the next day, Wednesday. A slump day in some aspects, in between the two newspaper days of the week. Cerb had vanished on my way to Papyrus People, to get some cute notebooks I had ordered to give the kids I worked with on Alumni Night at Neighborlee Children's Home. I was mentoring a group of kids of all ages who wanted to go into journalism. I didn't think anything about Cerb vanishing, once I gave him half my sandwich and he inhaled it. I figured he was just running off his lunch.

I picked up my order from the store, put it in my backpack, slung it on the back of my chair, and wheeled out the door. It was a gorgeous day and I seriously considered cutting my day short, getting right into my Jeep after I got back from lunch, and calling Conrad on my way down the street. I had vague plans to spend the afternoon in the park, just driving around. I could always access my work computer from home and finish the last few tasks I had, to proof and copy edit stories for next Tuesday's paper.

Cerb came at me out of nowhere.

Seriously. Out of *nowhere*. The air split in front of me, about ten feet down the sidewalk and he came barreling out. He leaped up on me and dropped an envelope in my lap and then went down on all fours to circle my chair. The envelope had a wax seal that showed the Wishing Ball. My hands shook a little as I opened it. Logic said Cerb had vanished because Angela had called.

But why hadn't she just called me? She knew my cell number.

The first line of her note explained that. She was getting interference when she tried to dial me. That reminded her of the same interference when London was trying to reach Athena to warn her. I looked up, fully expecting to see Freddie Grandstone come down the street, aimed at me, probably ready to demand I hand over "his" Athena.

Cerb growled and stopped his circling to stand in front of me. His fluffy fur vanished and the gold-silver-cream coloring darkened to something in between platinum and pewter.

My unwanted Romeo, Charlie came striding down the
~~~~~

sidewalk. *Strutting* would be a better word. He was grinning so widely I could almost see down his throat.

How come it seemed like he had pointed teeth?

"Darling! How wonderful to see you here. I was so afraid I would have to storm the castle gates to find you."

"You were told to leave me alone," I called, as if the power of my voice would stop him. "Don't make me file a restraining order. I will."

"Sweetheart, you don't want to do that." He slowed, and doggone it if his eyes didn't seem to kind of ... spin a little.

I gave a good hard mental shove, pushing my chair backwards. Cerb leaped forward, growling louder. Weird thing, but a good thing: my demented Romeo didn't see him. Cerb hit him, solid and square in his chest. Charlie staggered backward a step. A light flashed where they made contact. Cerb bounced off him and let out a muffled yelp. All I could think of was a puppy getting his paw stepped on. He landed crooked in the street, when I fully expected him to land on his feet. He went down and rolled, right into the path of an oncoming car.

I shrieked and braced myself to give a good hard yank with my brain to pull him out of danger. Too late. The car hit him.

But it didn't hit him. It passed through him. More accurately, Cerb passed through it. He was on his feet and grinning at me as he emerged from the back of the car.

Problem: in those few seconds of distraction, Charlie had time to recover. He lunged for me, arms spread, like he was going to pick me up from my wheelchair. I was still braced for the effort to yank Cerb to safety, so I turned it around and shoved him away hard with my brain.

Dang, that **hurt**!

Romeo staggered back a step. I got a definite stinging sensation in my head, like I had tripped and fallen face-first into an electric fence. I saw sparks. And that same flash from when Cerb hit him.

All I could think of was that he had some kind of weird body armor with a force field built into it, which didn't make sense.

"You don't want to do that." Charlie was only a few steps away from me. My head throbbed and I had the awful feeling another shove would give me a bloody nose. What was I up against?

"No, *you* don't," Daniel shouted from his green pickup truck.

He crossed the lane and pulled his truck up sideways across the curb, blocking Romeo for a few seconds.

In the time it took Charlie to get around the front of the truck, Daniel leaped out, leaving the engine running, and stepped between me and what I was suddenly afraid would turn into my personal version of *The Terminator*.

That light flashed again, across his chest, as Charlie shouted, "Get out of the way."

My head hurt a little. That light felt like a physical stab in my eyes.

"Nope." Daniel sounded like he might laugh.

"Get out of my way!" He took three steps closer, but his anger was crackling into confusion. Again, that light flashed. It was brighter and I had to close my eyes. Something in me wanted to …

Move aside? What the hey-ya was going on?

"You lose." Daniel reached out one hand toward the street and beckoned.

I turned my head and saw two men come from a car that had stopped on the other side of the street. They put long pipes up to their mouths.

Okay, this was getting freaky. Were those --

Yep. Darts flew out of the pipes and hit Charlie as he turned to look at them, his mouth falling open and his eyes widening with outright terror.

"No! They told me about you!"

Blowpipes? We weren't in the Amazon jungle.

"Sweetheart, don't let them. I was coming to rescue you!"

At least, the last few words were supposed to be a shout, but Charlie crumpled in on himself and went to his knees. Before he hit the sidewalk, the two men reached him, grabbed him under his armpits, and dragged him across the street to their car.

Funny thing. Charlie didn't look like himself anymore. He deflated, about ten times more than he had at the office. All that gorgeous dark hair receded and turned gray. All those weightlifting muscles flattened and those flat abs turned to an old man's paunch. Only his head didn't change. It was still big, the features still chiseled, now weirdly disproportionate.

"Come on." Daniel looked in all directions, even upward, as he stepped behind my chair and pushed me toward his truck.

"Cerb!" I staggered to my feet, looking for my bodyguard. He materialized up through the pavement and slammed into me and I flung my arms around him. I went to my knees. Cerb licked my face and shivered a little and then calmed down and looked over my shoulder at Daniel.

He stared at Cerb. I had the feeling he saw the real Cerb, the Egyptian tomb drawing sleek hound, not the fluffy, floppy, furry, huggable critter. Come to think of it, I could really use the furry Cerb right about then.

"We really need to talk," Daniel said. "Please let me get you in my truck and go somewhere safe, okay?"

"Where are they taking Romeo?"

"Somewhere he can't use his powers of mind control."

Okay, that made sense. And it scared me a little. I had the feeling that if Daniel hadn't been standing between me and Charlie, and I had gotten the full brunt of that light, instead of just flashes, I might have done something I didn't really want to do.

I saved my question for after Cerb climbed into the truck. I followed, and Daniel put my chair in the compartment behind the seats. I wouldn't have climbed in if Cerb had resisted.

"How come he didn't Svengali you?" I asked, when Daniel pulled away from the curb.

It all happened so fast, maybe ten minutes, max, no one seemed to have noticed yet. Or maybe that was one of Daniel's talents? Or one of Charlie's?

"You move things with your mind. I'm immune." He glanced at me and then focused on the road.

"Okay. Where are we going?"

"My --" Daniel cursed and slammed the brakes on.

A dark green sedan seemed to appear out of nowhere (I was getting really tired of that happening to me) and blocked the road.

Chapter Ten

Hayward leaped out of the driver's seat and pulled a gun. He pointed it at Daniel. "Lanie?"

"I'm fine." I looked at Daniel, who couldn't seem to pull his gaze off that gun. "I don't suppose you're immune to bullets?"

"Nope, just psionic attacks," he said, very quietly.

"How much did you see, Colonel?" I rolled down the window, and Hayward walked around the truck to the passenger side.

"Not enough." He caught his breath when he looked into the truck and saw Cerb sitting at my feet, with his forelegs up on the seat. "Okay, this puts a whole new light on things."

"You've run into him?"

"Or someone like him. Shows up when things get nasty." He raised his gaze to Daniel.

"I keep saying this," Daniel said, his voice quiet with strain. "We really need to talk."

"One question." Hayward holstered his gun. "Who are you allied with?"

"Please don't be a smart-alec and say Thanos," I offered.

Daniel laughed, a crackling kind of sound. "We're not allied with anyone. I assume you mean my family."

"I was considering calling off for the rest of the day. How about you take me back to the office so I can get my Jeep, then we go to Divine's? This is a conversation Angela needs to be part of. Colonel, he's got a fun new semi-pseudo-superhero power. Romeo tried to put a mental whammy on me, and Daniel turns out to be immune."

"You don't say." One corner of Hayward's mouth curved up. "Yeah, we do need to talk."

When we got back to the *Tattler* parking lot, Daniel made a call to the two guys who grabbed and tranquilized Charlie, and told them to bring him to Divine's. As a gesture of goodwill, he was turning my deflated, slumbering Romeo over to Hayward. In answer to the questions I could see building up in his eyes, I told him Hayward was working with us without the military or government's knowledge or approval. Then I got out of his truck and Cerb climbed out and ran across the parking lot and around a corner. I didn't doubt within five seconds after vanishing from sight, he was at Divine's and reporting to Angela in whatever way he communicated.

"Who is 'us'?" he asked, after thinking for several moments. "Sorry," he added, seeing me maneuvering my chair out of the back of the front cab. He hurried around to help me.

"We call ourselves Lost Kids, like your grandfather. And we also call ourselves the guardians of Neighborlee."

"Uh huh." He watched me take a few tottering steps to my Jeep, then hauled my wheelchair into the back seat when I had opened the door. "I have the feeling I'm going to need a business trip to report to Grandpop, and bring him back here to meet all of you."

"Like, duh."

That got another crooked smile from him. The last I saw him wear for quite a while that very long afternoon.

Angela was waiting by the gate, with Cerb and Col. Hayward, when Daniel and I got there. The car with the two blowpipe guys and Charlie pulled around a corner where I thought I glimpsed it waiting, and followed us to park on the street behind Daniel's truck.

"They'll stay and keep watch over him until you're ready to take custody," Daniel said.

"What did you use on him?" Hayward asked.

"It's a tranquilizer my aunt developed."

"How long will it last?"

"It won't wear off. It needs a reversal agent."

"Impressive," Angela murmured. She offered him a quiet smile and held out her hand. "Welcome to Divine's Emporium, Daniel Sheridan. I thank you for watching out for Lanie. And I have to ask why you didn't come sooner. Especially after all we went through at New Year's together."

"Ma'am … my grandfather has been living on the defensive since he shook free of some pretty nasty types who tried to draft him when he was a kid. I came here to put down roots and test the water, so to speak, and get a feel for the situation. See if we had possible allies here, or Grandpop's enemies were gaining power."

"Unfortunately," I said, "we've been trying to figure out if you were in the same army as the Grandstones. I think we've all been wasting a lot of time. Just like we decided with Jane, it's time to take that step of faith and trust each other. Especially since Daniel's immune."

"Immune?" Angela frowned, two thin lines appearing between her eyebrows as she tipped her head to one side and looked him over, head to feet, then feet to head. "To what, exactly?"

"So far, everything the creeps have thrown at me," Daniel said.

We went inside. Diane was there to tend the counter for the afternoon rush at the end of the school day, so Angela could take us up to her apartment. I got a raised eyebrow from Daniel when I hauled myself, legs shaking and gripping the bannister for dear life, up the stairs. In return, I watched him when we passed the long mural at the second floor landing. He looked at it, but didn't linger, didn't react in any way. So he saw only the swirling lavender and gray wallpaper and not the garden I had glimpsed hidden in it just once. Angela made tea and brought out fresh triple chocolate cookies, still warm and soft from her oven. That just reinforced my theory she could turn back time to handle emergency situations.

We discussed what had happened that afternoon. Wallace had been across the street, running errands, and spotted Charlie sitting on a bench, watching the front door of the *Tattler*. He called my cell phone, to warn me not to go out to lunch. He couldn't get through to me, so he called the office. When he heard I was already out, he called Angela, hoping she could get through to me. Then he contacted London to try to get through the interference. Neither of them could, so Angela summoned Cerb to warn me. At the same time, Col. Hayward had come to Divine's to check in with Angela before visiting the Longfellows. He wouldn't say why, and I figured it was personal, having to do with Athena. If she or Bethany were in danger, he would have told us. At least, I hoped so. Hayward headed into town to look for me and arrived in time to see me getting into Daniel's truck.

I related the story from my side of everything. Cerb sat on the floor, lying across my feet, perfectly still. I worried a little that I couldn't feel him breathing, just the warm weight of him.

Then Daniel explained his side of the story.

"We've built up a little army of people we've rescued from the influence and outright control of the people working with the Grandstones. It would have been easier if we had known the Grandstones were involved, but we weren't sure until the whole mess before New Year's. First it was just Grandpop, then my aunts and uncles, and now my generation. People with talents." He shrugged, paused, visibly waiting for us to ask what he meant by talents. Daniel obviously hadn't been in Neighborlee long enough to realize this was pretty normal for us. He caught on. I could tell the moment he did, with a slight flush on his cheeks.

"When that guy came after Lanie in our office, I felt something. A reverb, that usually means someone is about to use their talent. I saw a glow in his chest, and for a second it was like a mask slipped and I saw the skinny old ... fart," he snorted, glanced at the three of us, "underneath. But Lanie just exploded, and I saw the energy whiplash out of her and throw him across the room and ... okay, I got scared. I knew what I had to do, but I was praying like anything that she was on the right side."

"After what we went through with Sylvia at New Year's, how could you doubt what side I was on?" I said, my voice cracking with the need to both laugh and shriek at him.

"True. But see, it's been just us against the world, in a lot of ways. Grandpop escaped by the skin of his teeth, being enslaved."

"What's his gift?" Angela said.

"He calls it five-sight. A little more than foresight. Big, emotional or dangerous or complicated events, he can see multiple possibilities branching out from it, maybe about five, ten minutes before it happens. If he's fast, he can control reactions and outcomes. It's tricky, and he prefers not to do it. Except for important things, like saving lives." Daniel shrugged.

I had never seen him so uncertain before. Except when he was evading Sylvia, of course. I could see now why the Grandstones were so desperate to coerce him into marrying Sylvia and adding his bloodline to theirs. I had to wonder how Sylvia felt, if she realized she was basically being used as a hopeful broodmare.

"The talent helped him rescue my grandmother from the Grandstones' bosses. She's a touch healer. Not as great as it sounds," he hurried to add. "Whatever she heals, she suffers from it for a short time. Cuts, burns, dog bites, broken bones. Everybody who married into our family had some kind of talent, no matter how useless, that made them targets. Most of the time, they just tricked them and handed them over to these slugworts who had a school or camp or whatever that was pretty grim and controlled."

"Concentration camp," I said. Daniel flinched and his gaze locked with mine, then he visibly relaxed and seemed to catch his breath. "We rescued someone who was held there. He can set fires, and they were using him as a living battery, to power others."

"Ouch," he murmured.

"How did you know to bring your friends and the tranquilizer darts today?" Angela poured another mug of tea for him.

"I asked our researchers to look into this guy, and they dug far enough to find out his identity was faked. The old standby of using the identity of a baby who died soon after birth. They watched him. When he came back to town, I figured he was going to try for Lanie again. And I was right."

"What were you planning on doing with him?" Hayward said. "You're kind of stepping into the shadowy boundaries of the law with what you're doing." He snorted. "I ought to know."

"We have a place where Grandma and her team put the ones we rescue through a purification regimen, try to give them their minds and bodies back, set them free."

"And if it doesn't work?" Angela asked, voice softer this time.

Daniel shook his head. I had the feeling it wasn't a matter of not knowing, or even not wanting to know, but he didn't want to admit it to us.

"Definitely, it's time we joined forces," Hayward said. "Can you arrange a meeting for me with your grandfather?"

"I'd like to, but … Well, Grandpop has been sick. Something zapped him when he was out of the country, investigating something back in November, and he just hasn't been himself. I almost canceled the acquisition of the *Tattler* and implementing our plan to move in close to study Neighborlee, but he insisted. Kind of scary how important it was to him."

Hayward groaned and slumped a little in his seat and rubbed his eyes with the heels of his palms. "Sometimes I wonder if I'm doing any good here. By any chance, was your grandfather near the Bermuda Triangle at the beginning of November?"

"Yeah." Daniel looked back and forth between Angela and me, as if he expected to get some explanation from us. The second glance, he stared at me. I guessed that my expression had changed enough to worry him. Maybe I had gone white. I felt sick again, from the thoughts Hayward's words had triggered.

"You think maybe he was caught in the backlash from whatever made my folks vanish?" I finally asked, when it became clear Hayward wasn't going to explain.

"We won't know until we ask him," Hayward said.

We didn't talk much longer after that. We had turned the corner, made the decision to reach out and make contact and offer some trust to the Sheridan clan. Daniel instructed the two men to escort Charlie and follow Hayward to where Rodney and some of his allies were working. Then all of them would accompany Daniel to the treatment compound, where Charlie would hopefully be healed.

I went home and ordered the deluxe pizza and ribs combo from Mancuso's. Then I called Felicity and Jake, Kurt and Ford to come over, and I filled them in on my lunchtime adventure.

~~~~~

While we were waiting to hear about the proposed conference between Grandfather Sheridan and Hayward, we needed to move forward on the plan to make an alliance and join forces with Hoax. Jane didn't want to report to the Old Poops right away. Not until we had identified the source of that energy that had lashed out against Evan to protect Penny that night at the quarries.

Keeping information away from the Old Poops didn't include Jane's friend, Katie, whom Kurt had met last week. Sudden silence on Jane's part would alarm Katie and she would report to the Sanctum, the headquarters of Hoax. I totally agreed with Jane's reasoning of waiting to make her report, when she told me about her visit with her friend a few days after our big alliance meeting. Some good came of their discussion, because Katie had some ideas that Jane passed on for us to consider.

Such as the possibility that the Voice might be telling the truth, and he or it or them, whatever, knew where the Lost Kids came from. What if we could go back to whatever planet or dimension we came from, and we could hold onto our superpowers? Or what if it was like with Superman, and going home to our own version of Krypton meant we became ordinary? Then there was the theory we had discussed several times, that we Lost Kids were rejects, or sent to Earth because our home world was too dangerous for us. Kind of like the situation for Stanzer and the Hunt.

Katie brought up the theory that whatever doorway had
~~~~~

brought us to Earth, it was a one-way trip, so the Voice was stuck and we were stuck. So it didn't matter if the Voice was a liar or not. The important thing was that Neighborlee was our home and we were going to continue defending it.

So we needed to track down whoever was awakening to their Lost Kids semi-pseudo-superhero powers. We needed to find that kid before he or she caught the attention of the Rivals and got snatched from under our noses.

When Jane and I talked on Friday, we agreed she needed to join the effort to get close to the kids at NCH.

"You seem to be even more sensitive to powers at work than Kurt," I said. "Maybe the two of you together can kind of boost each other with the Geiger counter routine."

"What exactly do you have in mind?"

"Well, we can get you into the cottages easily enough. Just introduce you as Kurt's new girlfriend. The kids will flip."

"Is that a good thing, or bad?"

"Oh, definitely good. The kids love Kurt. He's kind of like Santa Claus, always fixing things for them, helping them with their science projects, making gizmos for them to play with."

"What about any little girls who plan on marrying big brother Kurt when they grow up?"

"Hmm, none that I know of." I snorted, muffling laughter at the idea. "Just our luck, the jealous one will be the one with the superpower and she'll try to zap her new rival."

"Well, if it brings her out of hiding, that might be good."

"How good will it be for you and Kurt?"

"I don't—" Jane looked stunned. Was it possible she hadn't been thinking along those lines, not even a little bit? Considering some of the looks we had seen Kurt giving her, she should have had some clue by now.

What was wrong with the guy, that he couldn't communicate all of a sudden?

"The guy is interested." Hey, I had to do my part for my big brother, right? "He's never been interested in us, but we know each other too well. No mystery. Kurt has been looking for someone like you for a long time. Of course, we always figured he wanted a top-heavy, single-digit IQ type of girl. Not someone smart and able to kick his butt when he needs it. If some jealous kid attacks, well, that'll wake him up, get him moving faster to strengthen whatever it is building between the two of you."

"That's a little too fast. Considering I loathed him up until a few days ago. Considering he was trying to drive me out of town up until a few days ago."

"Maybe the guy was scared."

Jane laughed. She looked a little relieved, a little uneasy.

"Of course, if the new superhero is a boy, he could have a crush on Penny," I had to point out, "which makes him protective of her, which explains him attacking that rich kid. All we can do is introduce you to the kids and see what happens."

~~~~~

The plan was easy. Jane and Kurt would handle crafts with the kids at the orphanage that coming Alumni Tuesday. Felicity and Jake volunteered to take care of the spa that afternoon while Jane was at NCH. I would join them in the evening for dinner. Hopefully the two of them with their combined superpowers would pick up something. Maybe Jane, being a new element, would notice something the rest of us had missed.

I started doubling up my prayers, because the situation with the Voice was getting ugly. Maybe he was Big Ugly, maybe he was another interdimensional troublemaker. Or maybe he really was someone like us, but had been caught between dimensions and warped by his long imprisonment. We had to deal with that problem and figure out some way to protect Jane.

Kurt called me soon after I got to work that morning to report that the Voice had been tormenting Jane in her dreams. If the Voice was Big Ugly, we were in trouble, because Jane theorized that the Voice had changed tactics. She had resolved not to trust her new friend, so now the Voice had taken to visiting in her dreams and apparently draining energy from her. The theory now was that the Voice had been doing it all along, only now it was multiplied in intensity because he wasn't trying to trick her into cooperating.

I told Kurt I would call our church's prayer chain, and that seemed to make him feel better. That was a big change, because while he appreciated my church's support over the years, he had never really applied it to anything that mattered to him. I also promised I would be talking with Stanzer and the Longfellows and Felicity, to figure out how we could help set up protections for Jane.
~~~~~

The shield she could erect around her shop obviously didn't keep Big Ugly or the Voice, if they were two separate beings, from getting to her while she slept.

I had to wonder later if Jane's return to Neighborlee was a warning sign that the intensity of the whole situation with Big Ugly and the Rivals and the Grandstone threat and other problems was about to get turned up to the equivalent of chop-and-liquefy.

We needed Jane in Neighborlee, because that night she and Kurt proved what a powerhouse team they made. By the time I arrived at NCH to have dinner with the kids, the two of them had solved the mystery of Penny's defender.

First of all, they were defenders, plural. Twin girls, Kory and Kelley. They had latched onto Penny from their first days at NCH, to the point that Kurt teased and called them the Octokittens. He caught chiming sounds when they activated their power, during a moment that afternoon when they took the teasing between him and Jane the wrong way. She saw a rainbow shimmer of power when the twins held hands and focused on him. As soon as she laughed, they stopped shimmering and chiming, obviously realizing he wasn't a threat.

Jane and Kurt met me with the news, out in the parking lot when they were putting away their craft supplies. We kept watch on the girls through the evening. Now that I knew what to look for, I could sense something. Of course, my sensitivity could be increasing now that the long-term power drain had been halted.

There really was only one thing we could do, with two sensitive little girls coming into their powers years ahead of schedule. The twin factor was something that probably added to the power buildup. We had to get them out of Neighborlee before the Rivals swooped in. I toyed with the idea of offering to adopt the girls, but where would I put them? All the spare bedrooms in my house were full with my brothers. The paperwork would take months, and during that time someone with more powerful connections could swoop in and yank the girls out of our grasp. Those thoughts led me to the only logical conclusion, which Jane and Kurt agreed with when I brought it up.

We had to ask her teachers, Demetrius and Beauregard, to snatch the girls away to the Sanctum and start their training ASAP. We needed to get into the NCH records and find out about the twins' background, first. They might be Lost Kids, or they might be descendants of Lost Kids. We needed to get all our paperwork in order to make the snatch-and-vanish operation as successful and swift as possible. So we went to Angela right after we left NCH that night. She agreed with us. The simplest plan of action was to call Athena Longfellow and ask her to work her magic, dig into the records and maybe even manipulate things a little to tear down any barriers. Anything Athena couldn't handle, London and Sherwood could.

When we left Divine's Emporium later that night, Kurt and Jane headed for the Sanctum to finally meet with the Old Poops and include them in everything we had been learning. I would have loved to have gone with them, but I had a job. Someone had to report to Felicity and the Longfellows. Besides, we needed to stay in Neighborlee in case Big Ugly panicked or had a temper tantrum when he realized he wasn't going to be able to drain more energy out of Jane that night.

~~~~~

I didn't have any odd dreams of warning, and neither did Felicity. Ford and Doni reported they didn't sense anything strange or have warning dreams, when we talked over the situation later.

Still, we should have expected something to happen. Our enemy had to be panicking, because pretending to be a helpful friend had failed so spectacularly. When interdimensional monsters got panicky and had temper tantrums, they got nasty. They got unpredictable.

They struck at little kids, which certainly wasn't fair -- but who ever said interdimensional monsters had to play fair?

The first I knew of it was a strange rippling in the air and coming from deep below Neighborlee, when I was sitting in the *Neighborlee Tattler* office the next morning. Nothing moved, visibly, but I felt something shift. My fingertips tingled just a little bit. I called Angela. She didn't answer the phone. I dropped my phone and snatched it up with my mind, without checking first to see if anyone was looking. I called Gordon next. If there was anything dangerous going on in Neighborlee, he would know. First, because he was a cop, and second, because he had grown a whole lot more sensitive to the background weird-and-wonderful in our town since his strong exposure to it at New Year's.
~~~~~

Before I finished asking my question, the radio in Gordon's car erupted with all sorts of voices. Something about a call from the schools. He put me on hold. Of course, with Gordon, that meant he just put down his cell phone while he handled the radio. Everything was a jumble, but I caught enough to piece together an explanation. When he picked up again just a few minutes later, he didn't have to explain.

The school bus coming down Overlook Road, on the long stretch that ran along the drop-off down into the Metroparks, had simply vanished between one house and the next. It was a gap of maybe a quarter mile, with lots of trees. There was nowhere for the bus to go except over the edge into the former sandstone quarries, but a crash like that would make a loud noise that people could hear up at Eden north of the site, or south at City Hall. But no one heard anything. The Fitzgeralds were the next house on the route, and the bus schedule ran more reliably than clockwork. When the bus was two minutes late, Grandpa Fitzgerald knew something was wrong.

The bus had stopped at Neighborlee Children's Home before heading down Overlook Road. Kory and Kelley were on that bus.

Big Ugly, the Voice, whoever our enemy was, had struck at the twins.

"Lanie, whatever you can do, do it." Gordon's voice cracked a little.

"I'm getting hold of Kurt. Anything having to do with machines, he might have a better sense of trouble."

"Yeah, sounds good. Thanks. I'm heading over there."

I hung up on Gordon without saying goodbye, but chances were he had already hung up on me. I really wished that our little team had telepathic powers, because going through the phone took way too long, even with speed dial.

Kurt answered on the first ring. He and Jane were at Divine's. He told me to meet them at the park. For just a second, I had a flash of them standing outside of the fence at the shop, shivering in a gust of wind that I could hear outside the office. They didn't have coats. Fortunately, we had a Goodwill box by the newspaper office, and it was full of coats. I snagged some that I thought would fit Kurt and Jane and used as much brain power as I could spare to make my chair whiz down the sidewalks to meet them. It was just faster to go straight there in my chair, rather than get in my Jeep, drive there, find a parking spot, and get out of my Jeep. Suddenly, though, the newspaper office didn't feel like it was close enough to the center of town, the pulse of events. When I reached them, I could see a flicker of the power Jane was using to keep off the worst of the wind and snow. I knew she couldn't hold up that shield for much longer. Not if she wanted to have anything left for the battle coming up. Whoever had snagged two innocent little girls, they were in for a battle. The guardians of Neighborlee were primed for bear.

I threw the coats to Kurt and Jane, and as soon as she let down the Ghost field to take the coat, she went to her knees and gagged.

"Getting the signal." She shuddered. "Duh. My field cut off the connection." Then her gaze went vague, and I had this creepy sensation like cold, dirty motor oil trying to soak through my clothes. It was easy to guess the Voice was talking to her, and he wasn't pretending to be friendly anymore. A second later she tipped sideways. Kurt pulled her upright and got her on her feet.

Jane was only out for a few heartbeats, but to her, when she told us about it later, it felt like she had been exploring the cavern the bus had fallen into for nearly half an hour. We settled on a park bench and she described the place to us. I got colder just thinking about the kids being trapped in that darkness and pressure and thickness that replaced the air. Jane picked up enough details, despite the warped impressions, to give Kurt an idea of what had happened, where the bus load of children had gone.

Chapter Eleven

"There's a legend, rumor, whatever you want to call it. Back when the town was still growing, while the quarry was still a quarry." Kurt turned and gestured out the western side of town, past the city hall and the slopes down into the park, toward the quarry. "There's an old sewer system. It got abandoned when they rebuilt the town." His expression grew grim. "When sinkholes opened up in the middle of streets."

"Previous attempts by Big Ugly to get through?" I asked, thinking aloud.

"Who knows? The thing is, they covered up a lot of it, threw reinforcing material across the holes. Ford Longfellow knows all about the town history, and he has schematics and blueprints and old surveys. Some parts of town never should have been built on again, but people did, because a lot of records were lost in a fire around the turn of the century."

"Big Ugly just yanked the school bus down through the street, into a cavern that's already there," Jane said. "You have an idea where that cavern might be?"

Kurt went to check with Ford. Jane stayed with me and I got on the phone to check the bus route, just to be sure. He didn't want to leave Jane, who still sat a little crooked. I really wished we had time for me to appreciate this new side of him, and to tease him about it. Maybe later, when the kids were safe.

Fortunately, I knew a lot of people in key positions throughout the city, and they confirmed what I had picked up from the panic calls I overheard on Gordon's radio. We headed out of the park and north, to Overlook Road. It didn't take us very long to get to the spot. I wasn't sure what I felt to see the stretch of road and the open ground on either side of it completely undisturbed. Relieved there was no physical damage? Worried that we had to deal with dimensional gateways again?

Jane's eyes got hazy and her mouth flattened in a cold fury that made me very glad she was on our side. The Voice was talking to her, and as she told me later, he was very smug, convinced he was already in power and she had no choice but to play along. The really ugly part was that for the moment, Jane did have to play along. She confirmed when we found the spot where the bus vanished, sinking down through the pavement without leaving a ripple.

"He's slowed down time itself. Everything is frozen, but if I don't go down there, he's going to let go of time and everything's just going to go back where it belongs. Pipes bursting. Pipes puncturing the bus. Drowning the kids. Crushing them." Jane gave me a terrified and yet furious look, then she went transparent and dropped straight down through the ground.

In the next few seconds of silence, as I waited for something to happen, I recognized and remembered that expression. She had worn it when she stood up against some awful, Grandstone-backed bullies when we were children. The quiet little shadowy mouse of a girl had become something fierce, just for a few seconds. I could only hope she would send the Voice running today, like she had done to those bullies way back then.

Of course, the bullies got over their fright before they were more than a dozen yards away. They circled back and got a few good punches in while our backs were turned and Jane was alone. Because she was alone so much, fading into the background. That day, she didn't fade. The rest of us saw her, and we leaped into the ruckus and gave those bullies triple what they handed out.

Angela appeared then, breathless, her cloak hanging crooked, looking rumpled and hurried. But not worried. Not like she had been when we faced down whatever nastiness had settled into that house on the border of Darbyville. Today she looked determined and her smirk hinted she had found something the enemy hadn't counted on. Angela carried a painting. She put it down in the snow next to the spot where Jane had vanished into the ground. While I told her what we had learned, what Jane had seen of underground, she straightened her clothes and caught her breath. She pointed at the painting.

Whatever had been painted there before, it now looked like the surface of the Wishing Ball. That had to be a good thing, right? I shivered, remembering the bits and pieces she had hinted at over the years. The dimensional doorways and inimical creatures kept prisoner in those paintings in the attic. The magic contained by the frames. The hints of how much damage could be done to the world, the chaotic power that could be released if the canvas were ever torn, the frames broken, or the paintings burned.

Right now, the painting was like a security monitor looking into the bus. It showed Jane staggering through the school bus, fighting her way through a hazy substance that resisted her. She pulled two girls from one seat, a boy from the other side of the aisle. And leaped upward.

Jane erupted through the ground with the children clutched in her arms. She rose up like I had seen dolphins leap from the waves, but there was no grace in her energy, just desperation. Jane landed on her knees, coughing and gagging. We had to fight her for a few seconds to get the children from her arms, then she rolled onto her back, struggling to breathe.

She had to go back. There were more children to rescue, and the driver. Who knew how much time remained before the Voice got nasty and let time and those tons of dirt and rock and rusty pipes go back where they belonged? Angela showed Jane the painting and I went down on my knees beside it, ready to help with the next batch of kids.

"We could see you in it," I said when Jane just shook her head. "Maybe if you can see us, you can hand the kids up to us through it. I'll pull, and you push. There's no maybe about it working. It has to."

Gordon joined us before Jane could do more than take a few deep breaths, visibly bracing to go back down. I introduced him to Jane and good old Gordon just took it all in stride. She went back down, and he didn't flinch, although he did wince a little when Angela gave him the job of thinking up an explanation to cover everything in the official reports.

We also serve who learn to lie convincingly for the greater good, to keep everyone else's brains from imploding.

Angela and I knelt on opposite sides of the painting, which was certainly big enough to act as a doorway, and we watched Jane. She staggered a little bit and looked around like she couldn't figure out what to do. For a few seconds she struggled to get the bus driver out of the stairwell, then seemed to give up.

"It's strong enough to cloud her mind, make her forget what she needs to do. Why is it playing games?" Angela murmured.

"Maybe it's not strong enough to fight her and hold everything in place?" I suggested.

"We need reinforcements." She looked up from the battle displayed in front of us long enough to nod to me and press her hands together like she was praying.

Duh! I pulled out my cell phone and called the church. Pastor Rocky was there. All my years of cramming as much news as possible into the smallest space possible in the newspaper served me well. All I had to tell him was that we needed prayer, dealing with the missing school bus, and he promised to get the prayer chain going. I had my phone back in my pocket in fifteen seconds.

Which was good, because Jane broke through whatever was distracting her and got the bus driver heaved upward. Straight into the backside of the painting. As soon as she touched it, we were able to grab hold of the woman and pull her out.

After that, Jane seemed to break through whatever distracted her, and pulled up children from their seats, one at a time. She shoved them upward high enough to touch the rippling surface of the painting. Then we could take them.

The image in the painting darkened. The interior of the bus shook. Jane staggered a few times, and from the way she paused and looked around, I could tell she was having a hard time concentrating again.

Kurt showed up then. He didn't have to ask what was going on. All he had to do was step up to the edge of the painting and look down. He got a grim expression, took a deep breath, and turned half-transparent before he sank down through the ground.

"I did not know he could do that," Gordon muttered. A cracked little chuckle escaped him. "How long has he been able to do that?"

"Kurt borrows other people's talents," I said. "He can do it because Jane can do it, and he's close enough to borrow from her."

"Oh. Okay. Makes sense." He took a deep breath. "I guess."

Angela and I looked at each other and for a few seconds we were able to grin. I couldn't get enough breath to laugh, though.

"Hey, Gordon, bet you never thought that being a Trekker would be a big help in doing your job, did you?"

He regained a little color and managed to grin, shakily, and nod. Just as shakily.

We watched Kurt get close to Jane and his presence seemed to break through to her. Between them, they got the rest of the children out from under seats and lifted them up to us. All except the twins. I couldn't see them. From the furious expression Kurt wore, the panic twisting Jane's face, they couldn't see Kory and Kelly either. The two of them seemed to be arguing. Then Jane shook her head and took a step back, and it was like she had a moment of epiphany.

She turned to go toward the back of the bus. The image through the painting grew darker, and something creaked and shuddered in the frozen ground under my knees. Jane and Kurt seemed to be shouting at something, but I couldn't see anything or anyone. Then Jane lunged forward and she partially vanished into the thickening haze. I had an awful vision of a dimensional doorway snapping shut and cutting her in half.

Kurt grabbed her around the waist and lunged upward. Jane appeared. The twins appeared, limp in her arms. The four of them erupted through the painting. We grabbed at everyone we could get hold of. Gordon nearly knocked me over, reaching in to help pull.

We had to pull. It was like an enormous, sticky tug-of-war. A horrendous creaking erupted from the ground underneath us and it rippled, like it had suddenly turned into the La Brea tar pits and a gusher of gas was about to erupt.

Kurt was shouting. The knot of the four of them popped up and we all fell. Most of us landed in the snowbank next to the road, where weeks of city service trucks had piled snow and grit and cinders.

"Move, move, move!" Gordon shouted, and the ground heaved under all of us.

I flew, dragging one of the twins and Angela with me. Kurt must have borrowed from me, because in a few breaths we were dozens of yards away from the road.

Or rather, where the road *used to be*. The rumbling and the sound of falling dirt and rock and metal seemed to go on forever as we clutched at each other and watched the collapse.

For once, Big Ugly's antics helped us with the explanation and coverup. The sinkhole could only be blamed on the cavern worn through the rock over the years by ground water, eroding new pathways through the previously damaged structure that never should have been built over. The dazed condition of the children came from the fall and the same toxic fumes blamed for all the hallucinations and odd events at Eden at New Year's. All of us were gathered up and hauled to Eden. It was the nearest shelter that could handle the large number of children and parents and officials and medical crew who came to check on everyone. Gordon didn't even have to lie about what had happened and what he had seen happen. It wasn't really lying, was it, if he didn't mention that the rescuers used a painting to get down into the hole that swallowed the bus? Who would believe him if he reported that Jane and Kurt had the ability to pass through solid objects? Best not to mention it at all. It would save inches of paperwork and days of explanations and lots of invasive scientific examinations.

~~~~~

Whatever Jane and Kurt did when they got the kids and the school bus free, it really hurt Big Ugly. We didn't hear anything, but we felt the change in the energy throughout the town. We thought the extra boost of energy after ousting the Rivals and stopping the power drain at New Year's was great. Now, for a few days, or at least until we got used to it, there was a sensation like carbonation had been added to the air. Another tap root or tentacle or whatever had been draining Neighborlee's magical energy reserves had been cut off.

Demetrius and Beauregard showed up on Friday, using the newspaper story as their justification. Kory and Kelly, they claimed, were the image of a niece who had been kidnapped by a non-custodial parent thirty-some years ago. They conveniently had strands of hair from a hairbrush, which provided DNA match. The twins had attached themselves to Jane and Kurt after the school bus incident, so it was easy for Jane to have lots of private time with the girls. She prepared them for these "long lost" great-uncles who showed up to claim them and take them to a wonderful school and big, new family. A family who would spoil them in no time, Jane assured us, while teaching the girls how to grow into whatever abilities waited inside them.

Athena came home during all the fuss of the bus crash and road cave-in and led the cyber-investigation into Kory and Kelley's backgrounds. They were not Lost Kids, but great-granddaughters of a Lost Kids couple who had fled just before Grandfather
~~~~~

Sheridan graduated from NCH. The attempts by that generation of Grandstones to seduce, then threaten them into obedience had triggered Arthur Sheridan's first rescue mission. He had helped them run for their lives. Their granddaughter had started displaying some unusual sensitivity, and a handy gift for predicting numbers. Minions of a nameless group preying on people with talents started paying too much attention to her. She vanished. Neither the Sheridans nor her grieving family were sure if she fled or she had been snatched. We theorized now that she had come to Neighborlee, hoping to find shelter and friends. Perhaps seeking her grandparents' roots. So in some ways, Demetrius and Beau's cover story was a little scarily close to the truth.

Funny how things like that seemed to happen when it came to Neighborlee and the guardians.

I totally agreed with Jane's label for the two old men who had raised her. They were Old Poops, but in an entirely lovable way. Ford wasn't too sure he wanted to meet either of them, because after all, he had spent years on the alert for them returning to Neighborlee, so he could drive them away. They were kidnapping Lost Kids, and Lost Kids belonged in Neighborlee. There was grudging respect visible on both sides from the moment they met, and that was a good start. We had our meetings at Divine's Emporium. Angela scolded the Old Poops a couple of times over the four days of their stay, for never having the brains to come visit Divine's. The moment they walked through the door, she would have been able to read them, she would have known what they were doing, and so many years of essentially working at cross purposes could have been avoided.

Col. Hayward was busy meeting with Arthur Sheridan and slowly forging an alliance with the shadowy organization he had created. He deputized Rodney as his representative at the meeting with Hoax, to hand over more than a dozen flash drives full of the data gleaned so far from the records taken from the Rivals. Rodney went back with Demetrius and Beau, to oversee coordination between Neighborlee's forces and resources and the Sanctum. When Hayward and Sheridan came to an agreement, that side would be merged with our suddenly expanded organization.

Kind of weird to consider ourselves an "organization" now, after all these years. We had always just been the guardians, brought together by not-quite-normal abilities and hyper-sensitivity to otherness. We didn't need to worry about structure and hierarchies, because, duh, who would refuse to follow Angela's guidance and advice?

We kept in mind that the bigger we got, the easier it would be for the Rivals to find us, to target us. We had to act slowly, cautiously. It might be months before the three groups could start meeting up and communicating regularly. After all, with the Troublesome Trio and now the new mess with Charlie, we had proof that the Rivals knew enough about Neighborlee to at least target me. Hayward's research supported the uncomfortable theory that the Rivals were involved in whatever went wrong around the Bermuda Triangle and made my parents vanish. The Rivals knew the Sheridans were strong enough to resist them, so they had used the royal marriage alliance gambit, sending Sylvia to snag Daniel. The tactic had worked for generations, with Grandstones marrying for power, influence, money, and talents. The Rivals had naturally expected it to work this time, too.

It was nice to know they could miscalculate so very badly. It gave us hope. Then again, this new generation of Grandstones were a law unto themselves, selfish and spoiled, and apparently thumbing their noses at the older generation. We had to wonder how soon the Rivals would cut themselves free of the Grandstones altogether. How many more failures could they endure?

Which brought us back to the problem of Freddie Grandstone trying to romance Athena. Despite her ignoring all his texts, emails, voicemails, and what amounted to stalking on social media, the guy did not give up. Either Freddie really was that oblivious, or terrified of the consequences if he failed in his mission. The guy was poised to pounce when Athena returned from her long visit with Bethany.

Wallace was ready. I think after all the public moaning and pining Freddie did, trying to convince people that he and Athena were just minutes away from eloping, Wallace had a lot of frustration to work off. He did an excellent job of hoisting yet another Grandstone on his own slimy petard.

The day after Athena came home, she and Wallace went walking to be seen by Grandstone minions. Within an hour, Freddie tracked them down at the gazebo in the center of town. The moment he jumped out of his sports car, waving a huge bouquet of flowers, Wallace went down on one knee in front of Athena.

I was there, because London notified all of us and asked us to be there as witnesses. We were thinking witnesses, as in testifying in court, or witnesses as in finally getting a Grandstone back big-time, the ultimate humiliation and making him eat his words.

From where I was sitting, Athena just didn't react. She didn't even blink, as Wallace pulled out an enormous diamond. It looked like it should have come out of those coin-op machines in the mall, where little plastic cups disgorged costume jewelry and temporary tattoos or gumballs almost too big to put in your mouth.

"Minerva," Wallace began, loud enough, and timed perfectly to drown out Freddie's shout of, "Athena, my darling!"

Minerva was Wallace's pet name for Athena, and it was a good tactic because that got a grin from her. I think she started breathing again. She even blinked.

"You know I love you, don't you?"

Freddie staggered to a stop, his eyes widening with horror.

"So help me," Wallace whispered, loudly enough for me to hear ten feet away, "if you don't say yes, I will leave you to the dweeb's mercy."

"Yes!" Athena yelped, then laughed. "You tell me often enough, I ought to believe you by now."

"But darling!" Freddie shrieked.

He stepped forward. I mentally grabbed his foot and twisted, so he spun around and went down. In the grass, I might add.

"You love me, don't you?" Wallace hurried to say, flinching just a little, so I knew he heard Freddie's squeak and the splat he made when he landed. The grass was very wet from snow melt.

"Would I put up with your craziness this long if I didn't?" Some color touched Athena's cheeks now, which made it clear how pale she had gone when Wallace pulled out that diamond.

"No, no, no!" Freddie called, as he scrambled to his feet. He darted forward, waving those flowers.

"Kiss me, quick," Athena said, yanking the ring out of Wallace's hand and jamming it on her finger.

"Athena, how could you do this to me?" Freddie wailed.

The bozo just never learned, did he? I pushed on both feet this time, so he skidded where there wasn't any ice or even dampness on the pavement. It was a lovely picture, Wallace and Athena in a clinch, with friends clapping and cheering, and Freddie flat on his back, in a mud patch this time, blinking dazedly up at the sky maybe five feet away from them.

They were still kissing when someone, who looked suspiciously like one of the Grandstone minions who had tried to mug Athena weeks ago, stepped up and helped Freddie get to his feet. He staggered away, whimpering about his cashmere coat and the mud.

"Okay, okay," Ford said, stepping forward as the crowd finally quieted down and started to disperse. "Enough, already. Save something for the wedding."

"Huh?" Athena looked kind of dazed as Wallace released her enough to step back. But he didn't take his arms from around her.

"Yeah," Wallace said with a grin, but still looking a little dazed. "Double huh."

"Granddad?" She looked around at those of us still watching them, and blushed. "Well, I think that worked."

"Hope so. If the first time doesn't take, then we're sunk." Wallace caught hold of her hand and started tugging on the ring.

Athena yanked her hand free. "Hey, he's going to realize it was a trick if he runs into me and I'm not wearing it."

Okay, if it was a trick, why did she go so white when she saw the ring? Unless that wasn't part of the plan to torment Freddie?

"I'd rather you wear the official one," Wallace said, grinning so hard his words kind of warped.

I caught him and Ford winking at each other. Then over Ford's shoulder I saw Charlotte, and Doni, and Cosmo behind her. I think I caught on sooner than Athena did.

"Official?" She still resisted as Wallace continued trying to slide that fake diamond off her finger. She kept her hand clenched, so I thought he might have to break her finger to get it off.

"Just how are you going to work your keyboard with that huge thing getting in the way?" Wallace gave up and dug in his pocket. It struck me that while he was always a spiffy dresser, today he had outdone himself, with sleek lines and an ascot instead of his usual tie, and a diamond and emerald pin in the ascot that matched the glittering cufflinks and his watch. He pulled out a little, carved wooden box and tipped the lid back on its hinge. Inside was a thick silver band with writing in flowing script. "Trade you?"

"Wow." Athena took the ring from the box and started to read it -- then looked up, frowning, and finally visibly realized that her grandmother and cousin, and her Uncle Jinx were there.

"Just on the condition that you never take it off," Wallace added, with a bit of strain and threatened break in his voice. He cleared his throat. "Read it aloud?"

I should stop here and point out that computer geek Wallace was also very much into anything Tolkein.

"One ring to rule ..." Athena blinked and held the ring closer. "Their hearts?"

For Christmas, Athena had given Wallace a Beta-test package of a linguistics course in speaking and reading High Elvish. Both of them spent more time than was probably wise studying it. I was witness to how fluent they had become, how quickly, and how much delight they found talking in High Elvish in front of their detractors and irritating classmates.

"One ring to bind them," Wallace finished. He took the ring from her fingers. I had the feeling that was a smart thing to do, because she might have dropped it in a few more seconds. Wallace slid the fake diamond off her finger and put the new ring in its place. "So ... will you?"

"You're serious?" She said it so softly, I only knew what she said because I could read her lips.

Time for the rest of us to get out of there and give them some privacy. I glared at Doni and Cosmo. They followed me as I wheeled away. I looked back once to see Ford and Charlotte hugging Athena and Wallace.

"Please tell me he asked Ford's permission," I said, when we were far enough away I felt safe to talk.

"Better," Doni said. "He asked Gram, first, then they asked Granddad."

"Did anybody think to ask the Colonel, and Portia?"

Knowing that London and Sherwood had to be part of the whole plan to zap and humiliate Freddie, I figured they would know those details, too. I asked London. An hour later, instead of her responding to me, I got an email from Portia. Wallace had included her and Hayward in a Facebook group chat, after he first cleared everything with Charlotte.

The boy knew what he was doing. All those steps proved to

Athena he was serious more thoroughly than anything else he could have done.

But doggone it, engagements were turning into a contagious disease around Neighborlee!

~~~~~

Ford and Charlotte had an open house to celebrate Athena and Wallace's engagement and Doni legally changing her name. London took responsibility for making sure the Hallidays didn't learn about it, just in case they tried to file protests to stop the process or try again to gain custody of Doni. Considering she was going on sixteen, it was kind of ridiculous, but the Hallidays were notorious for stupid actions, despite their slavish devotion to their public image.

When Demetrius and Beau left with Kory and Kelley, Rodney went with them, to install a program that would allow London and Sherwood to enter the Sanctum's shielded network. Some of the Sanctum's residents were twice the geniuses as Athena, Wallace and Cosmo, and they had created what was essentially a one-way street of communications. The Sanctum could surf everywhere they wanted to go, even infiltrating the Dark Web when necessary, but nothing could get through the shield and return the favor. Not even London and Sherwood. Until now. From inside the shield, they would be able to study what had been done and find a way to duplicate it. Their ultimate goal was to apply it to the energy shield around Neighborlee.

Wallace was nearly foaming at the mouth for a chance to go to the Sanctum sometime in the near future and investigate.

I swear I felt something change in the atmosphere of Neighborlee as soon as the van with the twins, Rodney, and the Old Poops crossed the border. Part of that was a sense of relief. They were safe, and we had one less responsibility on our shoulders.

So that meant, joy ... we could start focusing on the weddings for Felicity and Jake, and Gordon and Mandy.
~~~~~

Chapter Twelve

By the beginning of March, Arthur Sheridan had recovered from the strain he suffered in Bermuda, but he still wasn't up to traveling to Neighborlee to meet with Angela. The gang at the Sanctum were too busy training and exploring Kory and Kelley's talents to attend a conference of alliance, anyway.

Daniel came back to Neighborlee with a major assignment: find and buy homes, with a goal of moving the Sheridan headquarters within the town shield. If the Rivals were gathering their strength to make another salvo against us, then it would be wise to have as many of our new allies under cover as possible. So I spent at least one evening every week, inspecting houses for sale with Daniel. When I wasn't inspecting houses with Mandy and Gordon. Or looking through bridal catalogs with Mandy and Felicity. Or fending off phone calls from Mandy's relatives, demanding I speak some sense to her and to Gordon. Yeah, the perils of being a commanding officer in Starfleet.

Then to increase the weirdness, the stolen Rivals records yielded details of the campaign to match me with Charlie. Yes, he was a Rivals plant. Yes, his talent was mind-control. The physical appearance of Mr. Heartthrob barbarian warrior came courtesy of another talent, who could reshape living tissue for a short period of time. After I threw Charlie across the office, everything in his physical system was knocked out of balance, so he went through several weeks of instability. That explained my reprieve. Charlie was ready to kidnap my heart when he tried to corner me on the street that afternoon. He didn't want to risk my throwing him around again and repeating the whole painful process.

Kind of scary to learn the Rivals had such deeply planted tentacles they could uncover a stupid college research project and warp it to try to convince me to lower my shields. How come all that brilliance couldn't pick up on the fact that I wasn't interested, and the harder they pushed, the more I resisted?

Why couldn't they take the time to find out what attracted me, and the approach that would work, and then send someone to really sweep me off my feet? How come they had to use the hardball, wacko extremist approach instead of the sensible one? Wasn't I worth the effort to do things right?

What am I saying?

Thank You, God, that egocentric, wannabe dictators and wacko extremists don't have any common sense, and they will always, one way or another, trip themselves up.

Next to be uncovered was the Grandstone family tree. They were heavily into breeding. The rare Grandstone females often went to the Rivals headquarters, married for power (a Grandstone family tradition), and bred for powers. Fortunately, they didn't succeed very often. They kept tight control on their daughters, because (no surprise there) the girls were the smart, rebellious ones. When a mother didn't want her daughter to go through what she did growing up, they both fled for their lives and sanity.

Daniel's maternal grandmother and mother fell into that category. His great-grandmother was a Grandstone daughter who went hunting for more power than she could find among the minions in Neighborlee. I had to wonder if the Grandstones knew about his genealogy when they aimed Sylvia at him. His grandmother fled when his mother was six years old. They ran into Arthur Sheridan and his growing army, took shelter, got totally new identities, and the little girl grew up to fall in love with Daniel's father.

I didn't ask the questions burning holes in my brain, because honestly, I figured Daniel was going through enough turmoil without knowing I knew some of his ugly secrets.

What was really scary was the thought that struck me during a drowsy moment when my head was full of wedding details. I started out by wondering how I could dance in my wheelchair. Then I wondered if my legs would have strengthened enough by Felicity and Jake's wedding, I could get out of my chair and dance like a normal, able-bodied person. That led to wondering what it would be like to dance with Daniel, and if he would want to dance with me and maybe ask me out on a date and then ... could I date a guy who had Grandstones for relatives? Could I get serious about a guy with Grandstone blood?

Ewwww -- was I thinking about *that* kind of a relationship? With my **boss**?

Then another report came from Hayward and pushed all other concerns completely out of my mind. Even Felicity's upcoming wedding and my chances of having a maid of honor dress that would look good with my wheelchair.

More proof that the Rivals had been closing in, trying to find out what my parents were researching near the Bermuda Triangle, when they vanished last fall.

For once, the news was good. Most of the data in the reports filed by their operatives went at totally incongruent angles to what my folks were actually doing down there. None of the Rivals got their hands on any of my parents' notes and equipment. They thought whatever Mum and Pop were working on would tie into their primary goal of harnessing otherworldly energy.

Whew! What a relief.

Sort of. After all, this was further support for the theory the Rivals were involved in whatever made Charlie and Rainbow Zephyr vanish.

Lesson learned here: Be careful what you pray for, and be specific, because asking for answers, any answers, is just too vague and wide open. We got answers all right, but they were not the answers that could have helped us bring Mum and Pop home.

~~~~~

Cerb moved out. I decided to take it as a good sign that the danger had gone down enough his constant presence wasn't required. However, that didn't mean he left Neighborlee. I saw him at least once a day, if I was out and about. As the weather finally shifted from the constantly changeable weather of winter to the utterly unpredictable weather of spring in Ohio, I got outside a little bit more often. We weren't up to picnics in the pavilion in the park, or on our favorite high plateaus at the quarries. While my legs were stronger and less tingly than they had felt in a couple years, I wasn't up to bike rides yet. Forget about hikes. Still, I was outside more. Maybe it was restlessness. Maybe it was needing to get out of the house so I wouldn't be witness to how much time Felicity and Jake spent together. I had no idea why it bugged me now, because hey, they were engaged. It was kind of expected.

So any day of the week, any time of the day, I could be sure of spotting Cerb skulking somewhere in the distance. If he was the big fluff-ball, then everything was good. The more I saw of the sleek
~~~~~

hound underneath all that fur, the stronger the indication that someone was trying to cause trouble. Maybe Big Ugly was stirring, spying on us, maybe sending out feelers to try to siphon some energy from Jane or find another Lost Kid awakening to his or her powers. Or Rivals were stalking the borders of our town, trying to tap into the growing strength of our defensive shield. Or Grandstone minions were preparing for mischief.

Speaking of Grandstones, Freddie spent far too much time playing at being the broken-hearted, jilted sweetheart. Several times, he tried to sabotage a date for Athena and Wallace. Cerb always showed up and tripped him up. Either literally, or sabotaged whatever the overgrown snot tried to do. His feigned disappointment affected his working life, which was kind of sad, because Freddie had been shaping up to be one of the more tolerable Grandstones who actually contributed something worthwhile to society.

Bottom line: Freddie had a growing habit of irritating the senior members of his architectural firm. Either he turned in slapdash work because of his "emotional suffering," or he turned in his work late. Same excuse. Or, using the same excuse, he embarrassed the firm when he was supposed to be doing PR or drumming up business.

He got fired.

He threw a hissy-fit that the people on the street heard, despite the windows in the building being closed. He declared they couldn't fire him, he was quitting, and they could (impossible physical actions) if they expected him to give two weeks' notice.

Freddie vanished two days later. Either he ran away from home or the family sent him away until he stopped embarrassing himself. Or maybe he triggered some dimensional door and got sucked into another universe altogether. (Oh, we could only hope.)

What mattered was that there was currently only one Grandstone remaining in my generation, and Reggie was behaving himself. Some people speculated that he had been frightened into behaving himself. Maybe Sylvia's demise and Freddie's banishment had terrified his IQ into rising about thirty points.

Too bad I couldn't enjoy all that peace and quiet. How could I, when I was regularly spotting Cerb and wondering when he would go into bodyguard mode again?

Then I got busy helping Felicity arrange her and Jake's wedding. They had reserved the gazebo in the park, and then stunned me by asking Pastor Rocky to officiate. Yes, Felicity had attended church a few times with me when we were kids, and in the last two years she had agreed to come to special events at our church, averaging about once a month. Jake was becoming a more regular attender than her, and he was probably the reason she went to church at all. I knew how Pastor Rocky felt about the sanctity of marriage, and insisted on counseling for the spiritual as well as emotional aspects of marriage. Probably the reason he agreed to officiate was because they didn't ask for the ceremony to take place at our church. I took it as a good sign. I knew better than to ask questions that might give me answers that would disappoint me, so I didn't ask, either Felicity or Jake or Pastor Rocky. But I did happen to be driving past the church a few times and saw Jake's SUV parked by the office door, so that had to be a good sign, right?

Jane was coming to our church at least twice a month, and at least once a month Kurt came with her. I stayed away from them because I knew he'd feel awkward. If he saw me, he might turn coward and leave. I didn't want to jeopardize Jane's spiritual growth or their relationship. The two of them were good together.

Every time I thought about the kind of girl I had always envisioned Kurt ending up with, and compared her to Jane, I just had to laugh. One "girl's night" of just the three of us at Jane's place, Felicity and I told her what we had been thinking about Kurt's plans to become the patriarch of a superhero dynasty. She laughed, and laughed more when I gave her a collection of comic book heroine action figures for her birthday.

All in all, after those concerns, life really was looking good, despite the stress of being maid of honor, and the growing disappointment when every lead promising answers to my parents' disappearance ultimately failed us.

The middle of June was a big moment on the calendar. Not just Felicity and Jake's wedding. The long-awaited conference between Hoax, Sheridan's private army, and the guardians of Neighborlee would finally take place.

The tension rising around the "other" big wedding of the year had reached the boiling point. The tug-of-war between Mandy's relatives and Gordon's had gotten so bad that the two of them followed through with what had once been a joke to preserve their sanity. After the third time that one gang of relatives chose a wedding date and reserved the reception hall, and the other gang managed to cancel the arrangements for their own preferences, Mandy put her foot down. She announced that she and Gordon were getting married at Eden, using the small gym, the Saturday between Christmas and New Year's. They were going to have a Star Trek-themed wedding and reception.

Our Trek club was in ecstasy over the chance to go nuts recreating dishes and beverages mentioned in Star Trek novels or seen in the movies, with homages to Star Wars, *Galaxy Quest*, and *Firefly*. Mandy and Gordon's families were finally united in one detail: they absolutely refused to have anything to do with "that ridiculous travesty" of a wedding theme. They all declared they wouldn't attend. Those who reluctantly admitted they thought a Trek theme was pretty cool were bullied until they toed the line and boycotted the wedding.

There were several betting pools going in the club and at Mandy's office and the Neighborlee PD, on whether the bridal couple would give in to the bribes already being offered them, to give up their plans and elope. Some rumors said the two of them had already eloped, but they were playing hard to get just to punish their relatives for making so much trouble.

Some of their relatives had been heard boasting about the silent treatment they were inflicting on them. They had no idea the silent treatment was a reprieve and blessed relief for Mandy, Gordon, and anyone who had been pulled into the middle of the whole ugly social tug-of-war.

Since I was known as the captain of their club, all their relatives avoided me like the plague, while giving me a lot of dirty looks when I passed them on the street.

However, the family drama felt like comic relief, compared to a changing atmosphere and geometrical progressions of weirdness around town, accompanied by a growing sense of, "Uh, oh." More prosaically termed: "I've got a bad feeling about this."

The increasing tension of eagerness to get the school year over with and release students to summer freedom partially masked the other buildups and rumblings of energy. Daniel rode with our team when we patrolled on Senior Prank Night. Actually, he drove, because Kurt and Jane spent the night invisible and flying via the Ghost field, leaving Daniel and me in one truck, and Felicity and Jake in the other truck. Jake provided the radios to keep us all linked, and we pretty much had the town covered from the semi-pseudo-superhero angle. Even if Big Ugly squandered energy influencing kids to do something stupidly fatal, or the Rivals managed to get past our watchful guards, we were pretty sure nothing would happen.

Which meant on Thursday morning after Senior Prank Night, a lot of people would be both relieved and let down. Relieved no one got hurt, there was no damage to buildings and property, no big messes to clean up. And let down, because there wasn't a crazy story to keep them entertained and give people something to speculate about and criticize for the next week or two.

Daniel and I spent most of our patrol time talking about previous Senior Prank Nights. The memorable ones. The frightening ones. The frustrating and exasperating ones. The silly ones. When he asked me for more details of the Senior Prank Night that put me in my wheelchair, I countered by demanding he relate how he learned he was immune to the gifts of others. Interestingly, Daniel blushed and said quietly that he would prefer not to talk about it. That meant something potentially embarrassing, or at least made him uncomfortable. I didn't mind if we didn't talk about it, but I made a mental note and a promise to myself that I would talk to his mother or his grandmother and get the inside scoop.

Around about 11, when we were starting to run out of stories and I had the feeling he was going to return to questions about me, Cerb showed up. We had stopped at the head of the road behind the municipal complex and had to decide which direction to turn. Go down the road into the park, go to the right and head north up Overlook Drive, or go left and head south, aiming toward Divine's. Cerb leaped up onto the hood of Daniel's truck. He waited until he had our attention, then turned and looked back to the right, over my shoulder.

"I don't suppose you speak dog?" Daniel asked.

"That's Felicity's department, but Cerb isn't exactly a dog."

I opened my door. Cerb jumped down to the pavement, up into the cab, into the compartment behind the seat, then over the back of the seat, to perch between us.

"Why do you call him Cerb?" he said, when I had closed the door again and he turned, heading the way Cerb's nose had pointed.

"Short for Cerberus."

"Uh huh." He glanced sideways at me, then Cerb leaned forward far enough to block eye contact, and we both laughed. "Is that his real name, or just something slapped on him?"

"Don't know, and yes. I figured, if he didn't like the name, he'd let us know."

At the next intersection, Cerb went forward, resting his forelegs on the dashboard, and kept pointing with his nose toward the center of town. We ended up at the stretch of lawn with the gazebo. Daniel pulled into one of the empty parking spots, and I caught movement from the corner of my eye. Cerb let out that growl-snarl sound I had only heard the first time he leaped at Charlie. Instinct had me shoving the door open and leaning as far back in the seat as I could. As it was, Cerb got me in the gut with a hind leg as he scrambled out of the truck and into the darkness.

"Think we stopped someone?" Daniel asked.

"The gazebo is a good target. Someone in Athena's class turned it into a carousel, with huge balloon animals."

"That doesn't sound too bad."

"No, and it wouldn't have been hard to clean up, except that Channel 5 came out and covered it, and there were requests to leave it up so some schools could bring the kids out to see it, and then some snots from Seven Hills came over and used their BB guns on it. Shreds of balloons all over the place, and damage to the wood and … Why do people always have to ruin something, just because other people like it, or because it isn't theirs?"

"That about sums it up." He shrugged. "About all the reasoning they do. Think we should look it over?"

Considering Cerb hadn't come back yet, I agreed. I was out of the truck and standing up pretty much on my own by the time Daniel got my wheelchair out of the back and brought it over. He gave me a look that was easy to read.

"Yes, the spells of feeling like I can walk on my own are lasting longer, but it's the same unpredictability that kept me in the chair all along. You do not want me suddenly going boneless when we need to run for our lives."

"Ouch." He held the chair for me, I settled down, then applied a little brain power to get it moving.

Professor X, eat your heart out.

We toured everywhere we could around the gazebo and the intersecting paths across the grassy open area, then back to his truck. Daniel had brought big, powerful flashlights, and we couldn't detect anything other than footprints in the grass where dew had been collecting as the humid day cooled down.

"Hate to say this, but I really doubt Cerb would get upset about ordinary high school kids playing pranks," Daniel said.

"Since when are any kids who grow up in Neighborlee 'ordinary'?" slipped out of my mouth before I could edit my thoughts.

Daniel just cocked an eyebrow at me. I could almost read his mind on this one, and I had to agree. I pulled out the radio and contacted the other two teams. Just in case Kurt and Jane were interested in coming over and scanning the area for energy signatures that didn't belong there.

My legs got more twitchy than normal before those two showed up, so I got out of my chair and paced for a little bit. It felt dang good, despite the pins-and-needles sensation. I regularly did what exercises I could, just to keep up my muscle tone. It wasn't like I had what some friends call "writer's butt." Still, there was something invigorating about being able to stand up. Maybe doing it in the moonlight, walking around, knowing no one could see me and call me out for a fake, had something to do with the this-is-kind-of-sneaky-so-that-makes-it-fun feeling.

When Kurt and Jane arrived, I felt a little tingling in the air, and that made my legs wobbly, so I hurried back over to my chair. It figured that it was more than twenty yards away from me. I leaped and did a low-level glide the last fifteen or twenty feet. Hadn't done that particular maneuver since that night at the quarries. That got another cocked eyebrow look from Daniel. I settled into my chair just as Kurt and Jane made themselves visible.

"Okay, that's new. And old," Kurt said with a grin, gesturing at me and my chair.

"What's new is I could feel you two coming," I offered, "and it affected whatever *isn't* affecting me. Maybe pulled on or disrupted the power flow or something. Leave it for later, okay? What do you guy sense?"

After a few moments of the two of them walking around, they responded almost in unison, "Nothing."

"So what got Cerb riled?" Daniel said.

"Maybe he sensed someone preparing to do something," Jane offered, "but you guys got here in time to stop it?"

Cerb came back while they were doing a second walk around the gazebo. He seemed a little smug, which probably meant he had had some fun chasing someone or something. When we asked him what he had sensed, he just gave us those blank looks dogs are so good at, which clearly say, "Hey, I'm a dog, don't expect me to understand you. I'm not Lassie, remember?"

He was such a liar.

He did ride with us when we headed out to resume patrolling. He alerted us to some kids hiding behind the Post Office, and then another group climbing up onto the roof of the NCH gym. That was written up as a whole flock of miniature weather balloons, when the police filed their report. Daniel and I stopped the Post Office kids, who had a badly thought out plan to fill the letter boxes along the driveway with gelatin. The look of horror on their faces, when I asked if they were planning to check there were no letters already in the boxes, was utterly believable, and nearly comical. At least they were trying to follow the unspoken and unwritten rule not to cause damage. That rule wasn't written or spoken because that would make it official, and would encourage too many of the more rebellious and stupid ones to cross the line.

Fortunately, Kurt and Jane didn't need our help to handle the kids setting up the tiny weather balloons on the roof of the gym. Daniel and I were tied up for about an hour, guiding the nowhere-near-geniuses in finding another target. Some careful questioning before we let them go home, just before 1am, revealed that a couple of them were children of the definitely-nowhere-near-geniuses who had tried to turn the high school swimming pool into a gelatin bath when I was in school.

And now along with feeling tired, I felt old.

Cerb left us somewhere in there, which I took as a good sign. Or else he was just bored. When Daniel and I went to Angela to report the next day, we found Cerb there, curled up on a quilt that I swore sparkled with several dozen winkies. He had made his own report.

By the following weekend, we knew someone was attempting to infiltrate Neighborlee to do something nasty. Cerb chased intruders away from the gazebo on five different nights. Kurt and Jane had listened to gut instinct and flew patrol every night, so they heard Cerb howling and responded each time. I was more snarky than usual from lack of sleep, because I was either waking up from dreams of someone trying to shatter the Wishing Ball, or from strong, near-painful surges of pins-and-needles in my legs.

Angela and Ford agreed with us. The gazebo was a target for some reason.

"Okay, this may be egotistical, and maybe I'm turning into a Bride-zilla," Felicity said, when we had discussed the incidents at our meeting that second weekend in June. "What if they're targeting the gazebo to disrupt ..." She blushed, and gulped a little. "Our wedding?"

"Babe," Jake murmured, and caught hold of her hand and interlaced their fingers.

"For one thing, you are the least likely Bride-zilla in the world," I hurried to say. "You're too easy-going, and the wedding is too simple, and we're all having fun."

"That's because they're using up all their nerves and nit-pickyness on that monstrosity of a house," Kurt offered.

Everyone laughed. It was true. With Angela's help, all the permits, waivers and slightly grudging cooperation from town officials, inspectors, and historical preservationists had slid through at amazing speed. Bureaucracy and small-town mentality, foiled. Jake and Felicity were speeding through the dirty stage of the renovations, ripping out decayed drywall and peeling up ugly, old-fashioned vinyl flooring and all the layers of disintegrating padding and carpet that never should have been installed in the first place. Soon Kurt and the teams handling the rewiring and reconfigurations of plumbing and ventilation and heating systems would be getting to work. Felicity and Jake would spend the first couple months of married bliss in her garage apartment, and the first rooms to be renovated in the Willoughby house would be the offices for Jake's security firm.

Bottom line: the wedding arrangements were almost an afterthought, when it came to all the work they were doing.

"But that is an entirely too logical idea," Jane said somewhat hesitantly. Like she didn't want to break up the light moment. "That sounds like something the Rivals would do. I just hope we're wrong, because that means they know you're a guardian."

"Well, duh, they targeted me, they targeted Angela, and they know Felicity has been hanging with me and with Angela since we were kids," I said. "While I really like the philosophy that you always give the enemy credit for more intelligence and more resources than he really has, so you don't underestimate the damage he can do ..." I shrugged. "They have to know. They're taking names."

"So what are they trying to do with the gazebo?" Jake said.

"Why don't we let them do it, so we can find out?" Angela chuckled when all of us just looked at her, some of us with our mouths hanging open. That was because none of us were stupid enough, or disrespectful enough, to ask her if she was crazy. "We will move the wedding, but not tell anyone until the last minute."

"That ... could work," Felicity said. "We didn't invite that many people. Where?"

"Here." She tipped her head toward the back of the shop. "I do have a lovely back yard, and I would be delighted to host your wedding."

"Oh. Oh. Really?" She made a little gasping sound and kind of wriggled in her seat, then she lunged and went to her knees next to Angela's chair, wrapped her arms around her and burst into tears.

"That's a yes," Jake said. "And thanks."

Angela gave a regal sort of nod, and her mouth twisted in that mischievous smirk that meant all was right with the world, as she wrapped her arms around Felicity and waited until the blip of tears died out.

Chapter Thirteen

So that was the plan. We kept watch, but we wouldn't do anything if we saw anyone sneaking around at night where they didn't belong. A variant of the concept of giving our enemies enough rope to hang themselves. We brought Gordon and Mandy in on the theory. He arranged for the Service Department to ignore a request to replace the light bulbs that had been popping and dying with suspicious frequency around the gazebo lawn. We hadn't even noticed that.

The only one who didn't seem to like the plan was Cerb. He cooperated with us by cutting back to a warning trot through the park at dusk and just before dawn. The rest of the time, he settled down with whoever was on watch duty on the second floor of the office building across the street from the gazebo.

Naturally, no one tried anything from that day onward.

Two things did happen, though.

My dreams got more intense, and the pins-and-needles sensation turned into two instances of sleepwalking. Cerb woke me up both times, but the second time I had my hand on the kitchen door, ready to go outside. I could only speculate, and cringe, imagining what would have happened if I had gotten out of the house. My sleeping shorts and t-shirt were decent enough, and I was in decent shape because of my superhero metabolism. The queasy feeling came from imagining how far I would get before my legs reverted to what was normal for me, and I collapsed somewhere inconvenient. Without a phone to call for help.

The other thing that happened was that the Wednesday before Felicity and Jake's planned wedding at the gazebo, a crew from a landscaping business in Darbyville showed up to plant new flowering shrubs around the base of the gazebo, spread mulch, create paths with those ground-up tires that looked like mulch, and paint the gazebo. They had all the right paperwork, so several layers of authorities had approved the work. What made us suspicious was that Gladys Wypnash was paying for the work.

Gladys was a Neighborlee resident, one of the gracious rich

folks who were related to the Willis family and never rubbed their wealth or historical roots in anyone's faces. She often did things like this for the town and didn't think anything of it. She was one of the reasonable members of the Neighborlee Historical Society and had talked sense (threatened blackmail) into the recalcitrant members who wanted to control what Felicity and Jake did with the Willoughby house. However, anything so conveniently timed for the trouble we had been handling had to be examined with suspicious eyes. Especially when Gladys was involved.

Why? Gladys had one of the few sensible Grandstone daughters in her family tree, four generations back, and a cousin had married a Grandstone. For a short period of time, fortunately for her. She had fled the state of Ohio when that particularly stupid Grandstone got himself killed by a stunt equivalent to the time Reggie tried to blow a hole in Blackwater Pool and destroy Pickle Falls. The Grandstones let everyone know they were extremely generous to consider Gladys a Grandstone. Translation: they "forgot" to ask her permission when they used her good name to sneak motions through during council meetings, or claimed she supported something they wanted to do. Or in this case, as a few phone calls proved, put the bill for the landscaping on Gladys' credit card without her knowledge.

Gordon again intervened with the right people and nobody stopped the landscaping work. Nobody but Gladys, Chief Tanner, and the guardians knew the whole sneaky project and all the lies instigating it had been uncovered. We kept watch on the landscapers during the day, and the project when it was left alone at night.

London co-opted the security cameras around town, especially the ones in buildings surrounding the gazebo and park. Surprise: someone was doing some fancy programming, trying to shut down those cameras or erase whatever they caught as soon as it was caught. Oddly enough, the activities being erased or ignored all happened during the day, not at night, when we expected an attack or infiltration. Meaning the landscaping had been arranged to sneak something in under our noses in broad daylight, since Cerb's presence was stopping the invaders from doing it at night.

In the battle to keep the security cameras working, London didn't catch the landscaping crew doing anything other than what they were supposed to be doing. Digging up old plants, planting new plants, and painting the gazebo. Gordon got some friends on the force to snitch samples of the paint, topsoil, fertilizer and mulch. Jane flew everything to Hoax on Thursday night to have it analyzed. No poison. No drugs. So what were they doing?

Wednesday night, I went sleepwalking again, and Cerb was busy keeping watch at the gazebo, so he wasn't there to stop me. I made it out of the house just as Jake arrived after a late security watch shift. He tackled me when I didn't react to him whispering, then speaking, then shouting my name. I finally woke up, which was a blessing, because Jake was ready to tie me down to get me in his SUV and take me to Angela. He was growing desperate enough, he might not have stopped at breaking an arm or leg -- mine or his, we weren't sure when we thought about it later.

Felicity called ahead and Angela was waiting with Dr. Theodius, the same purple-garbed doctor who had showed up a little late to help when I got darted by Jay Parker's keepers back at Christmas. He examined me, such as it was, and agreed with Angela's assessment. My restlessness and the tingling in my legs were side-effects of the fluctuating, tainted energy returning to what should have been normal levels in the air and soil of Neighborlee.

He speculated -- oh, joy -- that I was developing some sensitivity to the use of energy, but I only reacted to it at night when my conscious mind relaxed enough not to interfere. Double oh, joy. He theorized that I knew subconsciously something was wrong, and I was trying to get to the source of the disturbance and do something about it.

Part of his diagnosis was that as I adjusted to the slowly increasing levels of energy, I would lose the disturbing, irritating, and encouraging pins-and-needles. Eventually, once the disturbance was identified and dealt with, I would be able to sleep through the night. He also noted that if the taint in the increasing energy wasn't purged or at least the source of the taint wasn't blocked, I likely wouldn't regain my legs.

"Is there a time limit on purging the taint?" Angela asked.

She put into words what had been only partially framed in my thoughts.

"Time limit?" Dr. Theodius hesitated in answering just long

enough, I was pretty sure he knew what she was asking, he just didn't want to deal with it.

"How long can Lanie be exposed to the taint before it causes permanent damage? Or looked at from another angle, how long can the taint build up before any hope of healing is ended?" She rested a hand on my shoulder and gave me a look that was sad, a little apologetic, but not pitying. I appreciated that.

"Honestly, my dear?" He shook his head. "Only time will tell." A sigh. "And by the time we have that answer, it will be too late to do anything about it."

Okay, not the most encouraging of responses and answers, but I had to be grateful for his honesty and his sympathy. And yeah, he gave me some hope that the discomfort would fade.

It's just that, doggone it, I was really hoping I'd be on my feet again someday. I loved playing basketball from a higher level in the air, and getting speed that didn't depend on wheels. The Ezekiel's Wheels were a great team, and good friends, and I enjoyed freaking out people who clearly equated broken body with broken mind. Snarking and saying things that required working brain cells always knocked them off balance. I had enough weirdness in my life, and getting rid of my natural four-wheel drive would just streamline some of it, that was all.

~~~~~

Jane called in friends from Hoax to come stand guard for the wedding rehearsal and on the day of the wedding. We had a few tense moments, wondering what our enemy's reactions would be when they realized the scheduled mid-morning wedding wasn't taking place. How long would they watch from wherever they were hidden before they wondered why there were no refreshments put out and no people arriving for the ceremony? We lined up chairs for people to sit on either side of the newly mulched path to the gazebo. We strung crepe paper in pale green and yellow and white, weaving it through the latticework sides of the gazebo, and hung those honeycomb wedding bells, but didn't do much more for decorations. We wanted to trick the enemy, but we weren't going to waste gobs of money on decorations we couldn't return.

At 10 on the dot, Felicity came out the back door of Angela's house with Kurt, acting as big brother like always. They walked down a path of apple blossom and rose petals, to the rose-filled
~~~~~

trellis where Pastor Rocky and Jake and his two best friends, Tyrone and Sherman, waited. Maybe two minutes earlier, Tyrone and Sherman had walked arms linked with me, maid of honor, down the path, so I didn't have to wheel down and hope I didn't tangle my gauzy skirts in my wheels. The music came from the wind chimes Angela had hanging everywhere, and they all seemed to be playing a real tune, soft and shimmering and gently rolling up and down. Like how a sunny meadow would sound if it was music. I was leaning on a conveniently placed pole, wrapped in more of that crepe paper, that helped me balance. Athena and Doni and the rest of the Longfellows were sitting in the front row, and the girls had the task of bringing my wheelchair if my legs started to give out.

The only thing that was missing, dimming the happiness for all of us, was that my parents weren't there. Mum would have loved to have made Felicity's dress for her, and Pop would have pretended to fight with Kurt to walk her down the aisle. They considered Kurt and Felicity their kids, just like me and Harry and Pete.

Kurt and Felicity reached the little lectern that served as the altar, draped with gauzy, rainbow-streaked material. Jake stepped up, grinning so wide I thought his face would split. At the same time, he seemed a little pale underneath that gorgeous, natural deep tan of his. Kurt shook hands with Jake, and muttered something that had Felicity rolling her eyes and prompted a few sparks to appear on her fingertips. Jake grinned, then Kurt transferred Felicity's hand from his grip to Jake's. He stepped back and sat on the other side of the aisle next to Jane. Pastor Rocky opened his mouth to begin the ceremony.

Cerb let out a howl that buzzed in my bones and sent chills down my spine. He raced up the slope from where Angela's backyard gave way to the Metroparks. Winkies spun and sparked, streaming from his fur. He ran around our little group of maybe forty people. Angela just sat there, arms wrapped around herself -- for the occasion, she had exchanged her blue handkerchief print granny dress for a long, peacock blue-and-green mottled Regency-style gown and matching peacock-patterned shawl. She watched Cerb, not a flicker of concern on her face, as he circled us three times.

Then abruptly the sound cut off and he settled down at Angela's feet, put his head down on his paws, and closed his eyes.

"I'm going to assume it's all right to continue," Pastor Rocky said, after a few seconds, looking between Angela, Kurt, Ford, and me.

A soft tremor in the ground seemed to be an answer. Angela smiled and nodded at Felicity and Jake.

Pastor Rocky kept his homily short and simple, maybe ten minutes at the most. Four minutes into it -- yes, I checked my watch -- sirens sounded from the center of town. After all, we were just a few blocks away from the gazebo and the park.

"Guess they weren't paying that much attention," Ford murmured, and winked at me when I glanced at him.

Honestly, I had hope for a few seconds that wink meant he and probably Kurt, maybe some of Jane's friends from Hoax, maybe even Gordon had rigged some kind of trap to catch our enemies when they struck.

Felicity and Jake said their vows and I really wasn't paying much attention. They kissed, then they hugged and shook hands with me and Kurt, the Longfellows, and Mrs. Silvestri. Then it was time to throw the bouquet and enjoy all the incredible refreshments spread out on long tables on either side of the backyard.

Jane's friend, Katie, the speedster, popped in out of nowhere as soon as Jake and Felicity headed over to the flower-covered swing, for the first of their official wedding photos. I made a mental grab for my chair and dropped none too gracefully into it. Then another mental shove got me over to where Kurt and Jane were talking with her. Their smiles had nearly dropped off their faces with an audible crash. Fortunately, no one was between me and them, so I didn't knock anyone over.

"What happened?" I demanded.

"It shouldn't have," Kurt said, sounding a little dazed. "After that whole mess with the school bus, the council and service department did a deep dive into all the records, all the structural details. There shouldn't be anything even remotely resembling a cavern or a sinkhole under the park."

"But now there is?" I felt kind of queasy. And furious.

The Rivals were looking more and more like nasty spoiled brats, if this was their handiwork. How dare they try to sabotage

Felicity's wedding?

"Unless it was Big Ugly behind it all, after all?" Ford said, joining us. Athena was right behind him.

"It's not that bad," Katie said. "I have to get back and help with the cleanup and coverup. We have some people who are kind of … re-inflating things, I guess you'd say. Before people realize how bad it is." She winked at me. "That's what Hoax does best."

"What does that mean?" Athena said, and blinked when Katie just vanished, with a tiny gust of breeze tugging at our wedding clothes.

"We have some people who are good at repairs and illusions to hide what really happened," Jane said. "But re-inflating … that's a new term for me. We can't leave right away, I know, but I really want to head over there and do some energy scans."

"You and me both," Kurt said.

By mid-afternoon, Felicity and Jake had left for their honeymoon, a rental house on Kelly's Island and plans to hit Cedar Point at least three times that week. The winkies helped with a lot of the cleanup, and we didn't have that much in the way of decorations to begin with. We had calculated the refreshments pretty well, so there wasn't much left over. While we had hoped nothing would happen once the schemers realized there was no one at the gazebo to ambush, we were prepared to react and defend. All the guardians brought clothes to change into after the reception. Angela rode with me as we drove the couple of blocks to the center of town, to see what our enemies had done.

Re-inflate was a good word, because while a hole had opened up underneath the gazebo, the ground had somehow risen back in places. The gazebo looked like all the support posts underneath had been yanked out sideways, the walls had tipped inward, the latticework roof had split in five places, and then the support posts had been shoved back into place. Everything twisted sideways as the gazebo kind of tried to stand upright again. The emergency crews and service department and fire department and police had worked quickly, stringing yellow crime scene tape around the perimeter of the park. After more than six hours since the collapse, there was still a good crowd, standing around and staring and asking questions and speculating. They were gathered mostly on the sidewalks and pressed up against the tape barrier, or standing in the parking spots that didn't have cars.

Kurt and Jane did their Ghost thing, flickering out of sight and going up to the gazebo to inspect it. They reported later they walked around the wreckage and through it and sank partially down into the ground, testing and sensing and scanning. They took their time, and some of the onlookers were finally drifting away when they flicked back into sight and gestured for us to follow. We went to the Sipping Post and got drinks, then walked down to the pavilion on the other side of Overlook Road, where we could see down into the park.

"Someone has the power to compress matter," Jane announced, after we were all settled at two picnic tables and we made sure there was no one nearby to overhear what we discussed. "Under cover of that landscaping, they buried something that took in massive amounts of energy and collapsed it, like a black hole that lasted only a second. But that's not right, because it didn't suck in anything, it just ... squashed it. At least, that's my interpretation of the energy readings, the warping fields that are still struggling to go back to normal flows and waves." She shuddered a little. "They were planted in a precise ring around the gazebo, and the energy was focused on the support posts and the bedrock under the gazebo."

"My reading is that they were trying to open a hole in the ground and send everyone in the gazebo down, and then close the ground on them," Kurt said.

"Only we weren't there." Ford winked. "Like I said, they weren't paying attention."

"Maybe there wasn't even anyone to press the button. It was probably set up on a timer. Or if someone triggered it, they were far enough away they didn't realize the wedding wasn't taking place there."

"Whatever they tried, they only partially succeeded," Jane said. "I don't think they had any connection to Big Ugly. They were trying to duplicate what happened back in February, but the stubbornness factor fought them."

"Come again?" Ford said. That got a short chuckle from her.

"It's something Beau has been working on for decades, refining his own version of quantum physics, I suppose. The stubbornness of reality, of matter, resisted whatever they were trying to do, creating a temporary black hole, compressing matter. Cedric is one of our oldest members of Hoax. Not counting the Old Poops. His forte is convincing matter to go back to what it was before something chaotic hit it, helping it reverse the damage. I could feel his signature energy already at work before Katie came to report to us."

"Was anyone hurt?" Angela said.

"Nope. We kept them away," Katie said, appearing with another tiny gust of breeze. "Happy couple away, none the wiser?"

"Yes," she said, nodding, and summoning a smile that struck me as just a little weary. Even counting all the fuss of the wedding and the reception. "Thank you for your help."

"Hey, this is our newly expanded family." She tipped a salute off her right eyebrow with two fingers. "Delighted to give the nasties another poke in the eye."

"Speaking of which, how long do you think it'll take until they figure out they failed, and how long until they have another temper tantrum and strike back?" Ford said.

~~~~~

That was a big concern, since we were looking forward to the official meeting and negotiations between the Sheridans and the leadership of Hoax coming to meet with Angela. If someone was going to just drop a nuclear warhead on Neighborlee and wipe out all opposition to Big Ugly's plans for domination of multiple dimensions of reality, that would be the perfect time.

We had to delay, because Hayward and Rodney and some of the Hoax team had identified another Rivals holding. It wasn't a base camp or supply depot or records storage depot or training camp, or prisoner camp. Hayward called it a holding because no one was sure what it was. There just wasn't enough information for them to know if it was a decoy or bait in a nasty trap that would allow the Rivals to turn the tables on us, maybe lure guardians and Hoax operatives in and swallow them whole.

So while they were out creeping up on the location, somewhere on the border of Canada and North Dakota (that was all they would tell us), we settled down with two huge projects. The most important was continuing to wade through the mountains of data that had been taken from the Rivals, to determine what was true, what was theory, and what was evidence of massive, long-term
~~~~~

plans of deception. Daniel was working with us now. It took him a little while to get used to London and Sherwood popping in and out, jumping from computer screen to tablet to smartphone. As they helped us with the decoding and sorting and analyzing, Daniel grew increasingly upset with all the false histories and false documents the Rivals had created, focused on him and his family.

July headed for August, and then one day Daniel hit a turning point. He laughed. He came to the realization that one of the elder generation's theories was true. The Rivals were fractured into so many different factions, they were tripping themselves and each other with all the false stories and reports. The Rivals themselves didn't know what was true and what was false. They wasted lots of time, energy, and resources determining what they could rely on, or trying to destroy each other.

Most important: the Rivals didn't know Daniel's mother and grandmother were escapees from the breeding/training program. His sister and cousins were safe from at least that aspect of the Rivals' plan. There was still Reggie Grandstone to deal with, and a revived attempt to form a match between Sheridan daughters and him. We hoped that the fact all those women were married and had occupations that kept them on the move, surrounded by guards, frustrated the Rivals and wasted their energy and resources.

So what did we do for fun, as we monitored the increasing levels of energy and the strengthening defensive shield, and unraveled the never-ending insanity of the Rivals' machinations? Daniel joined our patrols and joined my church and spearheaded the biggest, loudest, craziest Shore Leave (summer party) our Star Trek club had ever enjoyed. He was constantly interviewing Ford and Angela about the history of Neighborlee and the guardians, and sending reports to his grandfather.

We were still house hunting. We had all the Sheridan clan and their allies to move to Neighborlee, after all. This project would take several years, because we didn't want the Rivals to see massive movements, put details together, and figure out all the things they had missed all these years. We started with a house for Grandfather Sheridan, to act as headquarters for the migration. Daniel's parents would move after Christmas. Then other members of the family. Some of the Sheridan allies were in the process of essentially going into Witness Protection: creating new identities, new faces, destroying their current lives, even faking their deaths, so they could move to Neighborlee and the towns surrounding us. Maybe in ten years we would have everyone together. Then the war would be inevitable.

War was a little difficult to imagine, when the six of us were soaring through the sky above the quarries on a warm, breezy summer night. Yes, I said six. Kurt and Jane provided most of the "lift," and made us invisible. They were in the middle. Felicity and Jake were on one side, Daniel and I on the other. I helped provide some assistance, since my broken semi-pseudo-superhero powers were definitely coming back. If slowly. Daniel provided earbuds, courtesy of the R&D department of Sheridan Communications, so we could talk in low voices and not have to shout to be heard over the breeze or any noises coming from the ground. We had a lot of fun, flying patrol in the darkness.

Cerb came to visit maybe once a week, which we all took as a good sign. If he wasn't feeling any threats, didn't sense or even find anyone unfriendly sneaking around, then we were in good shape. We were as safe as we had ever been, when it came to the general background weirdness of Neighborlee.

At the start of August, we heard from Hayward and his team. Some of Jane's friends came to town to deliver a highly distilled report on what they had uncovered. At first it had appeared to be a remote settlement of back-to-nature folk, tending toward survivalists. A cluster of six buildings sat on top of a massive underground complex. The tunnels extended from the United States side of the border, going for more than a mile into Canada. Kind of like the drug smuggler tunnels on the southern border with Mexico. However, these tunnels had living quarters and research labs. Some of them, anyway. Essentially, the complex had been built in fits and starts for more than seventy years. One faction would come to power within the Rivals and throw resources at the project, have more tunnels built, install the most up-to-date equipment, and relocate "breeding stock" and "trainers" from other locations. Then in four or five years, according to the pattern deciphered so far, another faction would gain power. They would stop the work, move people out, strip out equipment, and leave the place a ghost town. On and on through the decades.

However, the pattern seemed to have changed drastically

during the last shift in power. The faction on the ascendant didn't go to the trouble of removing people and equipment. They brought in a research team working on germ warfare and let loose their latest nasty creation within the tunnels. The infiltration team from Hoax, fortunately, had some of that invulnerability I had been griping about not having for years. They needed it. As far as they could tell, even the researchers had fallen prey to the germ warfare.

If the records could be believed, none of the virus or neuro-toxin or whatever they had created had been removed from the tunnels or had escaped into the environment. But that was the sticking point. Could anything the Rivals recorded be trusted? They lied to and manipulated their own people, after all. Look what they had done to punish people in their own organization who disagreed with them.

The exploration of the underground complex was being conducted with glacial speed to ensure that nothing and no one escaped. Yes, "no one." As in people. Either the tunnels were inhabited by ghosts, or there were people down there, terrified and living in the darkness.

Wow, I instantly repented all those times when I had silently complained that I was so useless and unremarkable that even the Rivals had overlooked me and didn't snatch me and Kurt and Felicity. Who would have wanted to work for and with and be brainwashed by nasty, homicidal, elitist whackadoodles like them?

Chapter Fourteen

By mid-August, we agreed to go ahead with the "summit" of the three groups, minus Col. Hayward. He was staying with the team in North Dakota until that nasty situation was cleaned up for good and for all.

"We need a name," Felicity announced that August Sunday afternoon. We were all together at Willoughby House, spending yet another blistering hot day happily soaking up the cool of the revolutionary air conditioning system Kurt had designed.

He was nowhere near ready to offer the design to any of the local heating-and-cooling companies, or try to patent and produce the unit on his own. It worked fine most of the time. The problem was the not-most-of-the-time incidents, when the unit gave off noxious fumes or funny sounds or emitted sparks of various colors. There was a chance of a magical energy problem involved in the miniaturized, super-powered cooling gizmo, which meant either it wouldn't work outside of the borders of Neighborlee, or it might turn into something dangerous or even semi-sentient when it got outside of Kurt's growing sphere of influence. Yeah, with the slow increase of energy in the shield, the diameter of Kurt's influence field was expanding for the first time in ten years. He now had to walk an entire block away from his newest gizmos before we could be sure they would work when he wasn't there to "nudge" them.

"Name for what?" Jake asked, coming into the huge living room.

After their kitchen, bathroom and bedroom, it was the most recently finished, fully renovated room in the huge old house. Golden-stained pine floors, built-in bookshelves everywhere there weren't windows -- or the gigundotron-sized TV, of course -- floor pillows everywhere, low-built sectionals in conversation groups, scatter rugs in brilliant rainbows of colors. This was a room for relaxing, and a nice display of balance between Felicity and Jake's styles. It reflected the comfortable, happy, clean, no-frills and no-baggage marriage they had.

"For the Superfriends?" Daniel offered. That got a wrinkled up nose and a giggle from Felicity.

And groans from my brothers. They and Daniel, Wallace, Cosmo and Athena were playing a game that filled up maybe a quarter of the room. The huge living room was one of the few places where they could play it, other than outdoors on a basketball court. Cosmo and Wallace had designed it, part role-playing, on a fiber-optic mat made of multiple squares that could be connected and disconnected, going from one-foot-square to ten-by-ten one-foot squares, all connected by Bluetooth and controlled from the Game Master's computer. The mat displayed the changing battlefield and terrain of the adventure being played. That meant if the Game Master said there was a flood or fire, it took place, and obeyed the dice, which were also linked by Bluetooth to the gaming computer, so no cheating or fudging. The villages, cities, forests, rivers, lakes, and mountainous terrain all looked realistic. If in the course of the game a sink hole opened up or someone discovered tunnels, such as dwarf or orc tunnels, the display would adjust to show what was going on underground.

Even if I didn't play, it was fascinating to watch. Kind of like an interactive TV show. Right now, all they had was visual, but in another four or five months, they hoped to be able to add audio to the game system. Athena and Doni and some of the members of our Star Trek club who were into fan fiction were trying to create interactive story lines that could be plugged into the system, so players didn't need a Game Master. A narrator in the computer would offer them options.

Yeah, these kids were going to be rich sooner or later.

And yeah, there were a lot of us in Felicity and Jake's living room that day, having multiple conversations. All of us were guardians or were related to guardians, so it was a natural thing to think she was talking about guardian business.

Felicity and Jane and I had been talking in one corner about the upcoming conference. Demetrius, Beau, and several other leaders of Hoax would be staying in the Neighborlee Arms. Daniel's grandparents and parents were expected to arrive with the moving truck the next day. The plan was to help them settle in, get the big things in place in the house we all had been helping to clean and paint for a week now, then go to Divine's for a picnic and a launch-the-conference meeting.

"The bad guys have a name. At least, a name Hoax gave them, not the one they gave themselves." Felicity frowned. "Have they found anything in all those piles of records to indicate what the Rivals call themselves?"

"The Organization," Daniel said. "My dad's impression is that it's equivalent to when a lot of ancient cultures referred to themselves as 'the People.' They considered themselves the only ones, or at least the elite or superior ones. They didn't need a name because they were the top of the food chain."

"Break the chain, please," Jane muttered. That got a grin and snort from Kurt. She turned to look at him, sitting against a bookshelf and balancing the control computer on his lap. They shared a look that had me fighting a sigh I didn't quite understand. Yeah, those two were made for each other. I could believe they could read each other's minds even when they weren't close enough to share the Ghost field.

"So we need a name?" Athena said. "Yeah, makes sense. Something to indicate or symbolize that we're not three separate groups anymore."

"Working against each other and not knowing it," Daniel said. That got mutters and grins and a few chuckles from the rest of us.

Ford had waxed eloquent and irritated a few times, evaluating the damage our separate groups had done to each other over the decades through simple lack of communication. He and Arthur Sheridan had actually lived in the same cottage at Neighborlee Children's Home for a few years. Arthur had been preparing to graduate and Ford had just arrived. Neither one had reason to recognize the other when Arthur brought his family to Neighborlee that summer the Grandstones started their campaign to marry Sylvia to Daniel. Even more ironic, Hoax had been there too. Arthur had confronted Demetrius and Beau, when his gift prompted him to stop them from approaching a child at a baseball game. It would have drawn Grandstone attention to that child. No one knew which child, because the Old Poops only had a few vague harbingers of a talent awakening. It could have been Kurt or me.

Yeah, Ford griped about the years, energy, and knowledge that had been wasted or delayed. I couldn't tell if he was looking forward to the picnic and meeting at Angela's on Monday evening, or dreading it.

"How can you mush together guardians and Hoax and Sheridan into one name?" Doni didn't look up from her notebook and the scattered piles of index cards, where she was organizing a game-controlling story.

"Don't suppose you'd want a name that means anti-Rivals, do you?" Pete asked.

"That gives them too much credit, like they're the reason we exist," Kurt said.

"Well, maybe we do, I mean, we are, I mean ..." My little brother sighed and shook his head. "Would we be teaming up if we didn't have someone to work against? I mean, would Hoax have been snagging kids away from Neighborlee if they weren't worried about the Rivals taking them and brainwashing them?"

"He's got a point," Jane said, nodding, and then grinned at me and Felicity. "Okay, anti-Rivals ..." A snort escaped her, and her grin got brighter.

"What did you think of?" Jake said, as he settled down on the edge of the long, L-shaped sectional where the three of us had been sitting and talking and making lists of food for Monday's picnic.

"Stargate."

"No. No. No," Kurt said. Jane stuck her tongue out at him.

"Calling us Stargate?" Jake screwed up his face, eyes sparkling. He knew that wasn't what she meant, but he was just being silly. Yeah, he was good for Felicity.

"Tok'ra," Kurt said. "In the TV series, Tok'ra were rebel Goa'uld, fighting Ra and the System Lords. Tok'ra means anti-Ra."

"Tok'rivals?" I said, testing the word. I knew it didn't work, even before the others groaned.

The others played with twists on the name, getting somewhat silly and moving further away from the original words with every rendition. It was nice, taking a semi-serious conversation into foolery. A good way to spend a hot summer Sunday indoors, relaxing with friends.

Pete thought of the name, near the end of the day, when we were cleaning up and packing up to go home. School was starting for the fall, for college students and high school students. I had to go in to the *Tattler* early to get my day's work done, so I could take off early and help with the move. Not that they really needed me until most of the furniture and boxes were inside the house, because in my wheelchair it wasn't like I could be of much use with actual moving. My talents tended more toward unpacking and organizing. A good number of our Star Trek club would be waiting at mid-morning to help, when the moving trucks pulled up to the big old house just two doors down from Felicity and Jake.

Nope, there wasn't anything special about my being part of the effort. Yet I had this niggling feeling. I had been getting flashes of ideas, and realized toward the end of the day, when I was starting to feel drowsy, that I was remembering dreams. So I didn't really hear Pete when he brought up his idea for the name, until everyone had tossed it around, verbally, and came to tentative agreement.

"So what do you think, Lanie?" Jane asked me. She frowned and reached down to grip my shoulder. "Are you okay?"

"Huh? Think about what?" I didn't blush very often, but my face got warm, and not because we were all outside, getting in our cars and trucks, dispersing for the evening.

Pete backed up and explained. He suggested we consider ourselves the Alliance, or Allies, like in WWII, fighting the Nazis. Considering there was a lot of similarity in philosophies and self-righteous justification of atrocities between the Rivals and Nazis, yeah, it made a lot of sense. And we were allied, finally, after far too long fighting the battle on our own.

Cerb let out a howl and darted into the big front yard and circled us three times.

"Yeah, that," Kurt said. "Anybody else been having fragments of dreams they can't remember?"

"Just a weird sense when you wake up that something is wrong, but you can't put your finger on it?" Jake shrugged and wrapped an arm around Felicity's shoulders when the rest of us turned to look at him. "Hey, it's not like we're getting a mind-meld or anything, but she talks in her sleep when she gets warning dreams, and I'm smart enough to ask her about it and … that's about the extent of our impressions."

"Oh … heck," I said, and pointed in the direction of where Cerb was now facing.

Remember, these big old houses sat on the high points looking down into the old quarries, what was now either off-limits to the public (in theory, if not in practice) or had been turned into Metroparks. Two doors down from Felicity and Jake's house, heading north, was the big old house Daniel had purchased for his grandparents to move into tomorrow. In nearly a straight line from Felicity and Jake's house, through the Sheridan house, heading north, sitting on the horizon and lit up nicely by the new parking lot lights, was the silhouette of Eden.

The location of one of the biggest showdowns with Big Ugly we had ever survived. The place where the Rivals had made a major offensive move back at New Year's.

"Cerb, where is it coming from? Earth or the other side? Do we cancel the move?" I asked.

Yeah, like I expected him to start speaking English and tell us?

"That'd just let the Rivals know we know." Jake used that flat, assured tone of voice of his security consultant and expert mode. He wasn't speaking as an associate of the guardians of Neighborlee, our friend, or Felicity's husband.

"I agree," Daniel said. "We've dealt with them enough, if my folks changed their plans at this late date, they'd be signaling that they suspect something. Besides, the house was packed up and emptied yesterday, and they're on their way."

I knew that. I had overheard when they called Daniel at 6 last night to let him know they had reached their hotel in Columbus. They were two hours away, give or take morning commute traffic on I-71.

"On a positive note …" Jake shrugged and pulled out his smart phone and started tapping data into a program. Probably something Wallace and Cosmo and Athena had custom-designed for him. "Chances are strong your folks aren't their target. Otherwise they'd be attacking tonight, when they're most vulnerable, between the old headquarters and the new. So whoever is preparing for the attack, they're focused on something or someone here."

"No," Felicity said softly, "that really isn't as positive a note as I'd like."

"We're warned, and that's to our advantage."

We ended up driving patrol that night, after sending the younger members of the team home. They had school, after all. Athena called Ford to let him know what we theorized. I called Angela. Athena contacted London and Sherwood, who weren't usually in communication with us because all their energy was focused on dealing with that germ warfare-devastated underground complex in North Dakota. She would leave it up to them to inform Hayward and the members of Hoax who were dealing with the problem. Jane called Beau to let him and the others who were driving up from the Sanctum know what we theorized, and let them decide what to do or not do.

It was perfect timing, after all, for the enemy to strike at us, while the nucleus of the new Alliance was gathering in Neighborlee.

Which gave me the awful suspicion that somehow, the enemy was spying on us, could eavesdrop on us, or we had a mole in our midst. Either that, or it was just incredibly bad luck in timing.

I let Pete and Harry take my Jeep to go home. I went on patrol with Daniel in his truck, with Cerb sitting on the hood like a huge, direction-finding hood ornament. He didn't even twitch as we passed the house waiting for the older Sheridans, as we drove north on Overlook. That was some relief, and I could almost hear the drop in tension radiating from Daniel as we headed up the street to Eden.

Cerb stayed on the front hood like he had been glued there. I tried to take some comfort in the fact that he was completely the fluffy, furry dog, no sign of the Egyptian-style hound I knew was underneath. I didn't point this out to Daniel. His knuckles were white from his grip on the steering wheel. Neither of us spoke, and I figured he didn't need any distractions.

Besides, experience had showed me that when I tried to point out the bright side of things, distracting the driver, that was when something happened. Like the forces of the universe felt compelled to prove me wrong.

We reached the parking lot of Eden. Cerb hopped down while the truck was still moving, only going maybe ten miles per hour, but enough of a surprise to startle a curse out of Daniel. In English. I would have felt better if he had used some of the Klingon curses Pete had been teaching him. Cerb trotted over to the sidewalk in front of the main doors into Eden. He looked back at us, then lay down and curled up with his head resting on his forepaws.

"Okay, what's that supposed to mean?" Daniel muttered. He looked at me. I shrugged. "He's your dog, isn't he?"

"Ah … no. I'd bet anything if you asked Angela, she'd say Cerb adopted me. And don't even try asking Felicity. Cerb isn't really a dog, so he isn't talking to her."

"This is such a freaking weird town," he groaned, some of his words muffled as he rubbed at his face with his open palms. But when he put his hands down, he had a crooked little smile in one corner of his mouth. "Gotta admit, I wouldn't want to live anywhere else, though."

"That's because you're one of Neighborlee's own." I grinned back at him when he just cocked an eyebrow at me. "Be afraid. Be very afraid."

"Oh, I am."

After a few more minutes of us watching Cerb and him watching us, relaxed and not giving any clues what we should do, I called Jane. She and Kurt had flown patrol and couldn't detect any energy trails coming from any direction over any of the borders. We were always worried about that residential section where Darbyville and Neighborlee touched. After all, some enemy had settled there on the border and lashed at Angela. We were still unsure who, exactly, if they were Rival allies or something more like Big Ugly. There had been no stirrings of energy or trouble from that direction ever since, but that didn't mean anything. Interdimensional invaders had a totally skewed sense of time, with no pattern or rhyme or reason to their attacks.

All was quiet on the borders. Jane and Kurt flew over to join us, and they took a walk through the walls of Eden to inspect all the weak spots where the enemy alliance at New Year's had played with the fabric of reality. Daniel and I went around the perimeter of Eden as far as we were able, on foot and on wheels, looking for anything odd with just our eyes and his super-powered flashlight.

We found something. But it made no sense.

Ten holes. Bored into the ground at equal distance surrounding Eden. Jane and Kurt scanned the holes a short time later and found nothing in them. No unusual energy residue they could detect. The holes were shallow, maybe going at a twenty-degree angle downward, all of them around ten feet in length. None of them pierced or did damage to the foundation of the building.

So we did what we had always done when there was nothing further the guardians could do, and we had to include the authorities. I called Gordon and told him what had happened, what we feared, and handed him the fun task of coming up with a story Chief Tanner would accept and act on. Gordon and Mandy should have been with us at Felicity and Jake's that afternoon and evening. However, the impending global thermonuclear war over the wedding arrangements had taken a positive turn. They had a chance to sweeten family relations on both sides, and they took it.

Mandy answered Gordon's phone, because they were still on the road, driving back from Kelly's Island, where her family had a cottage and the older generation spent much of the summer. We went back and forth for maybe twenty, thirty minutes, with both our phones on speaker and Gordon asking questions. He had learned after all the incidents we had survived together to be as honest with Chief Tanner as possible, and tell as much of the truth as possible. The story he came up with was that he had it on good authority that people involved in the New Year's Eve trouble were coming back for another strike against the city and against Eden. He recommended extra precautions for the next few weeks, along with trying to limit some of the activities at Eden. The start of the school year, the regular inward migration of students to the college, the extra traffic around town as students explored their new territory, made this the perfect time for troublemakers to strike. Unfamiliar faces wouldn't set off alarms like they would at other times of the year.

"The guy is good," Daniel remarked, once we had refined the plan and story, and Gordon and Mandy said goodbye.

"Yeah. Thank God he's a friend, because he could make life miserable if he was against us, with everything he knows and has seen."

Daniel grinned and let out a weary chuckle. Then he headed to my place to drop me off. Cerb rode with us, and climbed into the truck to sit in the passenger seat when I got out.

"I think you've got something of a guard until everything is settled with your folks," I offered, when Daniel looked at Cerb and back at me a few times.

"What does he eat for breakfast?"

"Anything he wants."

That got a more genuine laugh from him.

I admit, I slept better that night, knowing Cerb was there. Daniel's immunity didn't really extend to bullets or bombs. Gee, the more I thought about it, the more we had in common.

~~~~~

The Hoax delegates arrived around 10 Monday morning, about the same time as the older Sheridans, coming from opposite directions. I felt an odd little ripple of energy in the atmosphere, not so much an increase or decrease, but just a sideways kind of shift. I stopped the final proofread I was doing and called Jane. She confirmed the arrival. Twenty minutes later, the Old Poops walked into the *Tattler* office to meet up with me. Why me? What made them think I was the best liaison between them and the Sheridans? I accused them of being terrified of Angela, and they didn't really laugh, so much as they tried to smile.

Wow, was there something going on I didn't know about? Had something strange happened the last time they were in town, that Angela had frightened them?

Well, my work was pretty much done, because I had come in two hours early that morning. I shut down my computer and called out to Conrad I was heading out. He didn't look up from his work. Just replied that as soon as Clarice swung by, they'd be heading over to the house to help with the moving, and he'd see me there.

Demetrius and Beau sat in the back seat, and I drove to Angela's. She was waiting by the gate, with one of those old-fashioned, corrugated tin spigot dispensers that seemed to keep the liquid inside so much cooler than the more modern dispensers. I had experience with this antique, and knew it contained probably three times as much liquid as it should have. And whatever drink Angela had concocted, it would be perfect for everyone helping with the move. Demetrius and Beau had to work together to put it in the back of my Jeep, Angela settled in the front seat, and the four of us were on our way.

Daniel was out front with his mother and grandmother. We went through introductions and the ladies were thankful and didn't gush over the decorations Angela had found at Divine's and given as a housewarming gift. She commandeered Daniel to retrieve the cooler from the back of my Jeep. Demetrius and Beau went to look for the Sheridan men and the ladies walked around the back with Angela. They had questions about the park and the path down from the house. The movers were all men who worked for the Sheridans, and a couple faces I recognized from Hoax. All the heavy lifting
~~~~~

was going on. The best way for someone in a wheelchair to stay out of the way was to get into the house and find some place full of boxes, where no one was walking and unloading, to start unpacking.

The dining room furniture was in place, and around the perimeter of the room were stacked at least two dozen boxes clearly marked *dining room*. The perfect place to start. I got a bucket of water and ammonia and rags, and got to work unpacking, unwrapping all the pretty, old dishes from the newspaper, cleaning everything, and stacking it on the dining room table. No way would I presume to know where everything went in the cabinets and display racks.

"So you're the funny girl, eh?" a man said from the door into the kitchen.

I turned around, and there was Arthur Sheridan. I knew him just from a strong resemblance to Daniel. He was thicker, whiter, wrinkled. There was a lot of power in him, and I supposed all that energy sizzling in the air around him came from alertness. It had to be a pretty stressful life, knowing he was responsible for guiding a group of people he had to protect from users and schemers like the Rivals.

"Funny girl?" I wondered if that was how Daniel described me, or if Arthur Sheridan was testing me. "Gee, I've never been compared with Streisand before."

He took a second to catch on. That moment of confusion in his eyes was priceless. Then he tipped his head back and laughed. The sound brought Daniel and his father and Ford running.

"Watch out for this one. She's going to be running things one of these days," he said, and winked at me.

"Nope, too much responsibility. Ask anybody, they'll tell you how lazy I am."

He thought that was funny, too. I caught him giving me thoughtful looks through the day, every time he passed me in the moving and unpacking process, and then when we had caravanned over to Angela's for that picnic. He and Angela, Ford, Demetrius and Beau had their heads together three out of every four times I looked around and found them. Angela looked as serene as always. Ford wavered between amusement and a somber, serious look that had me worried. I couldn't read the Old Poops, but when Jane joined us after she closed down the spa for the day, she said her teachers were pleased with how things were going.

However … all good things have to come to an end.

The late summer twilight was turning to charcoal and long shadows and it was impossible to tell the difference between swarms of fireflies and swarms of winkies. They liked the Sheridan gang and everybody from Hoax, but I was pleased to note that not all of them could see the winkies. Maybe that was childish of me, but I liked knowing there was some magic that not everyone could sense. Cerb hadn't showed up yet, so that was a good sign. I figured if something was going wrong, he would come get us, right?

Of course, as soon as I thought of him, Cerb whooshed up the slope from the park and ran to Angela. I was the only one who noticed, because no one else reacted. Good sign or bad?

Chapter Fifteen

Gina called me. I almost didn't hear my cell phone ring, with everyone talking and laughing about different things. There was a general debate on whether it was too warm to build a fire and roast marshmallows for s'mores. I almost didn't answer her, because I was turning my chair with one hand, watching Angela as she excused herself and stepped aside, with Cerb following her. Maybe she couldn't hear him, or however they communicated, with all the background noise.

"Hey," Gina said, when I answered. "Gordon told me to call you first, if anything odd happened here."

"Like what?" I looked up and that communication that has nothing to do with telepathy made Kurt and then Felicity turn to look at me.

"Well, there's a fire truck and an emergency truck and a city services truck outside. No sirens or anything. They claim some gas detectors I didn't even know were installed have gone off, but they didn't order us out of the building, and they didn't even come inside. They're walking around the outside and fussing with these long tubes attached to their trucks. I wouldn't have even known they were here, except the Mulrooney boys tried to climb up into the fire truck -- you know how they are -- and one of the firefighters blew a gasket, shrieking and swearing at him. And here's the weird part. I don't know the guy."

"Get everybody out of there, and make sure you call Gordon. As fast as you can."

"Do you think there's something dangerous?"

Did I think there was something dangerous? What was wrong with her? I knew Gina had a ton more common sense than to tell me those things and *not* think something was wrong.

Then I knew what was going on, and I felt sick and cold in the core of my bones. And furious.

"Gina," I said, trying not to shriek at her, because this wasn't her fault, "remember how people didn't notice weird things at New Year's? They said it was some toxic gas, remember? I think it's the same gas affecting you now."

"Oh. Okay."

"Get everybody out, and don't forget to call Gordon," I said, a little louder, waited for her to agree, then hung up.

"What?" Ford demanded, joining Kurt and Felicity, Jane and Daniel as they gathered around me.

"Something is messing with people's brains at Eden. Again." I told them what Gina had just told me.

Felicity got on the phone to call the fire department to see who had gone to Eden. Kurt and Jane started to go invisible.

"Not without me!" I shouted.

They linked arms with me, and in seconds we were in the Ghost field and on our way to Eden. We went without consulting Angela, because duh, this was obviously what Cerb had come to tell her was happening. Stopping for mother-may-I would just waste time.

Felicity called just as we got to Eden and did a fly-over to assess the situation. Nobody from the fire department had gotten a call to go to Eden. There were no special detectors installed to deal with the toxic fumes that had supposedly affected everyone at New Year's. All the city's emergency vehicles were still in their parking spots.

So those weren't our city fire trucks or emergency vehicles. Why did Gina think they were?

Long black hoses connected with the trucks, positioned around Eden, feeding into the holes we had found drilled into the ground last night.

People were coming out the front doors, kind of straggling, looking around, not at all worried. We landed, and nobody noticed when Jane shut down the Ghost field and we became visible again. Gina came out, herding them, wobbling a little, pressing a hand to the side of her head and blinking like she couldn't focus. She straightened up a little and hurried over to join us.

"Is that everyone?" Kurt demanded.

"Oh, yeah. We were clearing out early because of school starting up and ..." She shook her head. For a second I was afraid she forgot what she was saying. "This shouldn't be happening again."

"Did you call Gordon?" I asked.

"Yeah, he said what you did, get everybody out. What are they doing?" She pointed at the hoses.

Then three fake firemen came around the left side of the building. Five more came hurtling out of the building. They had guns. They saw the people getting into their cars or getting on their bikes to leave, and they did not look happy.

That was not a good sign. My first theory was that they wanted hostages, and we had foiled them.

Well, bully for them.

"What did you do?" one of them shouted, and stomped over to us, focused on Gina. His gaze met mine and he staggered. Then he shrieked something that sounded like one of those old European languages full of gutturals and a lot of spitting.

And he aimed that gun at me.

Kurt threw himself in front of Gina. Jane spread her arms and the Ghost field snapped into place with a crackle of energy that kind of sizzled across most of my nerves. We went invisible, and the three bullets in rapid succession passed through us.

The people who had been lingering in the parking lot let out screams and shouts and dove into their cars and got out of there. More fake firemen came running from around both sides of the building. There was more shouting and cursing and weird languages and what I was pretty sure was some vile cursing, and gesturing at the fleeing people and guns going off. Did they honestly think that shooting at people would make them *stay* and go back inside the building?

"That's not good." Jane pointed at the building.

Thanks to the Ghost field, I could see what was going on.

Something was churning in the floor of the lobby, right where we had fought the Oil Slick monster at New Year's. There were all sorts of special effects, shimmers of a really nasty shade of blue, edged in black, and some poisonous shades of green that I could easily imagine as either the slime coating a monster's fangs, or toxic, deadly radiation.

Sirens shrieked, coming from down the street, probably at the city service department. It sounded miles away. Gordon and maybe half the Neighborlee police were on their way. The question was if they could do any good. It was less than two miles from city hall to Eden, but that felt like the other side of the county.

We were alone in the parking lot, facing the fake firemen, who were doing something to their truck, with the engine running and probably pumping more noxious gas into the building.

"Can you turn it off?" I asked Kurt.

He grinned, baring his teeth, a totally nasty expression I loved right then.

With a loud *snap-bang-crack-thud*, the engine died. The fake firemen -- heck with that, call them what they were, Rivals -- screamed and swore and some of them fired their guns in all directions, even up in the air. None of them fired at us. Maybe they couldn't believe we'd be so stupid as to stay exactly where we were when we vanished? That was a pretty good sign they didn't understand Jane's Ghost field, how she phased us out and bullets passed through us. And we could pass through other things.

"Maybe we should go inside and get the vents open or do something to clear that stuff out of the air?" I said.

"Hey, what's going on?" Gina didn't sound loopy anymore. She did look a little green as she gripped one handle on my chair and wobbled.

"Those are the creeps who worked with Sylvia to sabotage New Year's and they're trying again and you're inside a force field that protects you from their guns and makes us invisible to them."

"Uh … huh …" She looked at Jane and Kurt, who had flashes of silver-blue light racing up and down their arms, writhing around their outstretched hands, and filling their eyes. "Either that stuff has totally messed with my brain --"

"Or you just got drafted by SHIELD. Try not to blow some circuits, and we'll explain later when we keep the town from being blown off the map, okay?"

"Not blown off the map *again*," Kurt said.

Tires squealed, cutting through the sound of approaching sirens, and Daniel's truck tore into the parking lot, followed by Jake in his black SUV, with Felicity. The SUV skidded sideways and Felicity leaned out of the passenger window with rainbow lightning swirling around her. Everything slowed as the Rivals aimed and fired at the newcomers. I held my breath as all those streaks of multi-colored light lashed out, and each one hit a bullet and killed it with a blinding flash and explosion in mid-air. Then more lightning flashed out, while Felicity shrieked her fury, and slashed at the Rivals.

Some of them went down, their guns going off and bursting open in their hands. Others were smart enough to throw down their guns before the lightning hit, and they ran. A few gathered up their fallen friends, dragging them along.

The only place for them to go was into the building.

Where they had wanted to keep people I knew, my friends, residents of Neighborlee.

Okay, that worked for me. Too bad Kurt had killed the truck pumping whatever that gas was into the building. But the other two trucks, around the side and behind the building, were probably still pumping that stuff.

Would it do us any good?

"I didn't know she could do that," Gina murmured.

"Hey," Jane said, wrapping an arm around her, "it's okay. We're all friends here. Just trust us, okay?"

"Yeah, trust us," she said, and nodded.

Jane shut down the Ghost field and Jake, Felicity and Daniel came over to join us. A few more of the Rivals darted out and dragged their fallen, either dead or unconscious, into the lobby.

Behind them, the energy of that dimensional vortex glowed brighter, sharper, and the dome of it, flashing and streaked with lightning of a totally not-nice, not-Felicity kind, got big enough to rise up through the roof now. I really hoped we weren't going to have a hole in the roof when we closed down that gate. If we could.

"Yeah, we gotta close it," Kurt said, when I said what I was thinking.

"What did you mean before, about 'again'?" Gina demanded. "What is that stuff?" She pointed at the building.

"We fought that thing at New Year's. That's what was snagging people and making them sick, and what killed Sylvia." He gave her a doubletake. "Uh … Gina, can you still see it?"

"Yeah."

"Okay, that's interesting." Jane seemed to know what he was thinking about three or four seconds before I caught on.

"Maybe being exposed to your Ghost field … makes her sensitive?" I guessed.

"Maybe it zapped something that was blocking her brain, like fighting that thing did for me," Felicity said.

"You guys do this a lot?" Gina said.

"Not a lot, but yeah, more often than we really want to," Kurt said. "Guys, it's getting bigger. I can feel it going down below the foundations. It's gonna break through. We don't really want to know what it's going to let in from the other side."

"Kill it permanent-like this time." Jane held out her hand to Felicity. "Girl power?"

Felicity bared her teeth, and I swear, they looked pointed for a few seconds. "Girl power."

"Make a circuit." Daniel snorted. "Like they did in *Guardians of the Galaxy.*"

I was just loopy enough from the tension, I almost kissed him. Then again, that probably would have blown a couple of his circuits, and we needed everybody's energy right then.

Kurt wrapped his arms around Felicity and Jane, pressing them close together. I held hands with Daniel and we both reached around Kurt to clutch at Felicity and Jane's lower arms. Jake guided Gina away. They were still walking, putting distance between them and us, and between them and the building, when Jane turned on the Ghost field and basically flipped off the safety switch. Cerb came out of a slit in the air and went with Jake and Gina. He trotted circles around them as they kept moving, and I knew they were safe in his care. If he wasn't focusing on us, that meant we were safe in the Ghost field. Right?

I closed my eyes, the light was so bright, but I could still see what was going on. I could also see five police cars and an emergency truck barreling up Overlook. They were going to get there and see what was going on in another minute. Or maybe they wouldn't see anything except the seven of us and the abandoned pumper truck in the parking lot.

Waves of energy blasted out of Jane and Felicity, in colors I had never seen before.

That was fine. Kind of fun.

Except -- scary part -- I felt something sucking at me, pulling something out of me. Now I knew how a milkshake felt.

Eyes still closed, I saw those pulsing waves of energy throbbing through the air. Concentric rings pounding at that growing dome of an interdimensional blister. Trying to expand into Neighborlee, into Earth, until something tore and let that oozing puss of an invader and noxious, negative energy get through to us.

Jane and Felicity cauterized it. They burned it. They sealed it.

A buzzing, rasping sound I hadn't even realized was there let out this subliminal pop that still wasn't audible, more felt than any other sense, and just … stopped.

The scream of the sirens was dang loud as the police cars tore around the shielding wall of bushes and into the parking lot. It hurt my ears, clashing with the almost musical, silent throbbing in my blood and bones.

I opened my eyes. The nasty blue and all those lightning strikes of energy were gone. The lobby was dark. Who had turned the lights out? We found out later all the circuit breakers had flipped inside the building, and some of them melted. Proof that something had happened.

But just like New Year's Eve, there was no indication that ordinary human senses and ordinary human equipment could pick up, to prove that anything had happened.

The lobby was empty. No signs of the Rivals. Just some bullet casings. Big caliber. Nasty stuff. Foreign-made weapons, we were told later. No guns. No people. Just an odd, sicky-sweet, chemical smell that was blamed on the strange gas the other two trucks were still pumping. But the people who had caused the evacuation and who had driven the trucks there?

Gone.

Jane and Felicity and Kurt saw what happened to them.

When all that energy the three of them commanded hit the bubble, the interdimensional blister collapsed, reversing, sucking downward when it had been reaching through the roof just a few seconds before. That downward pulse created a vacuum. The Rivals went down with it.

They didn't come back up.

"Roaches check in but they don't check out," Kurt offered, when we discussed it at Angela's more than an hour later.

Chief Tanner and the real Neighborlee fire and police departments were still dealing with the abandoned trucks and the noxious substance that had caused memory gaps and nausea and drowsiness in those who had been in Eden. They let us go once we had told them the absolute truth. Just not all of it. And by this time the Chief knew better than to probe for details beyond what we felt safe to tell him.

The official story: We had told Gordon about the holes drilled around the base of the building, and Gina called us to tell us something was odd when she called Gordon. We went to help evacuate the building because Gina seemed disoriented. The false firemen were pumping their gas into the building. They got angry when the people inside Eden listened to us and to Gina and evacuated. They shot at us, but we had to assume they were affected by the gas, because when Daniel showed up, they got scared and ran into the building. We were just standing there, waiting and watching, and hoping Jake wouldn't have to pull out his totally legal guns if those fake firemen came out and started shooting again. We didn't know where they went.

We could *guess* where they went, but we weren't about to share that speculation with the authorities. And the Chief, having dealt with Neighborlee weirdness for decades, knew better than to ask questions where he wouldn't like the mind-blowing, reality-straining answers.

He let us take Gina with us, to see if Angela could come up with something among all her specialty teas, to fight the effects of the gas. In fact, the Chief hoped Angela would be so kind as to provide her tea for everyone who had been affected by the gas. Of course, Angela was so kind, and more than happy to offer her skills to help. While Chief Tanner waited downstairs and met the Sheridans, and was introduced to Demetrius and Beau as Jane's uncles, Angela packaged up packets of the tea for everyone. She had me, Felicity and Jane help her, while giving Gina a little talk that could be labeled, "The Truth About the Magic of Neighborlee Without any Real Details."

Gina proved she belonged in Neighborlee. As Angela reminded her of all the odd little things she had seen and experienced for years, her color improved and she visibly relaxed. Essentially, she was convinced this was entirely normal for Neighborlee, and she was safe because Neighborlee liked her. By the time we were ready to go downstairs with the tea packets, she was laughing at herself for never having noticed before. Gina was one of us, and I really hoped that having been jolted by the Ghost field into being able to see, she would continue to be able to see the weird and wonderful.

"So, what's the verdict?" Jake said, when he joined us again.

He had stayed at Eden, helping to check the building, search for the Rivals, shut down the trucks, and disengage those hoses. This kind of work, dealing with emergencies, was what he did, after all. Cerb came with him. He had stayed with Jake. That made me worried, when I had time to think, that maybe some threat lingered around Eden. Nothing happened, though, and Cerb seemed calm enough when he climbed out of Jake's SUV and followed him over to join us. Maybe he just liked Jake?

"Considering that they wanted people to stay in the building when they activated the dimensional gate ..." Tiny frown lines appeared between Angela's eyebrows and around her mouth.

She glanced at Arthur Sheridan, then to Demetrius and Beau. Honestly? I didn't really like seeing her conferring with other people. This was Neighborlee. Angela was our ultimate authority. Why did she have to check with others, as if they were her equals? Yes, they were the leaders of their own anti-Rivals resistance groups, but if they had been more aware and if they had contacted her years ago, we wouldn't be having this meeting now, would we?

"Well, taking into account all the unsavory details we have been learning about how they treat each other, the safe assumption," Beau said, "is that they intended to feed those people to the being on the other side of the dimensional vortex."

"Big Ugly," Jane offered.

"Yes, quite appropriate. Thank you, Cookie." He winked at her.

"And quite appropriate," Angela said, "that it appears Big Ugly ate them, instead."

"Let's hope they give him a major case of indigestion." Ford and Arthur Sheridan locked gazes and nodded with flat smiles of satisfaction.

END

Neighborlee, Ohio

(Title, Original Title, Release Date)

Confessions of a Lost Kid (Growing Up Neighborlee) 05/20
Semi-Pseudo-Superheroes (Dorm Rats) 07/20
Virtually London (London Holiday) 09/20
Living Proof (that no good deed goes unpunished) (Living Proof) 11/20
Night of the Living Proof, 01/21
Quitting the Hero Biz (Hero Blues) 03/21
Bride of the Living Proof, 05/21
Shrunk: The Exile of Maurice (Divine's Emporium) 07/21
Return of the Living Proof, 09/21
Allergic to Mistletoe (Have Yourself a Faerie Little Christmas) 11/21
Dawn of the Living Proof, 01/22
Angela's Knight (Divine Knight) 03/22
The Living Proof Gets the Blues, 05/22

About the Author

On the road to publication, Michelle fell into fandom in college and has 40+ stories in various SF and fantasy universes. She has a bunch of useless degrees in theater, English, film/communication, and writing. Even worse, she has over 100 books and novellas with multiple small presses, in science fiction and fantasy, YA, suspense, women's fiction, and sub-genres of romance.

Her official launch into publishing came with winning first place in the Writers of the Future contest in 1990. She was a finalist in the EPIC Awards competition multiple times, winning with *Lorien* in 2006 and *The Meruk Episodes, I-V,* in 2010, and was a finalist in the Realm Award competition, in conjunction with the Realm Makers convention.

Her training includes the Institute for Children's Literature; proofreading at an advertising agency; and working at a community newspaper. She is a tea snob and freelance edits for a living (MichelleLevigne@gmail.com for info/rates), but only enough to give her time to write. Her newest crime against the literary world is to be co-managing editor at Mt. Zion Ridge Press and launching the publishing co-op, Ye Olde Dragon Books. Be afraid … be very afraid.

www.Mlevigne.com
www.MichelleLevigne.blogspot.com
www.YeOldeDragonBooks.com
www.MtZionRidgePress.com
@MichelleLevigne

Look for Michelle's Goodreads groups:
Guardians of Neighborlee
Voyages of the AFV Defender

NEWSLETTER:

Want to learn about upcoming books, book launch parties, inside information, and cover reveals?
Go to Michelle's website or blog to sign up.

Also by Michelle L. Levigne

Guardians of the Time Stream: 4-book Steampunk series
The Match Girls: Humorous inspirational romance series starting with **A Match (Not) Made in Heaven**
Sarai's Journey: A 2-book biblical fiction series
Tabor Heights: 20-book inspirational small town romance series.
Quarry Hall: 11-book women's fiction/suspense series
For Sale: Wedding Dress. Never Used: inspirational romance
Crooked Creek: Fun Fables About Critters and Kids: Children's short stories.
Do Yourself a Favor: Tips and Quips on the Writing Life. A book of writing advice.
Killing His Alter-Ego: contemporary romance/suspense, taking place in fandom.
The Commonwealth Universe: SF series, 25 books and growing
The Hunt: 5-book YA fantasy series
Faxinor: Fantasy series, 4 books and growing
Wildvine: Fantasy series, 14 books when all released
Neighborlee: Humorous fantasy series
Zygradon: 5-book Arthurian fantasy series
AFV Defender: SF adventure series
Young Defenders: Middle Grade SF series, spin-off of *AFV Defender*

www.ingramcontent.com/pod-product-compliance
Lightning Source LLC
Chambersburg PA
CBHW021147190726
48288CB00008B/2864